Praise for *Chances in Disguise*

"Though fictionalized, the novel is grounded 	:h saw
Mexican refugees and American-b	antes
and violent policing without due proc	is as
relevant to and important for contem	.y 20th
century. A timely and intimate first-per.

—*Kirkus Reviews*

"A vibrant and compelling story about a young woman's courage and the heroic efforts by a community of friends to save her. *Chances in Disguise* is bound to illuminate and inspire us in our present struggles for justice."

—Francisco X. Stork, author of *On the Hook*

Praise for *Evangelina Takes Flight*

A Junior Library Guild Selection
2018 Skipping Stones Honor Award
2017 Southwest Books of the Year
2018 Tejas Foco YA Fiction Award
2018 June Franklin Naylor Award for the Best Book for Children on Texas History
2018 Spirit of Texas Reading Program Selection
Runner-up, 2018 Texas Institute of Letters HEB Award for Best Young Adult Book

"Written in Evangelina's conscientious voice and containing parallels to some of today's current events, this hopeful, yet sometimes heartbreaking, novel is a fast and important read."

—*Booklist*

'Using the first person with Spanish sprinkled throughout, Noble propels the novel with vivid imagery and lovely prose, successfully guiding readers behind an immigrant family's lens. Loosely based on Noble's own grandmother's story, this debut hits awfully close to home in the current anti-immigrant political climate."

—*Kirkus Reviews*

"Honest in its exploration of xenophobia, and timely in its empathetic portrayal of a refugee family, *Evangelina Takes Flight* is a vibrant and appealing historical novel. As much as this vital work takes on social issues, it's Evangelina's coming of age that resounds. Her abuelito's maxim, 'Challenges are chances in disguise,' grows into a gorgeously woven message of hope."

—*Foreword Reviews*

"Noble's poetic yet accessible prose allows the reader to slip into Evangelina's world and understand that problems can be overcome with perseverance and bravery."

—*Latinxs in Kid Lit*

"Noble's compelling debut novel follows the life of a young Mexicana as she and her family escape the uncertainty and violence of the Mexican Revolution into a segregated Texas. It is through Noble's deeply poetic writing and deft depiction of 1910's Borderlands that we see the indignities of war, racism and discrimination; but it is Noble's humanizing point of view through the eyes of a girl that we witness the hopes, love and dreams inherent in any people engaging in the difficulties of a diaspora."

—National Association for Chicano/Chicana Studies

Chances in Disguise

Diana J. Noble

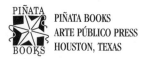

PIÑATA BOOKS
ARTE PÚBLICO PRESS
HOUSTON, TEXAS

Chances in Disguise is funded in part by a grant from the Texas Commission on the Arts. We are thankful for its support.

Arte Público Press is thankful to Mei Leebron for editing this work during her summer internship.

Piñata Books are full of surprises!

Arte Público Press
University of Houston
4902 Gulf Fwy, Bldg 19, Rm 100
Houston, Texas 77204-2004

Cover art and design by Mora Des¡gn Group

Library of Congress Control Number: 2021943472

Printed in the United States of America

October 2021–November 2021
Versa Press, Inc., East Peoria, IL
5 4 3 2 1

Acknowledgements

A thousand thanks to my husband, Russell, who provides the love, light and inspiration that nourishes me every day. And to Mom, Taylor, Tay, Adam, Sierra and Cora—your support and encouragement are the foundation for everything I do. Dad, your countless hours of reading, editing, collaboration and sincere belief that I have something to offer through my writing brought *Evangelina Takes Flight* and *Chances in Disguise* to life. We're a great team, you and me.

Dr. John Morán-Gonzalez, please accept my deepest gratitude for writing an afterword that provides essential history and meaningful context for Evangelina's story. To learn more about historical events along the Mexico-Texas border from 1910-1920, please visit www.refusingtoforget.org.

"It is from numberless diverse acts of courage and belief that human history is shaped. Each time a man stands up for an ideal, or acts to improve the lot of others, or strikes out against injustice, he sends forth a tiny ripple of hope, and crossing each other from a million different centers of energy and daring, those ripples build a current that can sweep down the mightiest walls of oppression and resistance."

—Robert F. Kennedy

CHAPTER 1

Dirty Field Rat

Ramona Healy, a woman I met just two hours ago, lays on a thin mattress in her one-room home, too tired to swat at the fly buzzing around her face. I grab the narrow handle of a corn husk fan and shoo it away. It moves onto a pair of pigs' feet in the cast-iron pot on the woodstove. The vinegary brine they cooked in gives off a sharp, repulsive smell. The wind whistles through the cabin sidewalls where the binding mud between the logs has crumbled and fallen away.

I hand Mrs. Healy a ceramic cup filled with tea that Mexican *curanderas*, or healers, have used for centuries to ease pain. She turns it a bit to avoid the chipped edges and sips.

After a thorough examination, I find no unusual bleeding or sign of infection, and her vital signs are stable.

"Do not worry. I will take care of you," I tell her.

The tea helps with the pain, but it can only do so much.

When the discomfort in her back increases, and she can no longer carry on a conversation, I give her another herbal remedy I made myself that should dull the worst of it. She slides her thin arm across the bed and rests her hand on mine.

Click, click, click, the pendulum on the shelf clock swings.

Beads of sweat appear on her forehead and lip, and her thin smile gives way to wild eyes and gritted teeth. The contraction starts as gentle as a spring breeze and grows like a twister picking up speed.

I ask if she would like me to pray for her. She nods, so I pull out my Rosary.

"Hail Mary, full of grace, the Lord is with thee. Blessed are thou among women, and blessed is the fruit of thy womb, Jesus." Her lips move silently with mine.

The cabin door swings open, *BANG*! A light-haired man with round spectacles and a goatee steps inside.

"I'm Doctor Jedidiah Morley. Who are you, and what are you doing here?" he barks and inspects me from head to foot through narrowed eyes. "Oh, dear God! You're nothing but a dirty Mexican field rat! How dare you masquerade as someone capable of treating a woman in this vulnerable state! Get away from her!"

I try to explain myself. Why I'm here, how many births I've assisted with, my training with Doc Taylor in Seneca, but the man turns away. He opens his bag and pulls out a stethoscope, bandages, scissors, tweezers and a syringe the length of a toothbrush.

"Evangelina?" Mrs. Healy murmurs. "Will you stay with me?"

"No, ma'am. This girl's not the least bit qualified," the doctor says, then points at the door. "Are you deaf, girl?" he shouts at me. "You don't belong here. You're a fraud and a danger to this woman. Get out!"

"I'm sorry," I mouth to her as I put my things away and run outside, where I get on my bike and ride for the two hours it takes to get home.

She'll be all right, I tell myself. She's with a real doctor now.

৬৯ ৬৯ ৬৯

I lay awake most of the night, wondering how Ramona Healy and her baby are doing. Childbirth may be the most natural process in the world, but it can also be a dangerous one. She would have done fine had I stayed. I've delivered babies myself without any problems and assisted Doc Taylor with countless others. Doctor Morley had no right to order me out of the way he did.

Of course, he's a licensed physician, and I am not. He's an adult, and I am just seventeen. But still, his abrupt entrance and insults startled the patient. And me.

৬৯ ৬৯ ৬৯

The early morning sun comes through the tiny holes in the lace curtains, and the smell of brewing coffee lures me to the kitchen.

Mamá wears an embroidered sky-blue house dress and an apron with a rooster painted on one pocket and chickens with eggs on the other. It's the only apron she brought from our ranch in Mexico. One long black braid hangs down her back. A rusty-colored pottery bowl with *machacado*, shredded beef sits nearby. She picks up the cutting board and pushes diced garlic and tomatoes into a cast-iron skillet on the stove. Next, she'll add the beef and cook it until it gets crispy, then fold in the raw eggs.

I love the sound of the sizzle and the instant steam that spreads a time-to-get-up smell that even sleepy heads like my little brothers, Tomás and Domingo, can't ignore.

"Good morning, Mamá," I say in Spanish, the language we use at home.

"Good morning to you, *m'ija*," Mamá replies, wiping her hands on a dishtowel. "You were gone longer than I expected yesterday. I was beginning to get worried. I couldn't fall asleep until I heard you come in."

"I'm sorry about that. I didn't expect to stay out that . . ."

"María Elena?" Papá calls from the living room. "The sheriff just pulled up in front of our house."

"Why would he come here?" Mamá asks as she pulls the skillet off the heat and sets it on a back burner.

My thoughts jump to my older brothers, Emilio and Enrique, working in the New Mexico coal mines. *Are they all right?*

Papá opens the front door. The sheriff, gray-haired, tall and thick around the middle, pushes past him.

"Excuse me, sir? What you want with us?" Papá asks.

The sheriff steps around Papá and faces me. "Are you Evanjellina duh Lee-on?" he asks.

"Yes, sir," I reply.

"You are hereby under arrest for the murder of Mrs. Otis Healy."

"What? Mrs. Healy is dead?" I ask.

Papá's eyes dart from the sheriff to me. "*M'ija*, what is he talking about?"

My older sister Elsa and younger brother Tomás shuffle into the room, Tomás in his rumpled pajamas, Elsa in her pink housecoat.

"You must be mistaken, sir. Mrs. Healy was alive when I left," I say.

"We can't verify that now, can we?" the sheriff retorts. "The woman's dead as a doornail."

"She asked . . . she asked me to stay with her!" I say. "There was nothing unusual about her labor. Her vital signs were normal!"

"Who is Mrs. Healy?" Papá asks.

"What about the baby?" I cry.

"Doc Morley saved the infant, a boy. That man's a hero," the sheriff says.

Mamá holds her palms up, her eyes wide as nickels. "I no understand. What she do—why you talk to my daughter like this?"

"Are ya feeble-minded? She killed Ramona Healy, a woman with child. Doctor Jedidiah Morley reported the crime to my office this mornin'."

Mamá shakes her head and looks at me to help her understand.

"Mamá, they think I killed the patient I was with yesterday. She died after I left the woman's home," I translate for her. "It must be a mistake."

"*¡Es una mentira!* That's a lie!" Mamá shouts.

The sheriff yanks me halfway around, claps the handcuffs on my wrists and walks me to the police wagon. Neighbors gather outside and stare.

"Where you take her?" Mamá pleads, following close behind.

"You people sure are stupid. Where do ya think I'm takin' her?" the sheriff snarls.

"Wait!" Papá yells as the sheriff pushes me into the wagon. "Evangelina never hurt no one!"

"Adán, do something!" Mamá shrieks.

"She just a child—she only seventeen!" Papá says, rushing towards me.

Sheriff Pearl grabs his gun with one hand and slams the wagon door shut with the other.

"Get back, seeen-yor," he says in a mocking Mexican accent, "or I'll shoot yer empty head clean off a yer neck."

The weight of the wagon shifts as the sheriff climbs upfront.

"Hi-yah!" he shouts.

My body pitches back as the horse takes off with a jolt.

"We come for you!" Mamá yells.

Thump, thump, thump, thump, someone's feet pound the road behind us.

"Where are you going?" Tomás yells. "Evangelina, don't go!" His voice trails off as he falls farther behind.

The clip-clop of the horse's hooves and the beating of my heart join together in terrifying rhythm.

Did I kill Ramona Healy?

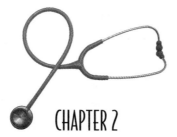

CHAPTER 2

Bronco in a Rodeo Shoot

Long after dark, the sheriff comes into my cell.

I know what he wants from the sinful look in his glassy, bloodshot eyes. He smells of sweat, liquor and cigars, and he breathes the low growl of a hungry dog guarding a bone.

"Sheriff? What are you doing here?" I ask him, trembling.

"You gonna git what ya deserve, girlie," he says, stepping to within an inch of me, then throwing me face first against the wall.

I try to twist away, but at 4' 11" and skinny as a corn stalk, I'm no match for his massive body, thick hands and broad shoulders pressed against my back.

He pushes my cheek into the brick with one hand and lifts my prison gown with the other.

"*¡Por favor! ¡Suélteme!* Please! Let me go!" I sob.

"Shuddup-ya-liddle-whore!" he says, his whiskey-coated words running together.

He moves his left hand off my face to undo his belt, and a silver band catches my eye.

His pants slip down his legs. His belt buckle hits the ground. *Clink.* He stoops over and puts his wet lips on my ear.

"I hear you Messican girls like it hot and spicy," he sputters.

"You're married!" I say in a burst of air. "Get off of me!" I throw my head back, but he just laughs. "You ain't goin' nowhere, girlie."

The night guard, Josiah, steps into the light of the open doorway, his eyes wide with panic.

"Help me!" I plead.

"Sheriff?" he says softly. Josiah's eyes shift back and forth from the sheriff to me. "Sheriff!" he yells.

"What?!" the sheriff bellows, turning toward the voice.

"Catherine came by earlier, sheriff, sir . . . said you should git on home. Ya missed supper, sir," the guard says. "Thass the second time this week she come lookin' fer ya."

The blood whooshes, whooshes, whooshes in my temples. Tears run down my tight, aching throat.

The sheriff lets out a long, raspy groan, leans back, and I crumple to the floor.

"Don'choo tell nobody 'bout this, Josiah, ya hear me?" he says, pulling up his pants. "What a shame id be if sumpin bad happen ta you an' Colleen way out in dem woods where nobody'd hear ya scream. You got my meanin', boy?"

The sheriff pokes my leg with his boot. "Ain't no differnt fer you, girlie. You don't want nuttin bad ta happen ta yer Ma and Pa, now, do ya?"

He opens the cell and storms out, angry as a bucking bronco in a rodeo shoot.

ॐ ॐ ॐ

I shake all night, curled up like a baby.

ॐ ॐ ॐ

My parents show up in the early morning hours. I hear their voices and pick up the faint smell of something delicious, maybe *papas con huevo*, potatoes with scrambled eggs. The daytime guard orders them to get out.

"*¡Te queremos mucho, Evangelina!* We love you very much, Evangelina!" Mamá cries.

Don't leave me here! I want to scream, but I can't find my voice.

ॐ ॐ ॐ

The jailhouse is no more than a square shape with a brick wall in the center that runs three-quarters of the building's length. An office area with three desks sits on one side, and two jail cells sit on the other. From where I am, in the first cell, all I see is part of the door and a bit of the front entry.

The metal hinges squeak as they rub past each other, and a slice of sunshine appears across the ceiling.

My heart pounds. Is it the sheriff?

"I'm goin' back there, Humphrey," says a woman. "And don't you try to stop me. I got heels on, and I'm not afraid to use one on that foot of yours."

"Whaddya wanna do with 'er?" Humphrey says.

The woman steps into view, removes her black velvet hat with its royal blue ribbon and pushes back a few flame-colored curls that have broken free of her loosely gathered bun. She sits down on a stool in the narrow hallway, pulls a pad of paper out of a leather briefcase and a silver pencil inscribed with "Cavanaugh Fine Fabrics." Her black and white pinstriped dress with its silver medallion belt, fine lace collar and pearly buttons contrast with my drab prison dress.

I've never seen her before.

"Go on, Humphrey," she says to the guard, shooing him away with a flick of her hand. "Why don't you leave us alone to talk? I'm not goin' to break her out of this here cell." She speaks like a southerner mixed with another accent I can't quite place.

"I'm Cora Cavanaugh," she says to me. "Doc Taylor told me all about you, and I knew right away that I had to get involved. Seneca's just a smudge on the Texas map, and we don't see the likes of a red hot murder case very often. You're in a world of trouble, darlin', but don't you worry. I told Doc Taylor I'd help you."

I wince on the inside but smile politely. *After what happened to me last night, I just want to be left alone.*

"I'm gonna write articles with your side of the story," she tells me. "*The Seneca Press* and *The Goldendale Gazette* said they wouldn't publish anythin' I write, but I'll find a way to make them bend. I'm stubborn and a damn fine writer, too. I know it sounds vain, but it's not braggin' if it's the truth. I was the head of my school newspaper and got an article published in the *Ladies' Home Companion* about a woman's right to a proper education."

I take my first chance to get a word in. "It was kind of you to come, Miss Cavanaugh, and I thank you, but I did not sleep well last night and feel very tired," I say. "Would you mind coming back another day?"

"Why don't we make a deal? You call me Cora, and I'll call you Eva. Evangelina's very pretty, but I like Eva for short, don't you? We women don't have to be so formal with each other. And I understand that you're tired. I didn't sleep well last night either, but time is of the essence," she says without taking a breath. "I want to publish at least two articles, maybe three, before your trial begins. I'll try to keep our time to a minimum, I promise."

"Yes, ma'am. Thank you," I say, shocked by this woman's unapologetic nerve.

"Of course, darlin'. I may not be a paid reporter yet, but I *will* publish this story. I'll spread the truth about this case across Texas—but first, I have a million questions."

She smiles and hastily writes the date on her notepad: *May 8, 1915.*

"For goodness sake," Cora says, wrinkling her lips to one side. "Where are my good graces? I haven't asked how you're doin'. Is that a bruise on your cheek? Did you get that in here? Are they feedin' you? Are they keepin' their grubby hands off of you? I swear that sheriff has horns under his hat and a tail tucked inside those saggy-bottom pants."

"Please do not worry about me, Miss Cavanaugh. I am tired but otherwise all right," I say, careful not to make eye contact. *I am nowhere near all right.*

"It's 'Cora,' remember? We have a deal. This place isn't known for its fine food, so I took it upon myself to bring an extra sandwich. I must say, you're awfully tiny for a child your age."

"I am almost eighteen," I say as if that makes me a wise old granny. "My parents came this morning with breakfast, but the man, Humphrey, would not let them in."

"Why is that?" Cora asks.

"It's against the rules," I shrug. "But they put a man in the other cell this morning. Then a lady came by and visited him. A few hours after that, someone else showed up, and Humphrey let the prisoner go."

"Anglos?" she asks.

"Yes, ma'am."

"Mexicans don't fare too well with the law around here, as I'm sure you know. I bet that's why your parents couldn't come in. Sheriff Pearl and his buddies are bigots, plain and simple."

Cora stands up and peers around the wall. "Humphrey! Get over here and bring me a chair. This damn stool is about as wide as a thimble, and it's not agreein' with my butt. And bring this child a chair, too. How dare you make her stand or sit on the floor? Didn't your momma teach you any manners?"

Humphrey appears, thin as sugarcane with wispy blonde hair that sticks to his head. One watery blue eye looks at Cora, and the other turns slightly upward and to the right.

"Momma says her kine don't deserve no manners," Humphrey responds. "Says they should go back ta where they come from or git on ta some other state that wants 'em. Texas is God's country."

"Well, your momma's an idiot. I'm sorry, Humphrey, but what does she expect? That 'her kind' will go back to Mexico to die? Or didn't you know there's a war goin' on down there? It's a revolution, like the one we had with England two hundred years ago and the one in Europe that's goin' on now. And, Texas is nobody's country. It's a state, like all the other states. It's just *big!*"

"Momma says Texas should be its own country again," he retorts.

"Texas was never its own country, you damn fool," she says, clicking her tongue in disbelief. "It was part of Mexico before somebody changed the lines."

"My momma wouldn't agree with that one little bit."

"You're a grown man, Humphrey; start thinkin' for yourself. Now, bring this child and me a chair before I thump you on the head."

"Gee, Cora, ya dohn have to git so nasty," he mutters.

A few moments later, Humphrey sets a wooden chair down, motions for Cora to take a seat and opens the cell door with a key hanging from a ring on his belt.

"Is Josiah coming back?" I ask.

"He does nights, an' I do days, and it ain't night, now is it? You can use the stool," he tells me. "Your skinny butt'll fit on the thimble-top jus' fine. Don't tell the sheriff I brung it in here, or he'll have my hide. And, Cora, from now on, I want ya ta leave my momma out of it."

"Thank you, Humphrey," Cora says, pulling a coin out of her purse and pressing it into his hand. "Go buy yourself a lollipop or somethin'. And if you treat this young lady proper from here on out, I'll leave your momma out of the conversation."

Humphrey drops the coin in his shirt pocket and disappears.

"Cora, you said *The Seneca Press* and *The Goldendale Gazette* wouldn't print your story. My family will talk to everyone they can, but I can't see how convincing people in our Mexican neighborhood will make much difference. How else are we going to get the word out there?"

"*The Gazette's* editor said he wouldn't hire a female writer. He said if I use a man's name, he might consider it, but I won't do it. If the story is good, who cares who wrote it?" she asks. "We've got to tell the truth, and everybody has to hear it. The right words put together in the right way can shift people's thinkin'. I *will* get one of those damn newspapers or some other one to take this story. It'll be too good to ignore, and I can be very persuasive. You're goin' to have to believe me on that."

"How long before the trial starts? I have to get out of here, Cora." *Before the sheriff comes back.* "I am no criminal, I promise."

"I went over to the courthouse this mornin', and Judge O'Leary wouldn't give me a straight answer about a trial date," Cora replies. "The prosecution needs time to build their case. If you were Anglo, they might never have charged you at all, bein' that they've got nothin' but hearsay and no motive. The judge doesn't like foreigners, especially Mexicans and Negroes. Since he took office, every one of 'em that's gone through his court has been convicted. And he gets re-elected time and time again. So does the sheriff. And those two are thick as thieves. You know, 'I'll scratch your back if you scratch mine.'"

Thick as thieves. Scratch your back. I've been here for four years, and I still don't know what some things mean!

"People think men like them are bein' tough, protectin' the town folk from some brown tidal wave of foreigners comin' here to take their jobs, their land, even their women," Cora continues. "For goodness sake, they're foreigners themselves! Just about everybody's family came here from someplace else! The judge hails from Ireland, and the sheriff's family came from Poland when he was a boy, although I heard he's the only one who made it alive."

"Did he tell you that himself?"

"Nah, I went to school with his daughter, Pauline. She's a talker, that one. She's not too fond of her father, neither, and that's puttin' it mildly."

"What happened to his family?" I ask.

"Pauline said his parents and little sister got typhoid on the ship that brought 'em here. Immigratin's a dangerous business, but you already knew that. Little Stanley Pedracki got raised by some lunatic uncle who lost a leg in the Civil War. Stanley took off on his own at thirteen and changed his last name to Pearl as soon as they'd let him."

"Maybe that is why he acts the way he does—so angry and mean," I say. *And violent.*

"Nothin' gives him the right to be like that, honey," she says. "Now, no more dawdlin'. I want to write the first installment of my story before gray hair sets in."

I study her face. *Can I trust her?*

"I see that look in your eyes," Cora says. "You're worried about talkin' to me, and I don't blame you one bit. I should have given this to you when I came in."

She reaches into her purse and pulls out a handwritten note on Doc Taylor's stationery.

Dear Evangelina,

This is Cora Cavanaugh. She's a patient of mine, whom you've probably never met. (She should come by the clinic more often!) She wants to help you. I've watched her grow up over the years and become a woman of strong character. She offers publicity for your case, and that could prove beneficial in the trying times ahead.

I stand with you, Evangelina, and I will do everything I can to clear your name.

Sincerely,
Doc T

I hand the letter back to her. "What do you want to know?" I ask.

"Excellent! I'll be takin' a whole lot of notes. I want to hear about your family, why you came to Seneca, and how you got involved with Doc Taylor. Most people will not understand why a young person such as yourself has been practicin' medicine. It's highly irregular. But, before you get to all that, tell me what happened with Ramona Healy. I need to hear it in your own words."

I picture Mrs. Healy, lying there, frightened and looking at me with her strangely pale blue eyes.

"I don't *think* I did anything wrong," I say. "This is all a mistake."

Cora arches an eyebrow. "You don't *think* you did anythin' wrong, or you *know?*"

I lick my dry lips. "I know," I lie. *Did I accidentally kill Ramona Healy?*

"Well, that's reassurin'," Cora says. "Doc Taylor told me the same thing, but I needed to know that you downright deny killin' that woman before I start shoutin' from the rooftops about your innocence."

"I visit patients who live out in the country, on farms or in the woods," I begin. "The day Mrs. Healy," I pause and exhale slowly through pursed lips, "died, I stitched up a boy's foot at the Garza farm outside Fox Grove. A woman came by asking me to help her neighbor who was having her baby too early. I finished the stitches on the boy's foot and followed her."

"What made you think you were qualified to help a woman in that condition? You're not even a fully grown adult, much less a physician," Cora says.

"My mother delivered babies in Mexico, and my grandmother did the same. When I was ten years old, Mamá started bringing me with her. I boiled water, lit candles, talked to the women to pass the time and cleaned up afterward.

"Here in the US, I studied medicine for three years with Doc Taylor before he let me assist him with childbirth at the clinic or in the ladies' homes. Mamá and I deliver babies in our neighborhood, but now, I do the midwife's work, and Mamá helps me. No harm has come to any of the mothers or babies."

"And you had no misgivings about assisting Ramona Healy?"

"Misgivings?"

"Worries."

"No, not at all," I reply. "Besides, I was the only person around with medical experience that I knew of, and there wasn't enough time to find Doc Taylor."

"What was her condition when you arrived?"

"She looked to be about eight months along," I say, remembering the sight of her big belly jutting upward from her thin body.

Cora reaches in her bag and offers a handkerchief.

"I still can't believe she's dead," I say, wiping my nose. "When I got there, she was still hours away from pushing. I lit a candle made with orange and cinnamon to cleanse the air, and we talked for a long time.

"When she got more uncomfortable, I calmed her nerves with massage and gave her chamomile and raspberry tea to reduce the pain and prepare her uterus for delivery."

"I don't know what 'prepare the uterus' means, and I don't wanna know. It sounds dreadful," Cora says. "In total, how long did you stay with her?"

"Three, maybe four hours."

"Doctor Morley's sayin' you were chanting to the devil when he came in."

"I beg your pardon?"

"He said you were doin' some backwoods Mexican sorcery and made her drink poison from a teacup."

"What is sorcery?"

"Witchcraft."

I suck in my breath. "Why would he say that?"

Cora leans over her notepad and writes furiously. "That Doctor Morley must be hidin' somethin'—like his guilt."

"He called me a 'dirty Mexican' and screamed at me to get out. Mrs. Healy asked me to stay, but he wouldn't have it. I felt bad leaving her, but I had to. She was scared but otherwise fine. I don't know what happened after that."

Cora sets her pencil down and looks at her watch. "I'm sorry you had to go through all that. And for the sheriff to arrest you the next day—what a nightmare. It's all kinds a'wrong no matter which way you spin it. Hey," she says, looking at her watch. "It's nearly lunchtime. Let's eat somethin' before we continue. I know *I'm* hungry! But it's gotta be outside. Smells like somebody sprayed 'Sweaty Man' cologne before I got here. Humphrey!"

"Now what?" Humphrey grumbles.

"I brought this young lady a sandwich, and she's goin' to eat it outside, with me. She needs sunshine and fresh air. Can't you see she's wiltin' in here? It stinks to high heaven! I'll be with her the whole time, and we'll stay right close to the buildin'."

"Are ya some kinda crazy lady? I'll lose my job!" Humphrey puffs out his narrow chest. "Jails rehabilitate sinners through displin and segrega . . . Ummm, we keep 'em apart from ever'body else, so they can think about all the wrong they done. Sunshine's not part of it."

"Humphrey, stop talkin' before you hurt yourself. I'll take her outside for fifteen minutes. You don't expect Sheriff Pearl in the next fifteen minutes, do ya?" Cora reaches in her handbag and sticks another nickel in Humphrey's shirt pocket. "Buy that ignorant momma of yours somethin' nice."

"Hey! You said you'd leave my momma out of it!"

"Give me that nickel back," Cora says, holding out her hand.

"Fine. Let me get 'er ready first," Humphrey says. "An' my momma's not pignorant or nothin' like that. You don't even know 'er, an' I think she's real pretty."

CHAPTER 3

More Than a Storyteller

A concrete bench backs up to the building. A can filled with rocks sits near the back door with five butts floating in rainwater and dozens more scattered across the ground.

Cora loops her arm through mine. The leg irons locked around my ankles drag across the ground. First step, jingle-clank, second step, jingle-clank, third step, jingle-clank.

Thank goodness Mamá and Papá aren't here to see this—they'd be devastated.

"I wish he didn't have to put those things on you," she says. "Dreadful!"

"I'm just glad to be outside," I say and sit down on the bench, which instantly heats my bottom like a tortilla on a griddle.

I take in the clear blue sky and listen to the joyful sound of the swallow's song. A row of bushy sycamore trees line up just past the alley, and purple flowers bloom on a jacaranda tree in the next lot filled with clumps of scrub brush and empty beer bottles.

Cora reaches into her oversized purse, unwraps and hands me a biscuit layered with creamy butter, slices of smoked beef tongue and sweet pickles, but I'm not hungry.

"I've got a peach for you, too, if there's time. I can just see Humphrey starin' at the clock in there, waitin' for the fifteen minutes to be up. He'll get tarred and feathered if the sheriff finds you out here," she says. "I can't say I blame him for bein' scared. That sheriff's an opposin' man, and he can be mean as one-a-them wild hogs—and about as ugly," she chuckles. "With you bein' a young lady and all, I assume he's been showin' you more of his good-mannered side."

"Yes, thank you for asking." I lie, squeeze my fists tight and shove them into my lap. "You suppose Humphrey will let me eat this inside? I had a big breakfast," I lie again.

"I don't see why Humphrey would care one way or the other. What are you gonna do? Use the peach as a weapon?" Cora says. "Let's stay out here until he forces us to go in. He may not let you do this again unless I give him another nickel."

A bully from school named Victor that I'd hoped to forget walks up the alley and turns toward us.

"Evangelina? Well, well, well—look at you, sittin' at the jailhouse with chains on yer ankles," he laughs. "Ever'body knows you people are nothin' but mangy dogs. The sheriff should do us a favor and lock ya all up."

A group of other schoolmates stands nearby, whispering in each other's ears.

"On second thought, let's not wait for Humphrey," Cora says. "Time to go in."

I stand up and dust off my backside. Cora and I link arms again. As we make our way toward the door, the group's laughter booms in my ears.

"You sons a bitches!" Cora yells before the jail door closes.

ↄ ↄ ↄ

"I got close to throwin' the peach at that nincompoop," Cora says. "Then, I remembered you're gonna eat it."

"Good thing the sheriff didn't come back," he says, unlocking my jail cell and pushing me in.

"Fine, fine, Humphrey," Cora says. "Now, if you'll excuse us, this child's gonna eat her lunch now, and we have some more talkin' to do."

I don't want to eat. I'll throw up if they make me.

"You women. All you do is talk," he says.

"Cora? If you don't mind, would you tell me a little about yourself?" I ask. "I appreciate your offer to help, but I don't know anything you."

"Good idea, darlin'," she says. "With me doin' all the askin', it's only right that you know a little about me, too.

"Well, most people would say I had a sad start in life, but it won't limit the middle or the end for me. My mother died when I was born, and my father's been mad at me ever since. He won't say it, but it's true. We came here by steamship from Scotland when I was three years old. My stomach turned inside out within an hour of leaving the dock, and I couldn't keep anythin' down the whole trip. I nearly died of thirst. When we got to New York, Doc Taylor was there tendin' to the sick as they came off the boat. That man saved me. We didn't know a soul in the US of A. My father thought we'd settle in New York City, but Doc Taylor convinced us to go with him to Texas—said there was lots of opportunity out west. I've been in Seneca ever since, although I have dreams of livin' in Boston or Chicago or maybe Philly. This place is too damn small for me.

"I graduated from the same school you did when I was fourteen, then studied English at a normal school—like a college—four hundred miles north of here. My father decided it was a waste of money and stopped payin' for it. I had no money of my own, so I had to come back. I'm workin' to become a writer now, so I'll never have to rely on that bastard again."

"I'm impressed," I say.

"Oh, don't be," she said. "I'm just tryin' to make my momma up in heaven proud by doin' something worthwhile with my life."

"When did Doc Taylor tell you about me?" I ask.

"I saw him yesterday. There's been a miscarriage of justice accordin' to him, and if he believes you're innocent, so do I. And I'm goin' to do everythin' I can to make sure you get a fair trial. Of course, we'll have to find you a qualified lawyer. I'm just the storyteller in this equation."

"You're more than a storyteller. You're brave, and you're bold! I've spent my life mostly try to get along—to make people happy—never breaking the rules."

"Is that right? Well, you're gonna have to be brave and bold to get through this thing. I'm sure you've got it in you somewhere."

I'm grateful for Cora, Doctor Taylor and my family. But Selim, the man I want to be with for the rest of my life, left Seneca twenty-six days ago with his father and hasn't returned. They sell everything from flour to blankets to eyeglasses and chicken feed out of their wagon-turned-traveling store. I have never needed Selim more than I do now. No one knows about the two of us, other than we're old school friends, so I keep my longing to myself. My sister, Elsa, knows of my feelings for Selim, but she doesn't know everything.

"All right," Cora says. "You can't just be an anonymous defendant in a murder trial. The public needs to see you as a whole person with a history. You have struggles and dreams, the same as any of them. Doc Taylor told me a little bit about you, but why don't you tell me about your background. Better to get it straight from the horse's mouth, as they say."

Horse's mouth? I'm not even going to ask.

"This was going to be a short conversation," I remind her.

"Oh, poo! Forget that. I don't want to interrupt what we got goin'. You're doin' great, Eva."

"Maybe just thirty more minutes," I reply. "Where do you want me to start?"

"Your life in Mexico. Tell me everythin', and I'll figure out which parts to include."

"Alright then. I was born July 1, 1898, on Rancho Encantado, outside Mariposa, a day's travel from the border. It was mostly a cattle ranch, but we also had orchards of tomatoes, onions, avocados, all kinds of citrus and pecans. My father grew up there, and so did his father and grandfather."

"What does 'Mariposa' mean?"

"Butterfly," I reply. "My *abuelito*, grandfather, said that not long after the Spaniards arrived in the New World, thousands of butterflies appeared, covering the sky in every direction. They soon landed on the great river, turning it into a moving ribbon of black, white and gold wings. When the cooler weather came, the butterflies disappeared. The people believed they were a blessing from God and changed the name of the town."

"I assume it was too dangerous for your family to stay when the war broke out."

"We heard General Villa's army was getting close to Mariposa, so we packed what we could and left. My mother's younger sister Cristina and her family lived here in Seneca, and we had nowhere else to go."

Cora looks up from her notepad with a furrowed brow. "Somethin' doesn't add up," she says. "Pancho Villa is fightin' for the Mexican people, and you're Mexican. Why would you leave if he was comin' to this butterfly town of yours?"

"Pancho Villa and his men were killing landowners all across Mexico, blaming them and President Díaz for the horrible conditions and suffering of the Mexican people."

"Jesus, Mary and Joseph! You must have been terrified!"

"Villa would have ordered my brothers and father to fight in his army or killed them if they refused. Women were . . . what's the word? Taken? Stolen?"

"Kidnapped," Cora offers.

"Yes, they kidnapped women and girls. And worse.

"My sister, Francisca, and her husband did not come. They are still hiding in an old cottage near an abandoned coffee field. Abuelito lives with them."

"Do you plan to go back to Mexico when the war is over?"

"They're still fighting after five years, and I don't see how I could ever become a doctor there. Here, I thought all things were possible if you worked hard enough. Now I'm not so sure."

ॐ ॐ ॐ

Three hours after she arrived, Cora finally goes home, but only because her writing hand hurts.

I finally get around to opening the wrapped sandwich she left for me. It smells good, and my stomach's rumbling, but I wrap it back up and set it aside.

It takes me until bedtime to choke down most of the peach. I give Josiah the sandwich and leave what's left of the peach on the ground, near my feet. There's nothing but the pit in the morning, moved half the distance between me and the wall. I'm sure the cockroaches enjoyed it more than I did.

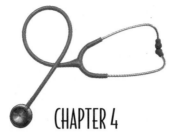

CHAPTER 4

Do You See Me?

The sheriff hasn't so much as glanced in my direction since he arrived. *Was he so drunk that he forgot what he did? Or is he too ashamed to look at me?*

I sit as still as I can, afraid to move or make a noise that could draw his attention.

"I'm back!" Cora announces from the front entry. "Oh! Sheriff Pearl, it's a pleasure to see you," she says with a helping of extra sweetness in her voice. "I'm here to see Eva, of course. Why don't you come on back and join us for a chat?"

She walks through the doorway, swinging her backside and holding one plate in each hand. "As you can see, I went to Lonnie's and bought Evangelina and me some lamb stew and cornbread. Would you be so kind as to open her cell, Stanley? I promised Lonnie I'd bring the plates back shortly. Or perhaps you'd be so kind as to take the plates back yourself. This young lady and I have important work to do," she says, smiling broadly.

"Are you outta yer cotton-pickin' mind, Cora?" the sheriff says. "This is a hangin' case. Yer no lawyer, so what exactly do ya think yer doin'? Yer on the wrong side here."

"I'm goin' to give this innocent child her lunch," Cora says. "You been near starvin' her. I see you prayin' at church every Sunday, Stanley, and here you are, treatin' one of God's creatures no better than a flea-bitten dog. Does Catherine know what you do in this hell hole? She'd be ashamed of you if she did. I see her at prayer circle sometimes. Come to think of it, she never speaks of you. Why is that?"

"You keep my wife out of it, Cora," he says. "Aren't you the same age as Pauline? I oughta put ya over my knee and spank ya." He fumbles with his keys before he selects one from the ring and unlocks the cell.

Cora hands me a plate and turns to face Sheriff Pearl. He's tall enough to touch the ceiling with his fingers. Her full head of red curls barely reaches the center of his chest. One bump of his stomach could knock her down.

"Stanley, this whole situation's as wrong as a two-headed pig, and you know it," she replies. "Now, what's it goin' to take to get Eva out of here while she awaits trial? She's no risk to the community. She has no prior convictions. Far from it! She's a seventeen-year-old girl, for Christ's sake. Let her go home to her family."

"I can't believe my ears, Cora! What does yer father think? He can't possibly support this!"

"I don't care what my father thinks, Stanley. You only like him 'cause he's rich, and he pays you to ignore the illegal shenanigans goin' on at the company. Besides, I'm goin' to be a journalist and stand on my own two feet. I won't need his help much longer. I don't even like the man!"

"You can call me 'Sheriff Pearl.' I work for a livin', and this here's my work," he says. "And, you? A journalist? In what life are you ever gonna be a journalist? You know any lady journalists 'round these parts?"

"Will you let Eva go home to her family or keep her here and starve her?" Cora asks. "I can get my lady friends from prayer circle to stand outside with picket signs demandin' her release if that's the way you want it. I can ask Catherine to join us!"

"Don't you threaten me, Cora! Yer just a little slice of nothin' with no say in anythin'," the sheriff hisses. "I'll let this girl out when and if her lawyer files a proper request with Judge O'Leary. If she has a lawyer, you tell him ta get busy, an' if the judge orders it, I'll let 'er go, under supervision. That is until she's found guilty an' comes back for her hangin'. Now, if you'll excuse me," he says and turns to Humphrey. "I'm headin' out. I heard them Kruger boys been stealin' from Mrs. Martinelli's melon patch again."

With his cowboy hat in hand, he throws open the front door and steps outside.

"Good riddance," Cora mutters. "Don't pay him any heed, Eva. Arguin' with someone with a lima bean for a brain ain't no use."

"Cora, about the lawyer—we don't have enough money," I say.

"Goodness gracious! Don't you worry your pretty little head; I'll be handlin' that."

"I don't know what to say."

"I wouldn't do this if I didn't want to, Eva, and I don't wanna hear another word about it." She sits down in the chair and pulls out her notebook and pencil. "Last time we talked, you told me a little about your life in Mariposa. What happened after you left? Did things back home turn out the way you thought they would?"

"Pancho Villa's men burned the ranch and stole our horses and cattle. I hate to think what might have happened if we'd stayed there. Thankfully, they didn't find my family in their little place near the coffee field. They're still in hiding. Three people in town got murdered."

"You've been through some awful times, haven't you?"

"Abuelito once said, 'Challenges are chances in disguise.'" I smile. "He always knew the right thing to say in every situation."

"You believe that, even now, with everythin' that's goin' on?"

"I'm tryin' to hear his voice in my head, to stay positive, but I must admit, I've been feeling pretty low. Honestly, I still can't believe this is happening to me."

k k k

Josiah drags an unconscious man across the floor and into the next cell, muttering something about "gettin' pickled an' startin' a fight at Slick's Saloon."

"Damn you, Frank. I was fixin' to take a nap before Slick brung ya here," Josiah whines.

Within ten minutes, both men snore loudly.

I search for stars through the bars of the narrow window near the top of my cell. Not a single one. Clouds blanket the sky. *God, do you see me through there?*

The front door creaks open. My breath catches in my throat.

The sheriff lumbers in and searches through his keys, muttering to himself. I grab the bucket I use as a toilet and throw up.

"Sheriff, I . . . I didn't know you were coming. Please you have to believe me! I wasn't even there when Ramona Healy died. I'm no killer; I swear it!" I cry.

"Don't talk back ta me, girlie! Doc Morley says ya killed her, and thass good enough fer me."

The lock turns.

His head bobs up and down as if a metal coil replaced the bones in his neck. He yanks me to my feet so hard that my head whips backward, and I bite my tongue. Blood coats my mouth.

I beat him with my fists and thrash my arms and legs. "Don't do this," I sob.

God, do you see me?

"Shuddup er or I'll go fine that pretty sister a-yourss. She's a sexy thing, that one," he says.

"Stop!"

He turns me around, holds my shoulders against the wall with his stubby fat hands and kisses my neck like a wolf devouring a rabbit.

Blood trickles down my chin.

God, can't you see me?

His hot breath coats my skin.

What do I do? What do I do? God, do you see me?

"*¡Me lastimas!* You're hurting me! Josiah, help!" I scream.

"Dohn fight me, li'l mamasita. I'm naw so bad," he says, reaching around to squeeze my breast.

I swing my leg until it connects with the bucket. Urine and vomit fly across the floor.

"*¡Quítate!* Get off me!" I scream.

I lift my right knee and shove my leg backward with every ounce of strength I have. My foot smashes his shin.

"You little bitch!" he screams, twists me around and swings at my head.

I duck and scramble to the other side of the cell.

He pitches forward, hits the wall face first and stands there, heaving in and out.

"Sheriff, you can stop this," I sob. "You're a man of the law! And a husband and a father! What if Pauline found out?"

His jaw hangs open as he catches his breath.

"They gone . . . leff me," he says, resting his head on his bent arm. "Mah wife ain't got no feelin' fer me; an' my daughter dohn love me neither. Wishes she had a different daddy."

"Sheriff, why dohn-choo come on outta there, an' I'll help ya outside," says Josiah, walking towards us. "You dohn really wanna hurt this young lady, now do ya?"

"Naw, I dohn wanna hurt nobody," he mumbles. "I'm a man o' the law," he says, wiping his hand across his nose and mouth.

Josiah opens the cell and puts his shoulder under the sheriff's arm to prop him up. The sheriff tilts slightly to his left and closes his eyes.

"Wass goin' on here?" the sheriff asks, his eyes unfocused and confused.

"Time to gitcha home," says Josiah. "I'll keep yer ole horse Shorty here, so you dohn fall off an' break somethin'. Yer gonna have to walk home this time. C'mon, I gotcha."

"Shorty like apples," the sheriff murmurs.

Josiah shakes his head in disgust before leading the sheriff out.

When Josiah comes back in, he stands in the doorway, shifting from one foot to the other. "I hope you can forgive me, Miss. My wife's fixin' to have a baby, and I can't be sure he won't hurt her. Please believe me; I really am sorry 'bout all this. I'm a God-fearin' man."

"I'm glad you came in when you did, Josiah." I almost want to thank him for helping me, but I don't. He let things go on far too long.

He brings in a mop and bucket and cleans the smelly mess off the floor. I don't even care.

I ask him for a dry cloth, a wet rag and a bar of soap. I apply pressure to my tongue with the cloth until the bleeding stops, then scrub every part of me the sheriff touched until my skin turns red.

Maybe God saw me and just didn't care.

♢ ♢ ♢

The morning sun shines through the little window. I sit on the floor, staring at my cold oatmeal breakfast when the front door opens.

"What're y'all doin' here?" the sheriff says. "I told ya before, this is a government institution, an' you got no rights here. What is it you people dohn understand?"

"Sheriff, we stay only short time," Papá says from outside. "My wife bring you sweet breads she make for you. Please, sir. We ask only short time."

"Yer kine don't get no favors here," he replies.

"Hello, Stanley." It's Doc Taylor! "Good morning, everyone. I'm here to see Evangelina. How is she today?"

"We not see her," Mamá says, her tone low and flat.

"Why is that?" Doc Taylor asks.

"It's against the policy, Doc," the sheriff responds. "I've already explained it ta these fools."

"And what policy is that?" Doc Taylor asks.

"The policy I'm referrin' to," he snaps.

"That's fine then, Stanley. Why don't you show it to me?" Doc Taylor counters.

"Show it? Shit, I don't know where ta find it in writin', if that's whatcha mean."

"Clean up the language, Stanley," Doc Taylor says. "I'm sure you don't mean to speak in front of Mrs. de León as if you're in some pool hall. Now, if we can't see the policy that precludes parents from seeing their wrongfully accused children in this place, then we'll head on back. I'm sure they're worried about her welfare, despite the tireless effort that I'm sure you and your staff are making to ensure her well-being."

"The girl is guilty, an' the whole town knows it. Nobody gohn believe the doctor in Fox Grove killed Ramona Healy. By the time he got to the Healy's, the woman was nearly dead from the poison this girl gave her an' some spell she was puttin' . . ."

"Thank you, Sheriff Pearl. We'll show ourselves in," Doc Taylor says.

"I'm givin' ya five minutes, and then I'm throwin' ya out. Like I said, these ain't visitin' hours," he grumbles.

"When is visit hours?" Papá asks.

"When I say they are!" the sheriff shouts.

"You have in writing?" Papá asks.

殂 殂 殂

The waist-length braid that Mamá usually assembles in a neat bun each morning hangs down her back. Tears fall as she approaches the bars of my cell and reaches in to grab my hand.

"*M'ija*, I so happy to see you. How you feel?" Mamá says in English.

"Ah fill fine," I say, my swollen tongue throbbing.

The muscles in Mamá's face tighten. "Why you sound like this?"

"I tripped and bit my thung. Iss nothing to worry about."

"*Ay, m'ijita.* Oh, dear child," Mamá cries.

"Let me take a look," Doctor Taylor says, coming in closer.

"Pleess dohn make a futh . . . iss awready healin," I say. "You can't put thtitches in a thung, anyway."

"You're right," Doc Taylor says reluctantly. "An injured tongue is more of an inconvenience than anything. It'll heal quickly," he tells Mamá. "Evangelina, has Cora Cavanaugh come by yet?" he asks.

"From the fabric company? Many from our church work there," says Mamá.

"Yes, Cavanaugh Fine Fabrics. Cora and her father have been my patients for years. Cora's taken quite an interest in Evangelina and intends to lay out her case in the newspaper. People need to know Evangelina's side of the story. If Cora can get more community support, it could put pressure on Judge O'Leary."

An angry V-shape forms between Mamá's eyes.

"Judge O'Leary," she huffs. "*¡Qué monstruo!* What a monster!"

Papá raises his eyebrows in surprise.

"*Es la verdad. Ese señor no es amigo de los Mexicanos.* It's the truth. That man is no friend of Mexicans," Mamá continues. "He puts Gregorio and Felipe Falcón in jail because they walk in a man's field to get to work, and he say they steal a cow. *Puras mentiras,* nothing but lies." She pauses and covers her mouth. "They find Gregorio and Felipe hang from a tree two days later," she says and turns away. "Their Mamá still cries. They was good boys."

"Such an outrage," says Doc Taylor, shaking his head. "I have no tolerance for leaders who fail to protect all citizens. We must secure an attorney to represent Evangelina in court, one with courage and grit. Cora and I are working on that."

"Thank you, Doc. Cora thed she hath some medical questions for you," I tell him.

"I don't know how much help I'll be. If I had done the autopsy, I might be able to prove your innocence. As it is, I'm only able to report on what you told me."

Mamá and Papá turn to me with a familiar look of confusion on their faces. They need me to interpret.

"Doctor Morley from Fox Grove did the autopsy—the study of the patient's body to find out why she died. He was there when it happened. I was not," I say in Spanish.

"Doctor Morley could not have been objective, given the circumstances and gravity of this case. I'm exploring other options, none of which I can comment on yet. Of course, I will vouch for your character and competence," Doc Taylor says. "I'll cite the many cases you've worked on with me. We'll bring in patients you've treated who'll sing your praises in court or at least have their written statements. The medical practices you applied with Mrs. Healy, without a doubt, did not cause her death. Something went wrong after you left, and only Jedidiah Morley knows what it is."

I feel nauseous just thinking about the autopsy. I'm going to have to tell Doc Taylor about the oleander sometime, but what if it proves that I'm guilty?

CHAPTER 5

Talk American

Elsa asks for two chairs. Humphrey gets them without a single unkind word. He brings the chairs over and smiles at her sweetly as he sets them down. He may not like Mexicans, but she's the Mexican exception.

"Here you go, Miss," he says. "Let me know if there's anything else I can get you."

"Please give the second chair to my sister," Elsa tells him.

I'm not surprised that Elsa walked in without question or disapproval, when just yesterday, my parents could only come in with Doc as their keeper.

My sister is so beautiful that people stare at her, then get embarrassed if she happens to notice. With her waist-length shiny black hair, cat-like, gold-brown eyes, long lashes and tiny freckles across the top of her nose, she's pretty enough for one of those advertisements in a magazine. Except magazines don't use brown-skinned ladies. And if her skin didn't exclude her, her accent surely would. "Go back to Mexico!" some people yell when we speak accented English. Or, "Talk American!" if we speak Spanish.

It's not like she's pretty, and I'm ugly. I'm not. I also have long black hair, but not as shiny as hers. My eyes and skin are brown, but I don't think they're exceptional in any way. A person might describe me as pleasant looking with no unusual feature other than I'm short. It doesn't bother me. I don't wear make-up or jewelry—too much money and too much trouble!

"I'm sorry I haven't come by until today," Elsa says, switching to Spanish. "I'm working two jobs now, from seven in the morning to nine at night. I assume Mamá and Papá mentioned it?"

"No—why are you working two jobs?"

Elsa dabs her forehead with a handkerchief. "It's hot and stuffy in here."

"Elsa, why are you working two jobs?"

"Ummm—Papá got fired from the brick factory last week."

"Why?"

"I shouldn't have told you," she says softly.

"Why did they fire him? Because of me?"

Elsa nods. "Fox Grove, Seneca, Goldendale—Ramona Healy's death has people very upset. Doctor Morley tells lies to anyone who'll listen, and you know how the gossip is around here. People are taking sides: the Anglos mostly on his side, everybody else on yours. Some of the brick factory's biggest customers threatened to go to the masonry in Goldendale if the owner didn't fire Papá," she says.

"But Papá has nothing to do with this!"

"He's looking for work as a horse trainer, a blacksmith, a butcher—he'll do just about anything. He studied with a tutor for ten years as a boy and ran a giant cattle ranch in Mexico! But no one cares about that around here. If he has to take a job in the fields, he will, but those jobs pay so little. He's worried we won't be able to make our rent payment."

"Doctor Taylor will loan us money," I offer but hate the sound of the words coming out of my mouth.

"Papá would never accept it. We will find a way through this."

"Tell me about this second job of yours."

"I'm at the dress shop most of the day, the same as before, and Señora Gómez hired me at the *tortillería* in the evening. She's a cranky old lady, but work is work."

I cover my face with my hands. "This is all my fault," I wince.

"Nonsense!" Elsa says. "None of this is your fault. You shouldn't have been arrested in the first place!"

Elsa pulls a section of hair forward and pinches off the split ends, a nervous habit. It's better than mine. I gave up biting my fingernails years ago but started again when I got thrown into this mess.

"Have you heard anything about Selim?" I ask.

"Like what?"

"When he's coming back."

"He travels pretty far out into the hills," she offers. "You're worried?"

"It's hard not to," I say. "I'll feel better when he's back."

"When are you going to tell Mamá and Papá that he's practically courting you?"

"I've been waiting for a sign that Mamá and Papá will accept him, but that means that I could be waiting forever."

"What would you do if they forbid it? Break it off with Selim?"

"No," I say. "I may not be here much longer, Elsa, and that's the truth. I want to be with Selim in the time I have left, and if our parents find out, then so be it."

"Don't say that!" Elsa says. "You *will* get out of here."

"You okay, Miss?" Humphrey says, suddenly standing next to my sister. He rests his hand on her shoulder. "Can I get you some tea?"

You've never offered me anything, you ass, and take your hand off my sister's shoulder!

"Please remove your hand," Elsa replies coolly. "And, we would like some water if you'd be so kind." She looks at his nametag. "Officer Chestnut, sir."

He looks at me with the face of a pouting child.

"I didn't ask if that killer wanted anything," he grumbles on his way through the doorway.

"I will ask about Selim's return," Elsa assures me.

"I haven't told you everything," I blurt out.

"Oh? About what?"

"Selim and I made each other a promise the day of my *quinceañera*."

"What kind of promise?"

"To get married." *There. I said it.*

A vein pops out on her forehead when she's agitated. I see it now, twitching.

"And you've been keeping this a secret from me? I thought we tell each other everything."

"I've known that I love him since the day we met in school. People would have laughed if I said it out loud. A thirteen-year-old falling in love? It sounds crazy, even to me."

"You're a Mexican Catholic, and he's a Lebanese Muslim. People will never accept it on either side. I wish it weren't like that, but it is."

"Which is why we haven't told anyone."

Humphrey brings us each a metal cup, hers with ice, mine lukewarm.

"Ya know, I been a sheriff's deputy fer almost a year now. Iss a good job, an' I make enough ta treat a pretty lady right," he says, casting one eye on Elsa. "We could never marry or nothin' like that, ya know, 'cause a who ya are, but we could have some fun together in private."

The vein in Elsa's forehead pulsates.

Humphrey waits a few seconds, clears his throat and slinks off, cursing.

"Can you believe that?" Elsa says.

"Unfortunately, yes, I can. That man's not too smart."

"Here, you take this one," she says, handing me her cup. "I can get cold water at home. Evangelina, I remember your *quinceañera* like it was yesterday. I don't know how you managed to 'make a promise' with so many people around."

ॐ ॐ ॐ

My family did not have enough money to buy a dress or the fabric to make one. I looked like a ten-year-old in the neighbor's daughter's ruffled sunflower-yellow dress, but at my size, most women's dresses hung on me like a potato sack. I took out the strips of rag I'd wrapped in my wet hair the night before, which left me with long sausage-like curls. Next came the stockings and fancy lace-up white shoes with a big yellow bow where the ankle meets the foot.

Mamá and Papá presented me to the congregation at a special Mass. They announced that I had come of age and wanted to dedicate my life to God and the Catholic Church. The ceremony signified I was eligible for marriage—to another Mexican, which no one said because they didn't have to—the people knew it as an expectation, a rule.

I stood by the altar with Father Amadeo. He recited a special blessing in my honor and offered me the Holy Eucharist.

We celebrated afterward at the house.

Our guests, dressed in their finest church clothes, ate in the crowded backyard and sang "Cielito Lindo" as Papá strummed and picked his guitar. When the next song began, I left quietly through the front door and met Selim behind the old mesquite tree in the little park around the corner. The air smelled of lilac and magnolia blooms. The sun warmed us from head to foot.

Selim looked around to make sure we were alone. He undid the top two buttons of his shirt, slid my right hand inside and pressed it to his chest. Tingles washed over me as his heart beat against my palm.

"My heart is yours," he said. "Forever."

It was then we made our promise. We talked of marriage, children and moving into a place of our own one day.

That night, I started climbing out a window to meet him, and many nights after that. I knew it was wrong, but being with him lifted me up more than the guilt weighed me down.

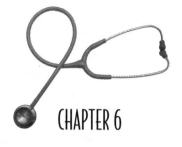

CHAPTER 6

Shrewd Negotiator

I sit in the corner and begin dozing off. In that foggy state between awake and asleep, a memory slips in.

My parents took us to a bullfight in Mexico City when I was five. We arrived early and walked behind the grand-stands to pass the time. Fat raindrops plopped into fat pud-dles. The dirt ground turned into mud, the air grew thick as spoiled milk, and the wet doubled the animal stench. A boy fed a carrot to a horse and spoke sweetly to it as a mother does with her baby. Two cowboys, a thin one and a thick one, sat in chairs facing a dusty mirror with dirty raindrops sliding toward the bottom. The men laughed as they put on their wide-brimmed hats to block the rain from their paint-ed clown faces.

I looked through the fence boards nearby and saw a white and tan bull pacing from side to side. Its ribs showed through its enormous chest, and greenish-yellow mucus dripped from its snout. I stared at it, unable to turn away. My heart hurt as if someone was squeezing it in a vise grip.

The bull begged me with its sad eyes to set it free.

Mamá said the bullfight would start soon.

Don't let them kill it! I screamed. It's hurt no one! It wants to go home! It wants its mother!

Papá pried my fingers off the fence door as I tried to climb up and unhook the latch. My oldest sister, Francisca agreed to stay with me outside the plaza as the crowd thundered in approval each time the bullfighter waved his cape, aimed his banderilla and struck his target.

How could someone, in a position of power, torture and kill a terrified, trapped, blameless animal?

🖢 🖢 🖢

I sit on the same stool Humphrey brought in before, at Cora's insistence. She sits outside the bars next to an impressive-looking woman she mentioned to my parents, and they, in turn, mentioned to me. I've heard of the woman but never imagined we'd have reason to meet.

Teresita Olmos wears a high-collared white blouse and a floor-length brown skirt. A fringed white shawl embroidered with yellow, orange and red flowers linked by brown branches and green leaves drapes across her shoulders. Her white hair falls in two braids, down to her waist. She leans oddly to one side in the chair as if someone folded her backbone into a boomerang shape. Her raven-black eyes look at me as if she's studying my insides.

"My name is María Teresa Olmos, but you may call me Teresita," she says in perfect English. "I've come from Loma, forty-five miles northwest of Seneca. Cora's description of your case was enough to bring me here, but there are many details to fill in. If the circumstances and facts are as Cora described, I will do all that I can to correct this injustice. I have numerous resources from which to draw that will aid in your defense."

"It is an honor to meet you, Señora," I say.

"The honor is mine, and please, call me Teresita."
She takes off her shawl and lays it across her lap. "Cora
tells me they're feeding you slop barely good enough for
a hog. I brought you a boiled egg, plums, two small
loaves of bread and a piece of cheese." She picks up a
paper sack sitting by her feet and hands it to me
between the bars. "Please help yourself. You look thin as
a broomstick in that dress, if that's what they call it."

I take the bag from her hand. "Bless you," I reply,
knowing I'll give most of it to Josiah.

The hairs on my arms and neck stand at attention.
Teresita's family is legendary. They moved from central
Mexico to Texas long before the revolution began. They
owned land on both sides of the border. When her father
died, she and her brothers turned their small cattle
ranch into an empire with the brothers running the
daily operation and her running the business side of
things. True gentlemen call her a shrewd negotiator.
The rest aren't so kind.

I set the bag of food aside.

Cora leans in. "Eva, Teresita brings good news. She's
hired someone to defend you!"

"A brilliant young man named Joaquín Castañeda is
on his way now," Teresita explains. "I spoke with him
before I left Loma. He was finishing a case against a sev-
enty-year-old man named Alberto Cantú arrested for
picking blueberries on the side of a road. They would
have hanged him if Joaquín had not convinced the
court to issue a sentence more proportionate to the
crime, in this case, a week in the Loma Jail. In most
cases, Mexicans and Tejanos accused of crimes in this
state have no representation and don't understand the
legal proceedings. Many speak little to no English, don't

know their rights and cannot aid in their defense. The organization I founded fights for those like Señor Cantú who cannot fight for themselves."

"It's the same here," Cora says. "I got a hold of the city records and studied 'em myself. I only had to twist a few arms," she says as she slides her thumb up and down her upturned fingertips as if she's counting out dollar bills. "The Mexicans who've gone through Judge O'Leary's court didn't even get a trial. They got arrested and sentenced, and that was it. And it's not just the Mexicans. It's the Negroes, the Orientals, the Arabs. A couple of years back, the City Council tried kickin' the foreigners' kids outta school as a way of tryin' to hold them down."

"They're doing it successfully in cities across the country," Teresita says. "Members of my organization are trying to stop it through legal means. Now, let's get to your story, Evangelina, if you don't mind. Do you prefer Eva or Evangelina?"

"Thank you for asking; I prefer Evangelina, the same name as my mother's mother."

"Oh Lord, you should have told me," Cora says.

"I just did," I say, smiling.

"Cora mentioned that a local physician has been an important part of your life since coming to Seneca," says Teresita. "And he'll be a key witness in your defense."

"I met Doc Taylor four years ago when my *Tía* Cristina delivered a stillborn baby. After a visit to check on her and the surviving baby, Tito, he asked if I would clean his house and clinic a few days a week after school. He worked long hours, and his mother, Agnes, could not get around very well. He paid me generously."

"And how does one go from being a housekeeper to practicing medicine?" Teresita asks.

"I became interested in medicine soon after I met Doc Taylor. As my English improved, I started asking questions like how to diagnose and treat illnesses, how his equipment worked and why he used different medicines.

"His wife, Susanna, and baby, Evelyn, both died in childbirth. If Evelyn had lived, she would have been the same age as me now. I think that is why he's always treated me so special, like a daughter."

"That is quite a story, Evangelina," Teresita says. "You were fortunate to meet such a man."

She stands up, tips her head from side to side and arches her shoulders back. No stretch can change her posture, however. I want to say something but think better of it.

"I'm sure you are wondering about my crooked back," she says, eyeing me carefully.

"My apologies. I did not mean to stare."

"No need to apologize," she replies. "I've learned to live with it. Why don't I save you the suspense? Years ago, I had a heated disagreement with someone on our ranch. When I'd had enough of him, I threw myself over the back of the nearest horse, an untrained horse. It bucked, I fell and broke my back. I don't suffer much discomfort now, but I do have to stretch occasionally, or my muscles punish me later." She sits back down.

"I'm sorry to hear that," I say.

"Joaquín will go into greater depth with you, Evangelina," she says. "He'll get every detail from you and tell you what you can expect in the legal proceedings. I'll work with Cora to get the story into *The Gazette* and every other paper in this area. I'll also make sure it runs in *La Prensa de Loma*, a Spanish newspaper, and perhaps others. We have thousands of supporters who can push for your acquittal. Joaquín will help with the rest, but you're going to have to fight. Are you ready?"

"Yes, of course, Señora."

The front door swings open and bangs the wall behind it.

"I'm looking for Evangelina de León."

"Yer not allowed in here," Humphrey says.

"I am her friend. Please, sir."

"You can call me Deputy Chestnut," Humphrey says.

"Who is that?" Cora asks me.

"The man I love," I whisper. *Why did I say that? Did Humphrey hear?* "Please don't tell anyone!" I plead. "It's a secret."

In a blink, Cora's out front.

"Humphrey, there is no reason this young man cannot see Evangelina. You let Señora Olmos and me back there; why not him?" Cora asks.

"She was with you, so a'course, I let her in. You gonna stay with this guy, too?" Humphrey asks. "'Cause I ain't lettin' no Arab go back there by hisself."

"Excuse me, Deputy Chestnut?" Teresita says. "I am certain there are no official rules saying which law-abiding citizens can and cannot visit prisoners in the middle of the day. If you care to challenge me on this, I'll have every *mexicano* within fifty miles here by Wednesday to lawfully express their displeasure with your actions. Who knows? Many of them may like it so well they'll decide to set up homes here in your charming little town."

"Oh, go on then," he says. "Cora, you take 'im back there, but he can't stay no more than a few minutes!"

"Follow me," Cora says.

Selim rushes forward. "Evangelina! I just heard! Are you all right?"

"We'll be back. I'm sure you have a lot to catch up on," Cora says.

"Don't forget what I said, young man," Teresita tells Humphrey. "We will be back in less than thirty minutes. Evangelina's visitor won't cause any disruption."

"I'm gonna let Sheriff Pearl know about this," Humphrey says. "And he ain't gonna like it."

"Excellent," Teresita replies, unphased. "I look forward to meeting this sheriff of yours. He has a reputation well beyond Seneca as a racist and violent man. The twenty thousand readers of *La Prensa* will be interested in the stories I collect from area residents about his despicable and unlawful behavior. One such person is the daughter of the Loma Mayor, Nicolás Montemayor. He and his family lived in Seneca for many years and owned Montemayor Ironworks, a successful business with locations across the state. Have you heard of him? He and his daughter, Anarosa, live in Loma now, and we've become well-acquainted. She tells me that as a teenager, Sheriff Pearl caused her physical and emotional pain. Coming from such a well-regarded family, I'm sure the story of the sheriff's violent acts would have credibility and be of interest to our readers across Texas and beyond."

Humphrey rubs the back of his neck and swallows. His pointy Adam's apple slides up and down.

"Would ya say that again?" Humphrey asks.

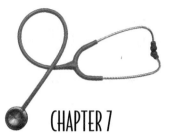

CHAPTER 7

Too Deep in the Ocean

Teardrops land on my un-washed, stale-smelling gown. Selim wears boots, a white and blue striped shirt and thick, tan work pants held up by brown suspenders. His loopy black curls frame his strong jaw and handsome features.

"Selim! You can't imagine how worried I've been about you!" I cry.

"Shhh, shhh . . ." he says softly. He takes my hands and moves his thumbs in little circles across the tops. His brown eyes glisten. I'm not the only one crying. "Had I known this was going to happen, I never would have left on such a long trip. How long have you been in here?"

"Nine days."

"I didn't know, or I would have come earlier. I'm so sorry."

"It's not your fault. Who would have ever thought I'd wind up here?"

"The wagon broke down on the way home, and it took a week to get the parts we needed. I promise I'll stay with you until this is over, no matter what my parents want."

"What your parents want?"

"No matter what my father *says*. We're supposed to leave again after we restock our supplies. But I won't go!"

I don't see Humphrey, so I take a chance and lean towards Selim. I stroke his cheek with the back of my hand. If only he could wrap himself around me, I'd feel safe again—safe as a pearl in an oyster shell, too deep in the ocean for anyone to find. *If only I could be a pearl.*

"Hey! Whaddya think yer doin'? You step away from there!" Humphrey screeches. "How do I know yer not slippin' her some kinda weapon? And, no touchin' her. This ain't no brothel. You do what I say, or I'll tell the whole town that an Arab's lovin' up on a seventeen-year-old jailbird."

Somebody's already been lovin' up on me in this hell on earth.

"Okay, okay," Selim says calmly, stepping back.

"An' dohn try no more monkeyshine," Humphrey orders. "I'll be listenin'."

I wait until I hear his desk chair scrape across the floor.

"The waiting has been hard," I say. "I'm so relieved that you're back."

"What happened?" he asks. "My mother wouldn't tell me much. I'll understand if you don't want to talk about it right now. We can . . ."

"No, it's fine. You need to know."

I tell Selim almost everything.

"What happened to the baby?" he asks.

"He survived."

"What happened to the neighbor who took you over there?" he asks hopefully.

"She left soon after I got there."

Selim stuffs his hands in his pockets and paces. "So, she can't be a witness for you."

"The only witness who knows what I did before Doctor Morely got there is dead," I say.

ॐ ॐ ॐ

Mamá and Papá know that Selim helped me during my first year of school in Seneca. I was thirteen years old and an easy target for the bullies to pick on. Older, taller and more muscular, no one bothered me when he was around. After my first year, he left to work with his father, but by then, my English had improved, and I could talk back to the bullies if I wanted to. But I never did.

If my parents knew about us, they'd forbid me from seeing him, and I don't know if they'd ever get over the shame it would bring on our family's good name.

Selim's not a devout Muslim, but to the outside world, he is. He goes along with the practices and traditions to make his parents happy but admits that he's not sure about Allah or God or any other spiritual being. He says that too many things don't make sense. Like, why do some good people suffer and die while bad ones go unpunished? Why are there so many religions, each believing they are right and frowning on those who think otherwise? They can't all be right, Selim says. Some use their faith as an excuse for hate and violence—and I can't deny it. How could a higher being allow it if that being is all-powerful?

Just because I've attended church my whole life doesn't mean I have all the answers, and I told him so. In the beginning, I struggled with Selim's lack of faith.

Would this become a problem as husband and wife? How would we raise our children?

The answer came back to love, God's most powerful and enduring gift. Selim's caring, generous and hard-working, and he does what he does because he is who he is, not because some higher power commands it. How many people say all the right things and do all the wrong things? That's not him. His actions match his beliefs—always.

Selim told his parents about us. They vowed to disown him if we married and ordered him to never speak of it again. They even threatened to move the family back to New York City, where they lived before coming to Seneca. They said they'd stop at nothing to keep us apart.

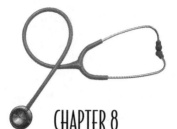

CHAPTER 8

Serious as a Murder Charge

The Seneca Jail has probably never had a female in here this long. Josiah breaks the rules and takes me to the outhouse, but only when it's dark. He can't risk someone seeing us, so he leaves the lantern behind. He feels the way with careful steps, and I follow closely. I persuaded him to take the handcuffs off after the first week.

I do everything I can to hold my bladder and bowels until Josiah arrives. Otherwise, if it absolutely can't be helped, I relieve myself in the bucket in the corner of my cell. I yell to Humphrey when I need privacy, and he yells back to me from the front office with promises not to look.

Most times, he looks anyway.

Change what you can; let go of the rest. That's what Abuelito used to say. The trouble is figuring out what I can change and what's out of reach. What do I want to fight for, and what's not worth the fight? It can be hard to know, but one thing is clear: I must fight for freedom, but how I if I'm stuck in here?

&ð &ð &ð

The mat they gave me is urine-soaked, lumpy and covered with mildew and holes on the bottom. Cora paid Humphrey to bring me a second smelly, lumpy mat to put on top of the first one. I share them with mice that come after dark and make off with the stuffing to build their nests. I can hear them scratching inside the walls. I sleep sitting up most nights.

I'm not allowed a blanket because they don't want me to hang myself. When I feel I must lie down, I lie on my side facing the open doorway, to watch for the sheriff.

&ᔥ &ᔥ &ᔥ

The young man dressed in a smokey-gray three-piece suit with a dark blue tie smiles, revealing a dimple in his left cheek. He removes his felt hat and bows with one arm behind his back. He has wavy black hair, freshly cut, and his eyes make me blink and look again: one eye is dark blue, and the other is blue on the top half and brown on the bottom.

"Good day, Señorita de León. My name is Joaquín Castañeda. Are you comfortable speaking in Spanish?"

"Yes, please," I reply.

"It will keep our conversations more private, no? I've agreed to represent you against Haller County in the death of Ramona Healy. I'm honored to meet you but regret that it's under such unfortunate circumstances."

"Please call me Evangelina."

"I will always be candid with you, Evangelina, so you must know that I am not an attorney as defined by law. There are no Mexican-American attorneys in the United States, to my knowledge. Still, I know the law and have worked alongside a highly successful attorney in Mexico

City for three years. While I don't have the title, I've been winning cases across the state for the past two years."

"The title itself is not important to me. Your ability to get me out of here is."

"Your case is one of many La Liga is fighting. Innocent Mexicans and Tejanos are under attack, and it's my privilege to get justice for you and others when I can. It's become my passion and life's work."

"Sir, I must also be truthful with you," I say. "My family would have had the money to pay you in Mexico, but our circumstances are different now."

"Your friend, Cora, offered to pay, but there is no need. My services are paid for by La Liga Protectora Mexicana in Loma, Texas. Donations from across the US and Mexico fund our work."

"What is La Liga Protectora Mexicana?" I ask.

"Yes, good idea. Let's start with what we do and why we agreed to represent you. The harassment and murder of innocent Mexicans and Tejanos have become commonplace across Texas and the greater Southwest, especially in the last five years. The perpetrators can be ordinary citizens turned vigilantes. Without the benefit of an official charge or trial, innocent Mexicans and Tejanos get arrested, thrown in jail and executed, although many are tortured or murdered on the spot and left to rot where they fall."

"That's murder! Why are their killers not arrested?"

"The Texas Rangers don't just look the other way when these violent acts occur, they commit them at increasingly alarming rates, and they answer to no one. Teresita Olmos formed La Liga because we are more powerful when we work together. The board members are newspaper publishers, legal experts and prominent business owners, and we have a growing number of volunteers.

"In your case, they arrested you but have no proof that a crime occurred," Joaquín says. "Doctor Morley says he has autopsy results that prove his assertions, but his findings are suspect. You are exactly the kind of person the league wants to defend. This will be the first time we've gotten involved in a female's trial. So you see, it's a bit unusual and could bring substantial publicity and change in the broader sense as well as justice for you."

"The judge, the sheriff, the doctor who accused me say I'm guilty, and most Senecans agree," I say. "It may be impossible to win my freedom here."

"Evangelina, I am sorry if I alarmed you. The facts are disturbing, yes, but we have an excellent record of restoring justice to those we represent. I cannot promise to clear you of all charges—that would be irresponsible. I can promise that I will fight for you with everything I have and bring the resources of La Liga to bear. I may be young, but I can be a tough opponent in court."

The look on his face is not one of arrogance. It's as serious as a murder charge.

   扛 扛 扛

After two hours discussing how Joaquín will build the defense's case, he leaves, promising to return soon. I spend the rest of the day and night thinking about the things I have the power to change. One of them has everything to do with Selim.

   扛 扛 扛

"I'm here!" Cora announces.

She removes her wide-brimmed bright blue hat with pink fringe and smooths the folds of her ankle-length pink dress with its blue- and pink-flowered belt. "Has Joaquín come by to see you yet?"

Humphrey steps in. "I let 'im come in here this mornin', if that's what yer askin'," he says. "I ain't never seen no Mexican dressed fancy like that before. Who does he think he is?"

"I'm not askin' you; I'm askin' her. And stop listenin' to our conversation. Don't you have somethin' to do?" Cora retorts. "Try readin' a book."

"Readin's for lazy bums who ain't got nothin' better to do," he says. "Real men don't read books."

"That explains a lot," I say before I can stop myself.

"Who asked you?" he snarls at me, then squints at Cora. "Ya act all high and mighty, Cora, but yer just as dumb as I am," Humphrey grumbles. "I mean, yer dumb. Not like me. I ain't dumb," he says and shuffles out. "But that jailbird's dumb. Everybody knowed that," he yells from his desk.

"His momma must'a dropped him on his head," Cora offers. "And I like hearin' you talk back to that do-do bird. I knew you had some sass in you somewhere!"

"Joaquín came by earlier, and we had a good talk," I tell her.

"I met him myself yesterday. He seems bright, and he's got good experience. He's easy on the eyes, too," she adds with a whistle. "In fact, he's downright gorgeous!"

"He looks young," I add, "not much older than Selim, and Selim's twenty-one."

"Mister Castañeda's twenty-five. I asked him myself. And speaking of Selim, that most exquisite specimen of a man, I brought you a present." She walks away and opens the front door. "Don't you give him any guff, Humphrey," she says sternly. "I'll be next door havin' a cup o' coffee. I'll even bring you back some food, *if* you don't give these two any trouble. Do I have your word?"

Humphrey escorts Selim in, holding him by the upper arm as if Selim's a four-year-old in for a spanking.

"I see that scowl on your face, Humphrey," Cora says. "I'll take that as a 'yes.' Now, what can I get you?"

"Liver and onions. And some'a that Lady Baltimore cake," Humphrey answers. "But it's gonna take more than food to let this Arab stay. Gimme ten cents."

"I gave you a nickel the last time I was here, and liver and onions stink like cow pies. If I hear you haven't treated them kindly and stayed out of their business, I'll toss that pile of innards you call food in the garbage."

Cora turns to Selim and me. "And you two? What would you like to eat?"

"Thank you for the offer, ma'am, but I just ate," Selim says.

"An she dohn need nothin'," Humphrey says, pointing at me. "I gave 'er potato mash this mornin'."

"I'll bring you whatever they have on special," Cora says to me. "I'm tryin' to make sure you eat at least one decent meal a day. Besides, you're lookin' skinnier all the time. You gotta eat, darlin'! I'm worried about you!"

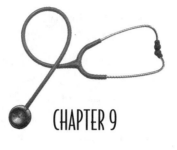

CHAPTER 9

Strong-Willed

Selim waits until we're alone, then sits on the chair Humphrey brought for Cora.

"How are you today?" he asks.

"I'm better now that you're here," I say, reaching for his hand.

But he doesn't reach back.

I pull my arm back, puzzled. "What's wrong? We held hands last time you were here."

"I know, and I thought about that after I left. Someone could have walked in, like your parents or Humphrey. It's not that I don't want to hold your hand; I do," he says. "But not now. It's risky, and you're in enough trouble as it is."

"Our whole relationship has been a risk," I whisper. "Why else would we sneak around and lie all the time?"

"Yes, but we did everything in secret," murmurs Selim. "Doing it in the wide-open is not the same. I don't want to make things worse for . . ."

"I disagree," I interrupt. "I want to get married. I mean it. We can do it in here, late at night. Josiah won't stop us. It's my dream, and we can make it come true."

Selim leans back. "This is a surprise," he says.

"I don't care what people think anymore," I continue. "My family will just have to accept it. What are they going to do? Deny their daughter her dying wish? There may not be much time left. We've got to face the facts."

"Of course, I want to get married, but not like this. If I could change places with you, I'd do it in a minute, but I can't, so I'm doing the next best thing. I've offered to help with your case. Doc Taylor said I could collect written statements from some of your former patients. They'll present the letters in court. After they clear your name, we can have the wedding you've always wanted. We can have something to look forward to."

I tip my head back, close my eyes and sigh.

"All right, but I'm not giving up on my wish just yet. I'm going to find a way."

"You are one determined young lady," he smiles.

We sit silently with our thoughts for a few minutes.

"Do you remember the first time you took me on a picnic?" I ask. "It's one of my favorite memories ever— maybe my very favorite."

"How could I forget?" he replies.

    ⅋ ⅋ ⅋

I was fifteen years old that summer. Selim was nineteen. We agreed to meet behind the schoolhouse, which required me to lie, a skill that got easier with use. I told Mamá that Doc Taylor needed me to interpret at the clinic. She waved goodbye and went about her business.

Naturally, I felt terrible, but with Selim's arms around me, his sweet musky smell, deep voice and body form-fitted against mine, the guilt quickly dissolved.

I climbed inside the small, covered wagon he and his father used to peddle their merchandise. Surrounded by bundles of kindling wood, soap, packaged linens, horse-shoes, saddles, cookware and clothing, I sat on an old sofa cushion with my back against a sideboard. Selim made me promise not to peek outside. My mind ran through a list of possible options. The library in Goldendale? Lucky's Arcade just outside of town? Or the ice cream parlor next to the Go Ahead and Blow It Smoke Shop?

After a long and bumpy ride, the horse slowed down and stopped. Selim untied the back of the wagon bonnet, looped his arms around my back and under my knees and carried me down to a meadow full of wildflowers.

He went back and grabbed a blanket and a basket from the driver's box and led me to the edge of Penelope Creek, a place I'd never seen. We talked, teased, laughed and remembered our childhoods, his in Beirut and mine on the ranch. We ate flatbread stuffed with bulgur wheat, minced lamb, onions and tomatoes, and a flaky pastry baked with sharp cheese and drizzled with honey.

Selim read to me in Arabic. I didn't care what it meant. Hearing him speak in his native language fascinated me. He taught me a few Arabic words. Na'am for "yes," la for "no," rajaa'an for "please," shokran for "thank you," and huub for "love."

The sun started to set, and he grew quiet. The sound of the birds and the rushing creek faded. Our surroundings blended into the background, and all I could see was him.

"I want very much to kiss you, Evangelina," he whispered.

"What are you waiting for?" I said, leaning in.

The more time we spent together, the more I knew that I couldn't live without him.

ॐ ॐ ॐ

The business of the jailhouse begins early. Men come in to pay fines. Others get hauled in by the sheriff for petty crimes, like fighting in public or stealing tobacco from the general store. None of them stay for long. If a relative pays the sheriff off, the prisoner's sentence disappears. Some people come to visit the sheriff socially or to exchange favors such as, *"I'll give ya a jug a moonshine if ya forget whatcha heard from that fish-eyed bitty Mrs. Greene. She can't prove it was my boy throwin' rocks at 'er house anyways."*

℮ ℮ ℮

I sit on the floor, counting my rib bones through my gown. The thin fabric doesn't hold in my body heat. When the sun sets and the temperature drops, my fingers and toes turn purple.

"Can I have something to read?" I call out to Humphrey. "Please? I need something to pass the time. I'll take whatever you have. And a blanket? I'm so cold."

Humphrey slips a magazine between the bars with painted pictures of ladies dressed in revealing bathing suits and thin nightgowns.

"You dohn git no blanket," he says. "I dohn know what yer gonna do with it. Besides, I'm sweatin' in here."

He props open the front door and stands just outside to light up a smoke, something he does at least ten times a day. I can't see him, but I smell the smoke and hear him talk to passers-by.

"I go back there, sir," I hear Mamá say. "We come to get Evangelina!"

I bounce up and down on my tiptoes as Mamá and Papá come inside.

"Are you sure?" I ask them as they enter the building.

"She ain't goin' nowhere till Sheriff Pearl says so," Humphrey snarls.

"That is correct, sir," says Joaquín, entering the building. "A court official is on his way with signed papers from the judge. You will release Evangelina into Doctor Russell Taylor's care."

"I'm not going home?" I ask.

"The request was to release you to your parents," Joaquín responds. "You've never had a run-in with the law. There are no witnesses to the alleged crime, and Doctor Taylor and Miss Cavanaugh vouched for your character. The doctor assured the judge that you are not a danger to anyone and that he would personally ensure that you remain on house arrest."

"I appreciate this, I do, but is there any way I can go home to my family?" I plead.

"The judge doesn't know your parents, and he doesn't trust them. He knows Doctor Taylor. It's the best I could do."

"We visit you," Mamá reassures me. "I bring you clothes from home and other things: a hairbrush, comb, toothbrush, everything I think you need."

"It didn't hurt that Miss Cavanaugh said she's writing a story about your treatment here since the arrest," Joaquín continues. "The sheriff and judge want no negative publicity with their re-elections just around the corner."

&ous; &ous; &ous;

I change into the long-sleeved dress Mamá has brought for me, thankful that she is around the corner and cannot see my body shape. Never before has my ribcage been so visible. I stopped eating to protest what the sheriff did to me. Now my exposed ribs look like bars on a prison cell, a cruel reminder of the very place he tormented me.

An hour passes before Sheriff Pearl comes in and looks over the judge's signed paperwork. Joaquín, Papá, Mamá and Doc Taylor stand nearby.

"I want all a you out!" the sheriff barks. "This ain't no social club. I got things ta take care of 'fore I let this criminal go, and I dohn need ya standin' around cloggin' up the place. You too, Doc. It's a damn disgrace you got caught up with these mutts. An' this girlie? She's guilty as the devil. Why yer puttin' ycr golden reputation on the line is beyond me."

Doctor Taylor glares at the sheriff. "I'm worried about you, Stanley. You've got broken blood vessels in your eyes, and your nose is red, swollen and bumpy. These symptoms are often associated with sustained alcohol-related impairment, known to weaken judgment. Perhaps you should come to the clinic for an exam. If you weren't on the job, I might think that you're impaired right now by the smell of you."

"Get out, you sons-a-bitches!" the sheriff shouts.

"Wait outside, please," Joaquín says to everyone. "I will stay with Evangelina."

"You can get out, too," the sheriff says. "She got some paperwork ta sign, and she dohn need ya ta do that. That is if she can read an' write English."

"As her legal representative, she will sign nothing unless I've read it first," Joaquín says.

The sheriff shrugs and shakes his head. "Girl, get over here. I'm turnin' ya over ta Doc Taylor, who's lost his mind. You need ta sign here agreein' ta stay with 'im at all times an' keep from practicin' medicine. An' that means yer witchcraft, too." He looks at Joaquín. "You can read it before she signs, but Doc Taylor's also gotta sign it. My mistake. I shoulda let him stay. Why dohn'-choo go get 'im for me."

"Evangelina, I'll be back in a moment," Joaquín says. "Do not sign anything until I return."

The sheriff moves in so close that I can feel the heat coming off his body and smell the cigar as if I were smoking it myself.

"I heard ya had a visit from some Arab, an' he was touchin' you. You two lovers, hmmm? We got mobs 'round these parts. You wouldn't want him gettin' dragged off somewhere. Them mob boys are loco in the head," he says, twirling his finger at his temple. "They dragged some guy named Modesto behind a horse last week, just for lookin' at 'em sideways."

   ℜ ℜ ℜ

"You sure you understand all the agreements you made by signing this page?" Doc Taylor asks me. "You cannot go anywhere beyond the house, and you cannot see patients. I'll be seeing patients in the clinic downstairs, but you can't so much as take a person's temperature until all this is over and you're declared innocent. I am vouching for you."

"Yes, sir. You have my word," I say.

The sheriff widens his stance. "I'll keep an eye on you ta make sure yer stickin' ta the rules," he says, looking directly at me.

Doc Taylor frowns.

"That will not be necessary," he tells the sheriff. "Evangelina, there's a group of folks outside, and they don't look too friendly. We'll get you into my coach quickly and take you to the house. Sheriff, we'd appreciate your assistance. I don't know what the crowd intends to do."

"You can see yerselves out," he replies.

I step through the jailhouse door and shield my eyes from the bright sunlight. A crowd of about ten people stands just beyond the steps.

"Murderer!"

"Witch!"

"Go back to Mexico!"

"The fires a'hell are waitin' fer you!"

Papá moves in front of me as a shield. Doc Taylor runs down the steps to open the coach door. Mamá follows behind. Joaquín grabs my arm and leads me down the steps when a soda bottle comes at me, and I duck.

CHAPTER 10

A Place to Land

"*¡Ay, m'ija!*" Mamá says. "I cannot believe what just happened! That horrible man threw a bottle at you!"

I wrap my fingers lightly around Mamá's hand and rest my head on her shoulder. I may be almost eighteen years old and an accused murderer, but there's a kind of comfort only a mother can bring.

I look at the town passing by. A girl strolls down the street. A skinny yellow dog follows alongside, with its tongue hanging out. Spots of brown grass appear in every yard, a sign of the spring sun making way for summer. A butterfly flits past, looking for a place to land.

Abuelito said butterflies have something to teach us.

"*Each one breaks free of its cocoon, flaps its wings, rises into the sky, travels long distances and overcomes many dangers along the way,*" he said. "*But, in the end, it reaches its destination. It works that way for people, too, m'ija. Many small steps become long distances, with determination and hard work. You just have to know where you want to wind up.*"

Seneca's city plaza nears. We pass Neat & Tidy Barbershop, Millie May's General Store, the Seneca Post Office and Grand Hats that Mamá sews bonnets for each week. Next is a narrow three-story brick house with a green sign hanging over the front door, the place where Doc Taylor set me on a new path.

"Doctor Russell Charles Taylor, Physician. Since 1885," the sign reads.

Papá opens the door of the carriage and offers a hand to help me down the steps.

"Would you give me a moment with Doc Taylor? I'll be in soon," I say to my parents.

"Do not take long, *m'ija*. There are people inside who've come to see you," Papá answers.

Doc Taylor dismounts his horse, comes around and cocks his head.

"Why are you still in there? Go in, go in! It's a time to be with family and friends," he smiles.

"I will in a minute. Doc, I overheard a conversation at the jail about a man named Modesto who got dragged behind a horse. Can you ask around town? Whoever he is, he must need urgent medical attention."

"Yes, an unfortunate incident that was. His name was Modesto Domínguez, just twenty-two years old. The horse bucked and dragged him behind."

My heart thunks inside my chest. "Was?"

"A friend of the family brought me to the home shortly after they found him, but the young man had already passed. His backside got tore up, and his head— well, you can imagine his head."

They murdered him!

"Did anyone witness what happened?" I ask.

"Not that I am aware. I understand the family arrived in Seneca two weeks before. They were staying with friends, and Modesto went out looking for work."

"I wonder what spooked the horse? Someone should look into it but—but not the sheriff. He won't care about a dead Mexican; we both know that. Maybe I should mention it to Teresita and Joaquín."

"It was a tragic accident, Evangelina. There's nothing to be done about it now. We need to get you inside," he says, taking my hand and guiding me down the carriage steps.

ॐ ॐ ॐ

"We've been waiting for you!" Tomás yells.

"Evangelina! I missed you!" Domingo says and hugs me around the middle.

A swarm of people from the neighborhood crowds the house: the neighbors, my aunt, uncle and cousins. Smiling ladies bustle in and out of the kitchen with corn tortillas and a pot of *menudo* with all the mix-ins: radishes, cabbage, onions, tomatoes and spicy chopped pickled carrots. I usually go outside when the menudo's cooking, because it smells like a barnyard, but today, the smell brings happy tears to my eyes. And these Mexican ladies will try to feed me the whole time they're here. Food and love go hand in hand. When they make it, they give love, and whoever eats it feels love.

"Sit down, *m'ija*, you must rest," Papá says.

The living room has not changed: two gold chairs, a coffee table with heavily carved legs, the red and gold striped sofa and the china cabinet with the late Agnes Taylor's painted porcelain cups, vases, jugs, sugar bowls and figurines of dancing ladies in ball gowns and tutus. She moved in with her son after his wife and baby died and soon redecorated the house in her own style: uncomfortable and uninviting, in my opinion.

There's a light knock on the door.

"Who is it?" Domingo asks, running towards the entryway.

"I'll get it," Papá says. *"M'ijo,* go help your Mamá."

"Awww," Domingo grumbles.

Papá opens the door. I look, blink and look again.

"Good afternoon, sir," Selim says, standing outside with his cowboy hat in his hand. "I heard about Evangelina's recent troubles with the sheriff. I came by to say hello, and wish her well. She and I are old school friends."

Papá stands and lifts the corners of his mouth into a strained smile.

"Thank you for coming, Mister Na-ja . . . Selim." The muscles in Papá's jaw twitch. "You want to come inside? We having a party for our daughter."

"Thank you for the invitation, sir, but I must get back to work. I am sorry if I interrupted," Selim says, glancing my way. "Please know that you are in my family's thoughts, Miss Evangelina." He nods at me and bounds down the porch steps.

Papá shuts the door. "I didn't expect him to come by."

"Who came by?" Mamá asks, joining Papá in the foyer.

"Selim Nnn . . . jame. *¡Ay!* I can never pronounce that young man's name."

"It's Nuh-hyme," I say softly.

"That's strange," Mamá says. "Wasn't he a school-mate of yours?"

I nod, afraid my voice will crack if I open my mouth again.

"I didn't know you stayed in touch," Mamá says to me.

⅗ ⅗ ⅗

Guests line up to shake my hand or bend down to peck my cheeks. Some hand me gifts: flowers, candy, a too-big knitted sweater, a little bag of dried lavender, a child's drawing of a cow and a beautifully painted cross to hang on the wall. No one asks about my case out of respect. I see the curiosity in their eyes and open mouths with questions practically spilling out, but they think the better of it and stop themselves.

After two hours, the crowd thins, and I get another round of hugs and encouraging words.

"Stay strong, child."

"We love you, Evangelina. Let us know how we can help."

"It is you that we trust when we need a doctor, little one. You must not give up."

When things settle down, Domingo sits next to me with a square of his baby quilt, which he tucks below his leg. At age four, Papá told him he was too old to carry a blanket, so Mamá let him pick out his favorite square, a white one with a cowboy on a bucking horse with one hand on the horse's neck, the other in the air. She cut that square out, sewed the edges and let him keep it under his pillow. I haven't seen it for years.

"Why did you bring that out?" I ask him.

"I don't know," he says, reaching down to feel the soft edge of the fabric.

My situation has been difficult for him, too. I stroke his hair and sing "Siete Leguas," a song he likes about Pancho Villa's horse. I don't remind him that Pancho Villa burned our ranch house to the ground, and his men killed our neighbors back home.

ॐ ॐ ॐ

The dishes have been washed, dried and put away. Exhaustion hits hard.

"I prepared the room upstairs for you," Mamá says. "Would you like me to come up to make sure that you settle in?"

"No, Mamá, thank you. All I want to do is lie down and close my eyes. It's been a very long day."

"Of course, *m'ija*. Sleep well. We'll be by tomorrow," she replies and kisses my forehead. "*M'ija?*"

"Yes?"

"Selim seems to be a nice young man."

Oh, please. Not now.

"I presume you are not spending time with him alone, or at all, for that matter. It was fine when you were in school, and I know he was a good friend when we first arrived. One day soon, you will get out of this situation and find someone special that you care for and that will make your family proud."

"Good night," I say.

"Sleep well, *m'ija*," she replies.

CHAPTER 11

To Give Off Light

I open the back door.

"I hope the doctor still makes house calls on Thursdays," says Selim.

"He won't be home for hours," I say and wave him in. "Quickly, so no one sees you."

"I've missed you," he says, wrapping his arms around me.

My muscles tense up—not the reaction I expected. I've dreamed of this hug.

Selim is the oyster, I am the pearl, and I am safe, I tell myself.

"Evangelina! You're so thin!" He steps back, his eyes full of concern. "Did they starve you in there?"

"I couldn't bring myself to eat much of the food," I reply, moving toward the kitchen. "I'll make up for it now that I'm here and doing the cooking myself."

I stir a pot of hot water with fresh-squeezed lemon juice, a sprig of mint from the backyard and a heaping spoonful of honey. I pour two steaming cups and set them on the small table next to the kitchen window.

Selim sits down and motions me to sit on his lap.

I want to, but I can't. I won't. Not yet.

I turn away as if I didn't see it and grab a pear from the fruit bowl on the countertop.

"You're in trouble with me," I say, pear in hand.

"Why is that?"

"Your surprise visit yesterday! What were you thinking? You made my parents suspicious." I slice the pear, fan the slices out on a plate, add a few butter cookies and set it on the table.

"You need to share this with me," he says, gesturing toward the plate. "I thought it might help to remind them who I am. Maybe if we break the news in small steps, it'll lessen the blow when you tell them."

"I wish you'd asked me first."

He looks down at his lap and rubs his palms back and forth on his pant legs.

"Evangelina, there is something important I have to tell you."

I sit down in the chair across from him and narrow my eyes. "What is it?"

His cheeks flush red as he runs a hand through his hair.

Does he want to leave me?

"Selim, what is it?" I ask, holding back tears.

"I haven't wanted to tell you because you have enough troubles, but I must. It feels dishonest otherwise, and things are getting out of hand with my family."

"Tell me what? Please just say it."

"My parents want me to marry a girl from Lebanon. Our fathers met and agreed on a dowry. That's why I was gone so long on this last trip. We stayed with her family for almost two weeks while we waited for the wagon parts to come in."

"What?! Did you know about this beforehand?"

"No! No! Of course, not."

"What are you going to do?"

"I don't know yet. If I don't go along with it, my parents will kick me out, cut me off from the family and the business. I'll lose everything."

"We're supposed to marry and build a life together," I cry. "You've known all along your parents would disapprove. My situation is awful, I know. More than awful—it's terrifying, and I need you more than ever."

"I don't want to marry her, I promise."

"What is this girl's name?"

"It doesn't matter," he says softly.

"It matters to me. What is her name?"

"Fatima. We knew each other in Beirut. She has a younger sister for my little brother, Maier. My parents paid for her family to come here."

"How long have you known about this?"

"I found out on the trip with my father. I didn't tell you because Fatima means nothing to me, and you mean everything to me. I didn't want to hurt you."

"Is there a wedding date?" I ask.

"August 21st," he says. "They've invited the whole Lebanese community. They're bringing in musicians, planning the menu, all of it. On top of everything that's happening with you, I have to act as if I want this marriage."

"Selim, we don't have much time to stop this wedding." Part of me wants to bury my face in his shoulder, but I can't bring myself to do it. "Your father should never have made a promise to her family. Fatima will feel hurt, and the parents will be outraged, but we *have* to be together. It's the only thing that keeps me going. We have to get married before it's too late."

"I will tell my parents about us today, that we plan to marry," Selim says. "I've been hiding it too long, and I'm sick of it. I'm so sorry I didn't do it sooner."

"No, not yet," I reply. "Most people think I murdered Ramona Healy. There couldn't be a worse time to tell your parents about us. Maybe it's best to go on keeping it a secret. Not forever, just for now."

&ð &ð &ð

The worn feather mattress on Agnes Taylor's bed is so soft that my body frame sinks in the middle. *My life is ruined. No school will accept me to study medicine. Selim's family will disown him if he marries me—he'll lose the business he's supposed to inherit. It's selfish of me to ask him to give all that up. Will I be forgiven if Ramona Healy died on my account? Will I hang for my crime? The third and final syrup I gave to ease her pain might have poisoned her.* I sob into the pillow to muffle the sound. *Things can't get any worse than this.*

&ð &ð &ð

I tiptoe down the stairs to the basement. Bottles and jars of medicines and salves line the clinic shelves downstairs. I find the green bottle of sodium bromide. One dose will relax me enough that I won't care about my disastrous life.

"To give off light, you must suffer the flame," Abuelito told me one day, long ago, when I was feeling sad and weepy.

But what if I don't want to give off light? What if it's too hard, and I'm too angry, ashamed, tired and broken?

I swallow one, two, three tablespoons of the bitter liquid.

When I sleep, I don't feel a thing.

ও ও ও

A rocking chair with a ripped woven seat sits outside on the hard, cracked ground. The front door's hinges whine as I enter. The house gives off a pungent smell. A narrow shelf with a clock and two cans of chickpeas lean against the wall. A pot with pigs' feet in a vinegar and clove mixture sits on the cookstove. A plain wooden chest and a basket filled with kindling and spiderwebs fill a dark corner of the room.

I approach the woman, pull up the quilt and examine her.

"You're doing well. The baby should be here before nightfall. I'll give you three spoons of a special syrup that I prepared myself to make you more comfortable. I'm here to help and protect you."

She nods. A ring of wet surrounds her head on the pillow like a halo. Her eyes open wide as marbles, her jaw clamps down and she folds at the waist as her womb tries to rid itself of a new life.

The woman's face softens when the contraction eases.

I pour water from a clay pitcher onto a folded white cloth and lay it across her forehead.

The door opens. A caped figure glides in. It's her again: the woman of a thousand nightmares, wandering between this tormented life and the next, eternally wailing in a fruitless search for the children that she threw over a bridge to their watery deaths.

La Llorona's glowing white hair twists and jabs, and her black hole eyes pull me toward her.

"Where are my children?" she howls.

"They're not here!" I shout. "Leave us alone!"

Snakes drop from her eye sockets to the ground.

She turns to the pregnant woman, yanks the sweat-soaked pillow from under her head and holds it down over her face.

I pull at La Llorona's cloak and yank on the hood.

Snakes curl around my ankles and slither up my legs.

"Stop, stop! She's suffocating!" I scream, but my voice sounds like the rush of a strong wind.

The shelf clock booms.

La Llorona straightens up.

I rush to the bed and pull off the pillow.

The pregnant woman's see-through blue eyes turn up toward the heavens but do not see.

I walk to the window, open the curtains and wave both my hands toward me. "Come in," I say in a honeyed voice.

The sun's rays blend into a thick cord, shoot through the glassless window frame and start a fire on the braided rag rug in the center of the room.

I pull a bottle of oleander syrup out from my bag and pour it into her mouth as the flames spread and grow.

"This will make you feel better," I say to the body.

Dead people can't swallow, but this one does.

La Llorona reaches under the quilt, brings the baby boy to her chest and hums a lullaby in the most enchanting voice I've ever heard.

Snakes drop from my eye sockets to the ground.

ℊ ℊ ℊ

"Evangelina, it's time to wake up now. Wake up."

I open my eyes gradually, blink a few times and focus.

Doc Taylor sits on a chair next to the bed and pats my hand. "How do you feel?" he asks. "You've been sleeping for a very long time."

"I have? I'm sorry. I should get up," I say in a creaky voice.

"No, no—you must stay in bed for a while longer. I'll be back in a moment. I'm going to get you something to eat and drink. You stay right here."

I sit up and scoot myself back against the headboard. *What is happening? My head feels like it's full of cotton.*

Doc Taylor comes in holding a glass of milk and a banana. "Here, you need the nourishment."

"I'm sorry, but I'm a little groggy."

"Evangelina, Elsa came by to visit and couldn't wake you. You gave us quite a scare."

"Oh?" *The sodium bromide.*

His thumb and fingers come together and press outward along his forehead. Behind his spectacles, his usually bright green-blue eyes look dull and weary.

"I'll get right to the point," he says. "I found the sodium bromide bottle next to the washbasin downstairs."

Did I leave the bottle out?

"Evangelina? Did you hear me?"

I chew on the nail of my little finger.

"I bought it last week, Evangelina, and I have prescribed it to no one since then. A quarter of it is gone. Did you take it yourself?"

What am I supposed to say? That I drank some? That I thought about pouring it down my throat so I wouldn't have to face my life?

"If you took it to help you relax, I don't know that I'd blame you, with all that you're up against," he says gently. "You left the bottle out of its place, almost like you wanted me to see it."

I did?

"Talk to me, Evangelina. I want the truth."

"I could have left it out when I dusted the shelves," I say.

He rubs his whiskers. "You've been asleep for almost a full day, Evangelina, and some of the medication is missing. You've never lied to me before. Don't start now."

"I took some to help me relax, is all. I haven't slept well for weeks."

"You took more than 'some.' You drank three or four doses. Were you trying to end your life? You're not in any trouble. I want to help you through this."

"No! Oh, I don't know."

He crosses his legs and waits patiently.

"I don't want to die," I whisper and draw my knees up to my chest.

"Evangelina, what you're going through is overwhelmingly unfair and stressful, but there is reason to believe things will turn out in your favor. Joaquín and I are building your case, and it's coming together well. You'll get through this, but we must get you healthy first.

"When I couldn't wake you, I did an exam as best I could," he continues. "Evangelina, you are dangerously malnourished. I knew you had lost weight, but you've been hiding it well. When did you stop eating?"

I rock back and forth. "The food in jail was barely edible," I reply.

"Didn't Cora or Teresita bring you meals on most days? Cora said she paid Humphrey Chestnut to give them to you."

"I feel fine; I do."

"Poppycock! You've been starving yourself, Evangelina. Are you having your menses anymore?"

I stare blankly out the window.

"If you continue this, you could suffer any number of things: brittle bones, muscle loss, an inability to bear children, even heart failure. You know this, Evangelina. That's what scares me the most. You've known the risks all along.

"I will not tell your parents as long as you start regaining the weight. You know you can talk to me. I've always tried to be a good listener. Is there anything else you want to say?"

"No, sir," I say, still looking out the window.

"Eat the banana and drink the milk, and I'll come back in about twenty minutes." He pulls an envelope from his front pocket and hands it to me. "It's from Elsa."

Dear Evangelina,

I hope you are better soon! I got so scared when I couldn't wake you up. Doc Taylor tells me you will be okay, but I look forward to seeing you soon and deciding for myself.

Andrés Villanueva came by the dress shop begging for your help. We met him and his family at the county fair last summer. Do you remember? You treated his son's broken hand. His daughter, Mercedes, has a rash and terrible stomach pain, and his friend, Señor Salas, got burned badly in the Fox Grove shoe factory fire.

I told Señor Villanueva that you are out of town, but I don't think he believed me. People still need you, Evangelina. You must fight hard for yourself and them.

Hugs,
Your sister, Elsa

⅋ ⅋ ⅋

Doctor Taylor comes twice before dinner time bearing bad food: burned toast with runny eggs and warmed up beans that were delicious when I first made them but smell just on the edge of rotten now. I tell him I'll return to the kitchen tomorrow.

He also says he plans to order a locked cabinet to store medication. I wish I hadn't given him a reason to do that.

I look through old medical journals I've looked through a hundred times before and think about Elsa's note. *"You must fight hard for yourself and them."*

⅋ ⅋ ⅋

The smell of cigar smoke blows in through the bedroom window.

Doc Taylor does not smoke.

I peer outside.

Sheriff Pearl sits on his horse under my window.

He sees me and pulls his finger across his throat.

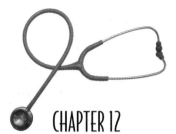

CHAPTER 12

No Cleanse from Heaven

Cora and I sip lemonade under a lemon tree in the backyard. Dusky gray clouds hang overhead. A heaven-sent shower could be just what I need.

Cora's red curls hang down her back in a loose ponytail tied with a black velvet ribbon. She wears a white blouse with long sleeves gathered in a ruffle at each wrist and pantaloons, which look like a skirt at first but separate in the middle like pants. *How freeing would it be to let my knees fall apart now and again?*

I wear my usual attire, a loose ankle-length cream-colored cotton dress with long sleeves and an apron tied at the waist, both of which hide my spindly limbs well.

"I stopped in to see Bill at *The Gazette* yesterday," Cora says. "Told him I'd have somethin' for him to review by Monday. He reminded me that I am not a reporter and that if he decides to cover your trial, he'll put one of his men on it. '*If* he decides to cover it? Yours is the first female murder trial in over a decade. He *has* to cover it. And, put one of his 'men' on it? What a surprise! There's only one female writer there, Ruby Roy, and she writes an advice column, 'Ruby To the Rescue.' Have you read it?"

"Doc Taylor gets the newspaper every day, but truthfully, I haven't picked it up," I say.

"If you want to know about useless nonsense, read her column. They bury it somewhere in the middle. Her last column covered the many uses of buttermilk, for Pete's sake! Women don't get to write about the more important matters of the day like some do in the big cities. I could just spit when I think about it!"

She spreads her pantalooned legs into a V and leans forward.

What is she doing?

A rumbling sound comes from her throat before she half spits, half dribbles on the grass, not more than two inches away from the tip of her red pointy shoe.

"Well, that settles it. I won't be winnin' a spittin' contest anytime soon," Cora laughs.

The smell of rain breezes in, and the first cooling sprinkles land on our heads and clothing. "We best go inside," she says, looking up. "I need to get more information from you if I'm goin' to turn the column in by Monday."

"You're nothing if not persistent," I tell her.

"Bill called me a 'vixen.' I told him that he could call me whatever he wants, as long as he agrees to what I'm askin'," she says.

Cora holds her notebook above her head and runs inside with me trailing behind her. There will be no cleanse from heaven today.

⇜ ⇜ ⇜

I lie in bed. Thinking back, I smelled the cigar smoke at least two other nights since leaving the jail. I just didn't recognize what it was, who it was or the message the sheriff wanted to send: "You can't escape me."

&ə &ə &ə

I don't have the energy to make breakfast, but I grab two balls of corn flour dough from the refrigerator and flatten them with my hands.

I cook the tortillas on the griddle and set them inside a basket lined with a kitchen towel, just as somebody knocks at the front door.

Cora stands on the other side.

"Cora! I didn't expect you," I say. "Would you like to join me for breakfast? It's not much, but I have tortillas and fresh coffee."

"Why sure, darlin', you're too kind," Cora says as we sit down at the kitchen table. "I got busy last night after we talked. My first piece is ready to go, and I brought you a copy."

She eats one warm tortilla with butter and a thin strip of salsa while I nibble at the edges of the other as I read.

The Truth Will Prevail—
Justice for Evangelina de León
Part I
Guest Opinion by Cora Kay Cavanaugh

In May 1911, thirteen-year-old Evangelina de León arrived in Seneca, Texas, from Mariposa, Mexico, with nothing but a suitcase the size of a Sunday picnic basket filled with two days' clothing, her Bible and a porcelain doll named Belinda. To keep Evangelina and five of her siblings safe from Pancho

Villa's rebel army and almost certain danger, or even death, her parents, Adán and María Elena de León made the only decision they could. Leave Mexico immediately.

Once prosperous cattle ranchers and citrus growers on Rancho Encantado, a massive property owned for generations by Mr. de León's family, they arrived in Seneca, Texas, with little to remind them of their once comfortable life. Adding to the family's worries, three relatives stayed back, unable to make the physically demanding and risky journey.

The de León's fears were not unwarranted. Within months of their departure, Pancho Villa's troops ransacked Mariposa, burned down the de León ranch and stole the livestock the family intended to sell to fund their new lives in the United States. Three innocent community members lost their lives during the raids, and numerous others got kidnapped by the rebels. The de León family members left behind, thankfully, were spared.

After settling in with an aunt and uncle, Miss de León enrolled at the local school. She studied hard, learned English and graduated with perfect grades. During this time, she worked alongside Doctor Russell C. Taylor and gained the knowledge and proficiency needed to become his trusted medical protégé.

Recently, Miss de León began administering medical treatment on her own for more routine ailments under the doctor's guidance and watchful eye. She also assisted him with childbirth. Patients who did not have the time or the means to travel into town and numerous Spanish-speaking patients found Miss de León's care to be an essential and sometimes life-saving service, often without charging the beneficiary for her time and expertise. She planned to attend Goldendale Normal School, then apply to the Texas University Medical School, where she could become the first woman of Mexican descent ever admitted. While these may seem like lofty goals for a young woman, Evangelina de León has never shied away from a challenge or hard work.

The unfounded and false charges of witchcraft and murder threaten to end her dream.

"I did not kill Ramona Healy," Miss de León said, behind bars at the Seneca Jail. "I helped Ramona Healy at a neighbor's request and with Mrs. Healy's approval and gratitude. I offered appropriate medical care using only natural remedies and was not present at the time of her death. The charges brought forward by Doctor Jedidiah Morley are false. I offer my sincere condolences and healing prayers to Mrs. Healy's family."

While Miss de León was not present at the death, Doctor Jedidiah Morley of Fox Grove was. Before his arrival there, Doctor Morley had a medical practice in Alden, Texas, where he had a troubling history of patient care.

Evangelina de León's legal counsel will show the charges against her are without merit and part of a disturbingly common string of racially motivated charges and killings of Mexicans and Tejanos throughout Texas. In time, Haller County will have no other choice but to apologize for this reprehensible miscarriage of justice and set young Miss Evangelina de León free.

Look for the next installment of The Truth Will Prevail—Justice for Evangelina de León in this publication.

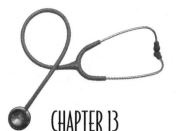

CHAPTER 13

Sounds Like Trouble

Teresita and Joaquín arrive. "Someone left you a letter," Teresita says, motioning to an envelope under the welcome mat.

I escort them inside and set the envelope on the hallway table to take upstairs with me later. Joaquín and Teresita sit down in the wingback chairs. I hurry off and come back with a platter of apricot *empanadas* and a pitcher of hibiscus tea. I take a seat on the sofa and wrap a light throw blanket around my shoulders.

"We've come to update you on a few matters," Teresita says. "Cora took her opinion column to *The Seneca Press* on Monday, and as expected, the editor refused it. As did *The Goldendale Gazette*."

She wears a long black skirt that hangs in flowy folds, a multi-colored woven belt, a loose cotton top embroidered with deep red birds and a thick silver necklace with large turquoise stones and matching earrings.

I've never been one to call attention to myself, but since crossing the border as one of the many brown "unwanteds," blending in has become a way of life. Dressing in bright-colored Mexican clothing would only invite angry stares and insults. Most Senecans are friendly and kind, but others have stirred up a strange mix of feelings in me: I'm proud of who I am but too afraid to show it.

"We'll make sure Cora's article circulates in the newspapers serving Tejanos, starting with *La Prensa*," Teresita adds. "That will reach twenty thousand readers in total. *The Goldendale Gazette* has a circulation of 1,000, and that's being generous," she says. "Communicating the plight of our people is essential," she sighs. "The acts of violence against us are getting more frequent and brazen."

"Did something else happen?" I ask.

"Nine days ago, the Texas Rangers forced ten Mexican men off a northbound train, lined them up and shot them as their wives and children looked on in horror. The Rangers claimed the victims had robbed a bank. Even if they had evidence of a crime, which they didn't, the law doesn't allow them to execute people on an accusation alone. That's cold-blooded murder."

I fold my legs under me and pull the blanket in tighter.

"None of the Anglo papers reported on it," Teresita continues. "There's no question who did it. A hundred passengers saw the crime. And yet, none of the killers have been charged or arrested. I'm leaving for Loma tomorrow. I'm going to publicize the hell out of the killings and assign resources to make sure the perpetrators pay. Every soul in Texas will learn of it before I'm through."

"It could have been any one of us," I say. "We put ourselves at risk every time we leave our homes."

"We must pull the curtain back on these monstrous acts, so ordinary people see what's going on, no matter how uncomfortable it makes them," Joaquín says. "A movement is starting, Evangelina, and your case represents what we're fighting for. The county's case amounts to nothing more than hearsay from a doctor with a record of patients suffering and dying under his care."

"I read something about that in Cora's article, but I didn't know what it meant," I say.

"We know of two patients so far, one of which was a woman in labor, like Mrs. Healy. We need to interview more witnesses to corroborate our findings. You can help by telling Cora more of your story, specifically how Sheriff Pearl and the two guards treated you while in their custody, and anything else you think will sway public sentiment."

How the sheriff treated me?

I throw off the blanket and stand up. "Would either of you like some more tea?" I ask, lifting the pitcher.

Doc Taylor opens the door from the clinic downstairs leading to the hallway, takes one look at me and raises his eyebrows. "Are you feeling all right?" he asks. "Your face is flushed."

"Please excuse me," I say as I scoop up the envelope with my name on it. "I have a terrible headache."

"Evangelina! Have you eaten this morning?" Doc Taylor calls to me as I run up the stairs.

ॐ ॐ ॐ

Someone taps on the door.

"Who is it?" I ask.

"It's Elsa. Can I come in?"

I open the door and hug her tightly.

"Oh, my goodness, that was a good hug!" says Elsa. "I finished with work and thought I'd stop by for a quick visit. The doctor said that you have a headache."

"That's not entirely true," I say. "I came upstairs to prevent one. All the talk about my case—it can be very upsetting."

"It's a wonder you still have your head on straight."

"I'm glad you came by. I could use your help."

"Anything," she says, squeezing my hand.

"Would you ask Selim to meet me in the barn behind old man Carlson's place?"

"When?"

"Wednesday morning, at 1 am."

"Sounds like trouble. What are you planning to do at that hour?"

"It's better if you don't know," I say.

"I was afraid you'd say that. It'll sink Mamá and Papá even lower if you get thrown in jail again. Are you sure you want to take that chance?"

"It's important to me, or I wouldn't even try what I'm about to do."

&⅞ &⅞ &⅞

When Elsa leaves, I plop down on the bed, open the envelope with my name on it that Teresita saw under the doormat and pull out a plain white sheet of paper with typed letters.

LITTL KIDS LIKE YER BROTHERS
GO MISIN ALL THE TIME

I weep until my sides hurt. *Who can I tell? He's the sheriff! And how would I prove that he wrote it? I must tell Elsa to make sure someone walks Tomás and Domingo to and from school and never play outside alone.*

CHAPTER 14

You're Not Serious

Elsa brought me an old pair of Enrique's pants, a shirt and a cowboy hat as a disguise.

I stand next to the bedroom window and lean over just far enough to scan the surroundings outside. Nobody there, or at least I can't see anyone. I creep down the stairs, avoiding the spots that squeak, and escape through the kitchen door. The three-quarter moon shines bright white. Not good for a girl who wants to go unseen. I step lightly down back alleys with my head down.

Old man Carlson lived with his son in the run-down house on Pine Street. They kept to themselves, but sometimes, old man Carlson would sit in his rocker on the front stoop and watch people going by. Some greeted him, the children teased him and none got a response. I couldn't tell if he was deaf or just uninterested.

Since he died and his son moved away, the windows serve as targets for rock-throwing kids and a place for people to dump old furniture, broken tools, cracked dishes and the like. The poor, the crafty, and the curious search through it and make off with whatever they want.

The wood posts holding up the barn have rotted away unevenly, making one side look shorter than the other. I step inside and wrinkle my nose at the smell of stale hay. A tall figure steps forward out of the shadows.

"Evangelina?" Selim whispers.

"Yes," I whisper back, relieved. "I'm glad you came!"

"How could I resist another chance to see you?"

He pulls me further inside the barn to shield us from the view of potential passers-by. He picks up a wooden stool from inside an animal stall, sets it down quietly, takes his hat off and motions for me to come closer.

I hesitate.

"Evangelina? What is it?" he asks.

"I've decided to do something, and you need to know because if it works out, I'll have to get you involved."

"It's making me nervous already, but you know I'll do whatever you need."

"Elsa says that patients are asking for help, and I'm going to see them."

"At the clinic?"

"In their homes, in the early morning hours when I can move around unnoticed."

"You'll get thrown in jail again!" he says.

"If I get caught."

"You're not serious!"

"No one will know except you and the patients, and I'll make them promise not to tell."

He stands up and puts his hat back on. "I'm sorry, but this is a terrible idea."

"Selim, you have to understand. I can't sit around waiting for things to happen to me anymore. I have to *make things happen*. People need me."

"Then let me come with you," he pleads.

"No, no—absolutely not."

"Then why did you tell me if you didn't want me to get involved?"

"There's no reason for you to risk it, and I can do it alone," I assure him.

"Nonsense. We'll do it together. You can't stop me. I am coming, period."

"Selim, the father of one of the patients used to be a priest."

"You mean . . ."

"That's exactly what I mean. Former priests can perform marriage ceremonies."

"Are you sure?" he asks.

"Mm-hmm," I nod. "That's why I had to tell you. If this goes as planned, we could wind up married, after all."

A flicker of light appears in the house and disappears.

"Did you see that?" I ask Selim.

"See what?"

"A light in the house."

"No one's been in that house for years," he replies, but I'm not so sure.

❧   ❧   ❧

The next night, a dense fog rolls in, providing the perfect cover as I walk to old man Carlson's barn. I reach Selim in the alley behind the barn and step into the smaller of the two Njaim & Sons' carriages. He managed to cover the name with a large piece of burlap he rigged up.

We near Andrés Villanueva's small cabin outside Fox Grove and stop a stone's throw away. I motion to Selim to stay with the horse. I tiptoe to the front door, open my bag and pull out a small canning jar with a note inside.

Dear Villanueva family,

Elsa told me you spoke to her about Mercedes. I will come by very early tomorrow morning, around 1:30 am, to do an examination. That is the only time I can safely see her. I will not need payment of any kind. I only ask that you tell no one about it. If you do not wish me to see Mercedes, or if her condition has improved, leave this note in the jar with an X through it. That way, I will know when I arrive if I should knock or not.

Evangelina de León

I set the jar down on the front stoop and head back to the carriage when a rifle shot rings out.

"Who's out there?" a man yells.

I throw my hands up. "It's Evangelina de León!" I shout.

Señor Villanueva strides over, rifle still at his side. Selim stands, his gun cocked and ready to fire.

"I'm sorry about the warning shot," he says. "I could only assume it was burglars or worse at this time of night."

"I apologize for coming unannounced," I say. "I left a note inside the jar by your front door. My sister Elsa said Mercedes has been ill. I hoped to return tomorrow, about this time, with your permission."

"What about now? I can't thank you enough for coming. We have no way of getting to town to see the doctor.

My horse went lame a week ago, and I can't afford to replace him. Please, come in. I'll let Mercedes know you're here."

"I'll stay out here with the wagon," Selim says.

Señor Villanueva and I step into the simple one-room home.

"Señor? Before I examine Mercedes, you cannot tell anyone that I've been here. There will be serious consequences for me if you do. I must have your word."

"Everybody knows they accused you of killing Otis Healy's wife. I don't believe it. The law around here finds us guilty for living and breathing. I will keep your secret, and I'll tell Mercedes and Serapio to do the same. You have my word."

"I'm relieved to hear that, Señor. Thank you."

"Evangelina, Santiago Salas lives not more than two miles from here. He got burned in the Wallingford Shoe Factory fire, which I'm sure you heard about. He needs your help as soon as possible. He is unable to work and in great pain."

"Yes, sir, Elsa mentioned that."

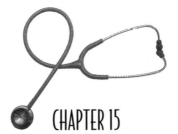

CHAPTER 15

Two Crucial Requests

"Please ignore the mess," Señor Villanueva says. "I've tried to keep the place clean since Paloma passed last year, but I find myself too busy with everything else to keep up. I do the best I can with Mercedes, but I am a poor substitute for her mother."

"The house is fine, Señor. Please don't give it another thought. And may I offer my condolences."

"Paloma went from having a headache one minute to collapsing the next. I had just enough time to give her last rites," he says, making the sign of the cross with his hand.

"You mentioned that you used to be a priest when I was here to see Serapio," I say.

"I have not been a priest for many years. I fought my feelings for Paloma and agonized over the decision to marry for the better part of two years. I decided that loving Paloma did not mean I loved God any less. Love is love; that's what I believe." He turns his attention to the loft. "*M'ija?* I know you're awake up there. I saw you peeking over the covers. Come on down, so the doctor can see you."

Mercedes, clad in a long white nightgown with stripes of tiny blue flowers, steps down the ladder. She climbs into her father's wicker rocking chair by the fireplace.

"I remember you," she says, smiling shyly. "You fixed my brother's hand."

"That's right! How old are you now?" I ask.

"Seven," she says, holding up her fingers.

"I understand you haven't been feeling too well. Your Papá says you have stomach aches?"

"And bumps on my belly, too. Do you want to see?"

I finish with Mercedes and ask Señor Villanueva to join me outside, where I make two crucial requests. He agrees to both, and I have to stop myself from doing a little dance right there in front of him.

"Is it anything serious?" Selim asks.

"She had an intestinal parasite, not uncommon, especially in children, but it seems to have died off. Her symptoms are improving, and her appetite has returned. I'll come back on July 1st to see how she's doing.

"I asked if he knew anything or anyone who might have information about my case," I say.

"And?"

"He's going to ask around."

"Will he marry us?"

It's the first time I put my arms around him in months.

I creep upstairs to my bedroom and light the oil lamp.

Tap, tap.

"Evangelina? May I come in?"

It's Doc Taylor at the door! What do I do? What should I say?

"Let me put on my robe," I say and rush to pull off the bulky clothes, stuff them in the armoire and grab my robe from the back of the chair.

"You can come in now," I say, sitting on the edge of the bed.

Doc Taylor opens the door a crack and peeks in.

"It's okay," I assure him.

He wears a dark blue robe over his nightclothes and well-worn black slippers.

"I thought I heard someone coming up the stairs," he says. "All is well with you?"

"I went downstairs for something to eat."

"Good, good. I want you to eat whenever your stomach tells you it's time. And since you're awake, you should know that the judge set your trial date. Cora came by earlier with the news when you were napping. She'll be by again tomorrow after lunch with Joaquín. He wants to review the defense strategy, witnesses and so on. And Cora's writing her second editorial. She has some questions for you."

"What is the trial date?"

"It'll begin on July 5th."

"That's so soon!"

"I'm feeling more and more confident about your case," he replies. "Joaquín is a wonder. He's . . ."

"Doc? There's something I must tell you," I say.

He lowers himself into his mother's old chair.

"I'm scared," I say softly.

"Scared of what?"

"That I killed her."

His hand slowly moves up toward his face, and he rubs his chin for what feels like forever.

"Evangelina," he says, looking over the tops of his glasses. "I care for you as a father would, and I want what is best for you. Whatever transpired with Ramona Healy will not change that."

I wipe the stream of tears from my cheeks with the first knuckle of my curled hand.

"Everything I told you before is the same," I tell him, "but her back pain became unbearable. She screamed for three hours and begged me to give her something else."

"Did you?" Doctor Taylor asks.

"My mother used oleander to manage pain, and I carried it with me. I'd never used it before."

"But you did this time," he says.

"Yes, sir. I didn't want her to suffer more than she already had if there was something I could do about it."

"And this is what you've been keeping from me?"

"I've told no one."

"Evangelina," he sighs. "Oleander is well-known for treating indigestion, even warts and sexually transmitted disease. I've used it with patients to relieve menstrual cramps, so it hardly seems like an improper or dangerous solution to manage pain. It's a natural remedy and not something that would harm the patient."

"If I had given her just one dose."

"Hmmm," he says. "How many doses did you give her?"

"Three. I started with one, but it didn't help. I gave the second dose thirty minutes later and the third one an hour after that."

"Look at me, Evangelina."

I search his eyes for signs of a guilty verdict.

"When a baby is in a posterior position like this one must have been, it can cause extreme back pain because the skull is pressing against the mother's pelvis, but it's not unusual and rarely leads to maternal or infant harm. Oleander can be poisonous if ingested in large amounts. I cannot imagine that three spoonfuls caused her death. I will research this and let you know what I discover, but I greatly doubt it was the culprit. Do you know the ratios of water to flowers and seeds?"

"It was equal parts water and plant material, with some added honey," I reply and heave an enormous sigh of relief.

"I will do some research, so you can put this fear to rest. Morley may have found traces of oleander in Mrs. Healy's body during the autopsy, which the prosecution could use against you. Joaquín will need to prepare for that.

"Tell me, at what point in this timeline did Morley arrive?" he asks.

"Fifteen, maybe twenty minutes after the third dose."

"If we can say with certainty that your actions did not contribute to her death, what did? That is what we must find out. Otis Healy has agreed to let me investigate further."

"How so?"

"I'm going to conduct a second autopsy, but no one else outside, you, me and Joaquín can know. The man who tends the graveyard will exhume the body tomorrow."

❧ ❧ ❧

Joaquín and Cora arrive in the early morning and sit on the living room sofa. She sits sideways, looking at him with softened eyes and flushed cheeks.

"Evangelina! We have good news," she says. "Teresita translated my first column and got it into six Spanish-speakin' newspapers, and two others are askin' for it."

"That *is* good news!" I say.

"We're thrilled," Joaquín says. "And the editor at *The Gazette* wants to pick it up. They're running it today with plans to publish the second piece next week. The editor couldn't refuse it any longer. He would have looked the fool otherwise."

"He's already a fool," Cora adds. "I hope the jurors read it before the trial starts."

Something bursts through the window. *SMASH!*

Joaquín throws open the front door and disappears down the steps.

"Jesus, Mary and Joseph! There's somethin' in my eye!" Cora shrieks. "Is it glass?"

"Let me look. Hold your eyelid open with your fingers and try not to blink," I order.

Cora holds her right eye open with her forefinger and thumb as I lean in.

"There's a little bleeding in the sclera, so yes, there must be glass or other material in there."

"What in God's creation is a sclera?" Cora asks.

"It's the white part of your eye. The bleeding is nowhere near the cornea, so that is encouraging. It might have just scratched the surface of the eye. Try to keep it open. Blinking will make it worse. I'll guide you to the washbasin in the kitchen, and we'll flush it out with clean water."

Cora rises to her feet, still holding the right eye open. "Am I goin' to be blind? I'm seein' a handsome young man now and don't want anythin' to stop me from lookin' at every inch of him."

"Take it slow. The last thing I want is for you to trip."

I grab her hand and lead her to the kitchen, where I scrub my hands in the sink and dry them on a clean towel. "Let me pour some water in the basin," I say.

"Awww damn, I feel somethin' wet. Is that blood comin' out?"

A pink-tinged teardrop spills over her lower lid and dribbles toward her nose.

"Cora?" Joaquín calls from the front room and heads towards us. "Good God, are you all right?" He puts his arm around her shoulders.

"She needs to flush out whatever she's got in her eye. Cora, lean over the basin," I tell her. "Splash the water into your eye. Multiple times," I instruct.

"Did it cut her?" Joaquín asks.

I'm surprised he's got his arm around her shoulder.

"Whoever threw that rock's a damn, d-d-d damned . . . jackass!" Cora says between splashes to her face. "Do I keep goin', Evangelina?"

"Yes, and keep your head down until I come back," I say and run downstairs to grab a hand lens. I find it exactly where it should be, on a shelf with other medical instruments, lined up by size.

Cora remains bent at the waist, her hair and face dripping wet. I drag a chair over and hand her a clean kitchen towel, which she dabs around the edges of her face, chin and neck.

"Sit here, by the kitchen window, where there's more light," I tell her.

I hold the lens up. "Keep the lid wide open. You're doing well. Look up. Down. Now left. Now right."

"Am I still bleeding?"

"No, but your eye could be watery and red for a while. I can't see anything in there with the hand lens," I say. "That doesn't mean there's nothing there. It just means I can't see it. What you're feeling in the eye is the best indication. I'll have Doc Taylor look at it when he gets back."

"I think it's out," Cora says.

"No more applying colored eye cream on your lids. You could get an infection if you don't keep the area clean. I'm going to recommend an eye patch for a week."

Cora turns to Joaquín. "Did you see who threw the rock?"

"The man rode off faster than I could run. His black horse had a white shape on its hindquarters, like an upside-down C. Someone in town may be able to identify it."

"Hell, I can do that," Cora says, using the towel to dry and scrunch her curls. "Humphrey Chestnut, that's who. I'm not surprised," she says. "I'm goin' to make him pay.

"And while we're on the subject of jail staff, I need to include somethin' about the conditions there in my next article. I wanna know everything. Now, if you two don't mind, I'd like to go home. I can come back tomorrow to ask my questions."

"You can't leave before Doc Taylor gets back," I say. "He should examine your eye as an extra precaution. Would you like to lie down here? You're welcome to use the bedroom upstairs."

"If I have any problems with it, I'll let you know," Cora replies, sounding somewhat testy. "Otherwise, I'll stop by in the mornin', say around 10 am to finish up with my questions. I have to submit my column soon."

"I could write down the conditions in the jail," I suggest. "I'll send a note with Doctor Taylor tomorrow. He can check on your eye while he's at it."

"That'll do just fine," Cora says as she stands up.

"Are you sure I can't convince you to stay?" I ask. "He could walk in the door any minute."

"No, no, I'm feelin' a bit ragged is all. There's been too much excitement 'round here."

"Don't take that patch off until Doc Taylor or I tell you it's safe to do so."

"Joaquín, will you be so kind as to escort me home?" Cora asks.

"It would be a great honor, but I am concerned for Evangelina's safety," he replies. "Someone meant to harm her. Perhaps we should stay until Doc Taylor returns."

"I do advise that he examine Cora's eye, but don't stay here on my account. If Cora wants to go now, I'll be fine. Doc Taylor won't be much longer, and I doubt Humphrey will come back anytime soon since you chased after him."

"Please, Joaquín, take me home," says Cora. "Maybe I'll hold your hand and bring you into the foyer. I'll even introduce you to my father." She winks with her left eye.

"I'm not ready to face the firing squad yet," says Joaquín.

"I believe I missed something here," I say. "When did you two start . . . ?"

"As soon as I asked him to take me to dinner, the day we met," Cora replies.

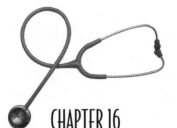

CHAPTER 16

What You Choose

"What is fate?" five-year-old me asked Abuelito.

"Fate is your future, the way your life is meant to turn out," he answered.

"Where does it come from?"

"It comes from inside you," he said, touching the center of my chest lightly with his fingertips. "Aquí, right here."

"Really?" I asked.

"Really! No one else decides it. It's not what happens to you, m'ija; it's what you choose to do with what happens to you that determines your fate," he said, then went inside to get me a buñuelo, *a cinnamon-sugared doughy treat.*

⚘ ⚘ ⚘

I light the oil lamp and pick up my pen.

Dear Cora,

During my first week in the Seneca Jail, I had to sleep on the ground. I was given no blanket, fed nothing but mush and beans and made to toilet in my cell. I caught Humphrey Chestnut watching me in my most private moments. I begged him to stop, but nothing changed.

I told the sheriff that I was getting terrible headaches, most likely from dehydration, but I was rarely given something to drink, not even water.

Humphrey Chestnut eventually gave me one, then two mattresses to sleep on, but only after you paid him to do it. They were both coated in urine from drunk men? Rodents?

My family members were regularly called racist names, yelled at, made to stand outside the jailhouse and speak to me through a narrow window. Anglo prisoners' visitors came and went as they pleased.

I barely slept and got regularly reminded that I would hang for a crime I swear I did not commit.

Cora, there is something else I want you to know. Can I please speak to you or Teresita in private?

I put the note in an envelope and seal it.

⅋ ⅋ ⅋

It's 12:30 am. I pull the men's clothes out of the armoire where I've had them hidden. With baggy pants, shirt and jacket on, I pull the cowboy hat over my ears, throw my bag over my shoulders, tiptoe down the stairs and out the back door.

Humphrey sat on his horse nearby earlier, watching my window, but he's long gone, or at least I hope he is. The sheriff must have enlisted his little helper to keep me in line. I'm sure he also told him to throw that rock. Humphrey doesn't make many decisions on his own.

⅋ ⅋ ⅋

Selim and I arrive at Santiago Salas's home, a tiny log house with horseshoes and antlers of various sizes nailed on each side of the front door. Selim dismounts and helps me down.

A man hobbles outside with crutches.

"Evangelina, welcome, welcome," he says as he approaches.

He appears middle-aged, judging by the wrinkles at the corners of his eyes and around his mouth.

"Señor Villanueva told me to expect you. He brought you a note," he says, reaching into his coat pocket with his unbandaged hand.

I stick it in my bag for later. "Thank you, Señor. Please allow me to introduce my driver, Selim."

"Good evening, sir," Selim says. "Or at this hour, perhaps 'good morning' is more fitting."

"Please, come inside," says Señor Salas. "It's just a little place, nothing fancy about it."

"I'll wait out here, but thank you kindly, sir," Selim says.

Señor Salas steps with one foot and slides the other using his crutches to support his body weight. With each movement, he grits his teeth, holds his breath and then releases it. The moment the door opens, the smell of cinnamon and citrus fills my nose.

"I made cinnamon tea for you. My mother made it when I was a child. I apologize I have nothing else to offer. I would have baked something for you, but the truth is, I can't bake." He shrugs. "And even if I could, I couldn't stand long enough to measure or mix anything."

"Why don't you sit and let me do the pouring?" I say.

He shuffles over to the bed and drops his weight onto the mattress. "You'll find two cups inside that cupboard there," he says, pointing with a crutch, fashioned out of two lengths of a stout branch, tied tightly into a T-shape and wrapped with cotton shirts to cushion the armpit.

"Do you live by yourself?" I ask.

"I had a missus once, but she left me a long time ago."

"I'm sorry to hear that, Señor."

"Don't be," he says. "I like living alone. It's peaceful. I have a cat that hangs around once in a while."

"Tell me what happened in the fire, then I'll take a look at your wounds," I say as I pour the tea.

"It started on the first floor of the shoe factory where I work," he begins. "I was on the second floor. By the time I smelled the smoke, flames were climbing high out of the windows below. A bunch of us got burned bad, and nine people died. I'm in terrible pain, and the burns on my legs and feet are looking worse all the time. My cupboards are bare. I haven't eaten in days except for what Andrés and his son brought over. I am grateful, but it only lasted a couple of meals. I'm hoping you can fix me up quick, so I can get back to work."

I hand him a cup and sit down on a stool near the bed. I sip my tea and feel the cinnamon slide down and warm my insides.

"I'll ask Señor Villanueva to speak with parishioners at your church. I am sure they would be happy to help with food. Let's take a look at your burns, and I'll see if you're ready to go back to work. I'll do the very best I can for you."

"I heard they put you in jail for killing some lady. There's no way you would have done something like that. I've been praying ever since I found out that the judge will let you go."

"You must promise that you won't tell anyone I've been here, or I could be in even more trouble."

He places his bandaged right hand over his heart. "I swear it."

"Thank you, Señor. Now, let's take a look," I say, setting my mug on the ground. "Are the burns just on your legs and feet?"

"I got one on my hand. See? But it's healing pretty well."

I unwrap the cloth. The burn on the palm seems to have blistered, popped and peeled. While still raw in the center, new skin is growing around the outside edges of the wound.

"I'll give you some aloe to put on it. I also have oregano oil in my bag to prevent infection. You'll put two drops onto your fingers and rub it in gently, twice a day. You can mix it with the aloe if you wish. I'll wrap your hand with a clean cloth now and give you some extra so that you can re-wrap it yourself. You must keep it clean. That's extremely important."

"I got the one on my hand when I tried to open the door to let people out. The doorknob was so hot that my hand stuck to it. As bad as it looks, it's not near as bad as the ones on my legs and feet."

"Can you roll up your pant legs, or do you need my help?" I ask.

"I can do it."

He gives me his cup, which I set on the floor next to mine. He bends down and carefully rolls up his left pant leg. As he pulls the sock off, he clamps his jaw, squeezes his eyes shut and wipes away a few tears.

"Don't tell anyone you saw me cry," he says. "I'll never hear the end of it from the fellas at work. Maybe a shot of whiskey would help?"

I nod. "I can get it for you before I go if you'd like. But you'll need to be sparing with it."

He drops the sock on the bed. The unmistakable smell hits me first. Then I look at his foot. Four of the five toes are black. The surrounding skin on the top and bottom of the foot has deep cracks. From the ankle to the knee, the leg appears bloated, red and purple. Open sores weep clear liquid and yellow puss. The flesh has rotted beyond repair.

The right leg looks better but not by much.

Gangrene.

Amputation.

Doc Taylor.

I'll have to tell Doc Taylor!

"I've got morphine in my bag," I say, touching his arm gently. "I'm sorry you've had to endure this for so long. I'll give you an injection to reduce the pain. It's strong medicine, but from the look on your face, it's just the thing you need."

"Bless you," Señor Salas says.

"You won't be needing that whiskey you requested after I give you this."

℃ ℃ ℃

Selim snaps the reins, and we're off. I explain the situation and ask him if he can bring Señor Salas enough food for a few days and deliver a note to Andrés Villanueva. The church community must be mobilized and soon.

I didn't tell Señor Salas about the need to amputate. Doc Taylor can do that after a thorough examination.

I rest my head against the carriage wall on the trip back to Seneca. Selim stops a block away. I hear the crinkle of paper in my bag as I move off the seat to exit. I sit back down and pull the note out from Señor Villanueva.

Ramona Healy's son Cyrus knows something. He told me himself. He agreed to speak with you.

CHAPTER 17

Buoy in Treacherous Waters

Doc Taylor sits at the kitchen table with his morning coffee, his once hot eggs and toast, cold and untouched.

"You see this lab coat?" he asks, pointing to the white coat hanging on the back of his chair. "Any person who wears this coat must demonstrate an unshakeable set of principles. I am shocked at what you've done. Your regrettable actions show that you are not ready for this coat. Do you know how many people are working on your behalf to prove your innocence? Do you know how many people love you to their very core and can't imagine a world without you? I'm one of them! I've treated you like a daughter, and you betrayed me."

"I am truly sorry, sir," I say. "I thought I was doing right to help others."

"Yes, but you didn't just risk yourself, did you? You risked Selim's future. You risked my good name and reputation. You made a promise when you signed the conditions of your release, and you broke that promise. You endangered yourself! You are in the fight of your life. Now is not the time for foolishness."

"I'm sorry a thousand times," I say, resisting the urge to run upstairs and lock myself away.

"I will cancel my afternoon appointments and see Señor Salas today. I'll have to get him to the clinic for surgery if it is as bad as you say, but I'll do my assessment first and decide what comes next.

"You realize that your case represents injustice for many! You must promise me that you will never do it again," he says. "Nothing is more important than clearing your name and securing your freedom. Don't make things harder to get you acquitted than they already are."

"I promise. I won't do it again," I say. *But I will have to if I want to marry Selim.*

☙ ☙ ☙

My family stops by the house bearing a bouquet of purple thistle. I set it in a white porcelain vase painted with tiny pink rosebuds. I say nothing to them about my moonlight patient visits or my conversation with the doctor.

Despite the outward pleasantries, the mood is somber all around.

Mamá and Papá can no longer stay in the house we've rented for the past three years. Papá took a job picking cotton. The owner of the dress shop let Elsa go. They'll move back in with Tía Cristina and her family by the end of the week.

We sit in silence, contemplating the reality before us. I search my memory for one of Abuelito's sayings to use as a buoy in these treacherous waters. Sometimes, what I can remember fits the moment, and other times, not so much.

Your conscience provides all the direction you'll ever need.

He who plants winds harvest storms.

"Do you want to hear one of Abuelito's jokes?" I ask my family. "We can all use a bit of humor right now."

"*Ay, m'ija*, his jokes were all pretty bad," says Papá.

"Tell us!" says Domingo.

"Okay. A woman invited her new neighbor for tea. Before going inside, she proudly showed him around. He saw the grounds, the goats, the chickens, the stables and the fields. After tea, the neighbor began his walk home. Halfway to the country road, the woman called to him. 'You have not seen my calf, good sir!'

'No, ma'am,' said the neighbor. 'I shouldn't be seein' nothin' higher than your ankle.'"

Domingo's the only one who laughs.

We exchange hugs and kisses before they leave. Elsa stays behind to visit a while longer.

"I know they were trying to cheer me up, but I feel worse now than before," I say. "Things are falling apart for everyone."

"The housing situation is hard, but we've done it before," Elsa says. "Tía Cristina said, 'Where there's heart room, there's house room.' The worst part of all this is how powerless we feel to help you."

"There is something you can do," I say softly. "But only you. You mustn't tell anyone."

"I'm rather enjoying these secret assignments," she says.

"I need to speak with Cyrus, Ramona Healy's older son. I don't know his last name, but it's probably not Healy. He's from her first marriage."

Elsa's smile fades. "Why would he talk to you? He thinks you killed his mother."

"Cyrus knows something about his mother's death that he wants to tell me. I'll be at the Villanueva's on Thursday to check on Mercedes. Ask Cyrus to meet me there at 1:30 am and no later."

"How will I find him?" she asks.

"I can describe how to find the Healy place, but make sure his step-father isn't there before you approach him."

"What should I say?"

"Tell him that I am innocent and need whatever he knows to prove it."

"What if he says, 'no'?"

"Elsa, you're the most beautiful woman within a hundred miles, and he's a teenage boy. I'm betting he'll say, 'yes.' Beg him if you need to. My life could depend on it."

"You may be losing your mind," Elsa says.

"I don't disagree with you," I reply.

"This whole thing scares me," she says. "What'll happen if the sheriff finds out?"

"Challenges are . . ."

"Challenges are chances in disguise," she says. "Yes, I know, but I don't think this is what Abuelito meant."

CHAPTER 18

For Every One There Are Four

Joaquín and Cora join me at the breakfast table. She holds out three pieces of paper, typed and double-spaced.

"Take a look," she says. "Pun intended! Ole Cyclops here had a challenge typin' it up with one eye, but you're worth it. It should be in this morning's paper."

"Cora, Doc Taylor stopped by your place to examine your eye. The woman who answered said you were unavailable," I say.

"That was Caledonia, our housekeeper. I didn't have time for an exam! I was busy writin'."

This woman can be so pig-headed!

"Cora's work has been a great help," says Joaquín. "Members of St John's Parrish in Loma plan to attend your trial in a show of support, and there will be others, many others. Teresita has been in communication with the Loma Mayor, Nicolás Montemayor. He and his daughter Anarosa may also attend."

"Is Teresita back in town?" I ask.

"Yes, she'll be here at the house shortly," Joaquín says.

"Enough chatter, you two," Cora says. "Read this, Evangelina. I'm dyin' to know what you think."

The Truth Will Prevail—
Justice for Evangelina de León
Part II

Guest Opinion by Cora Kay Cavanaugh

Seventeen-year-old Evangelina de León awaits her day in court. She faces the possibility of death by hanging for a crime the county contends she committed, but for which it has no conclusive proof. The trial relating to Mrs. Ramona Healy's death will begin Wednesday, July 5, 1915, at the Haller County Courthouse.

Evangelina de León is innocent of the charges of witchcraft and murder. Her experience while at the jail under the management of Sheriff Stanley Pearl was nothing short of appalling. Corroborating testimony from eyewitnesses indicates that Miss de León was nearly starved and driven to dangerous dehydration under the county's blatantly insufficient care. Made to sleep on the ground and with no blanket, this otherwise healthy young woman suffered from headaches, dizziness, stomach pain and other ailments while in custody. She reported these disorders to the sheriff to no avail.

Despite having no written rules regarding jail visitors, the sheriff barred her family from entering the premises. They arrived on multiple occasions bringing Miss de León much-needed food and comfort. Instead, Sheriff Pearl and Deputy Humphrey Chestnut ordered them to leave and called them racist names too offensive to include here. Anglo visitors came and went as they pleased with no objection by the sheriff or his staff in the same time period.

While Evangelina de León now resides in Doctor Russell Taylor's home as mandated by the court, she is, in essence, still a prisoner, ordered to stay within the confines of the home's four walls. Patients she might have treated over these past seven weeks have presumably gone without medical care.

Charges against Miss de León center on Doctor Morley's word that Miss de León poisoned and placed a witch's hex on Mrs. Healy. Miss de León's legal expert, Joaquín Castañeda, will prove this to be nothing more than speculation. In court, he will make clear the exact measures Miss de León took to provide appropriate care, and the jury will come to agree those measures could not have caused Mrs. Healy's tragic death.

Teresita Olmos, the founder of La Liga Protectora Mexicana, a league that promotes civil rights and justice, and the owner of the renowned Olmos Ranch, supports Miss de León's quest for an acquittal. Her organization, which provides expert resources to Mexicans and Tejanos falsely accused of crimes, has been, to the best of its ability, investigating injustice and violence against their people across Texas since 1906. The league's records indicate that ninety-two wrongful executions have taken place at the hands of ordinary citizens and law enforcement alike for no other reason than the victims were Mexican or US citizens of Mexican descent.

The majority of the dead were never charged with a crime and did not have an opportunity to defend themselves in a court of law. The few who went before a judge could not speak English proficiently and were, therefore, unable to testify on their behalf or challenge the process or content of the legal proceedings.

La Liga Protectora Mexicana estimates that for every murder they come to know about, there are four more unreported cases. The blood of innocent men, women and children stains the great state of Texas. Perpetrators must be held to account.

The false charges brought against Evangelina de León and the vile treatment inflicted by Seneca officials are nothing more than excuses to perpetuate hollow justice for yet another Mexican, a worthy and loved human being under the eyes of God.

Evangelina de León and her legal team are mounting what should be an impressive defense with scientific findings and witness statements to prove her innocence. Ultimately, they will uncover the racist injustice in a county and state that claims to be proud of its American ideals but does not exemplify them.

"Very persuasive!" I exclaim. "You are an incredibly talented writer and good friend, Cora! I couldn't be more thankful that you came into my life."

"Teresita agrees about her writing," Joaquín says. "She's asked Cora to help with communications at La Liga in the future."

"Well-deserved! Now, Cora, why don't you sit on that kitchen chair so I can look at your eye," I say.

"Oh, fiddlesticks, that won't be necessary," she says.

"It was not a request. Take the eyepatch off, Cora," I tell her.

"Ummm, you should know that I have not been wearin' the patch like I should have."

"Cora, take off the eyepatch."

"It's been bothering me some since I was last here," she says. "I was plannin' to tell you."

"Uh-oh," I mutter.

She slowly pulls the patch off, revealing a swollen, puffy eye with nothing but red in the area that should be white and a crusty substance around her lashes and tear duct.

"Heavens! What happened?" I cry.

"I didn't care for that patch very much," she says.

"You ignored my instructions?"

"I couldn't write very well with it, now could I? My sense of near and far was off completely. If I'd kept that patch on, I think I woulda fallen down the stairs and broken my pretty li'l neck."

"I said to come back if your eye turned red, became painful or showed signs of infection. Doc Taylor stopped by your home, and you turned him away! Can you see out of it?"

"I hoped it would improve on its own."

"Hope was not in the treatment plan I described," I scold.

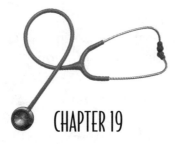

CHAPTER 19

A Dangerous Mix

Teresita arrives at the house at the same time Doc Taylor does. I describe the condition of Cora's eye. He does a quick exam and accompanies Cora and Joaquín downstairs for a thorough check with his equipment.

"Why don't we move to the back stoop?" Teresita suggests.

"May I get you some coffee or tea?" I offer.

"No, thank you," she says, heading through the kitchen to the back door. Her twisted torso might make her look vulnerable to some, but I know better.

She takes a seat on the white wicker bench on the covered porch enclosed by a mesh mosquito barrier. I sit on one of the outdoor scrolled metal chairs.

"I can't help but think of Doc Taylor's mother when I'm on this porch," I say. "The memory haunts me to this day."

"Why is that?" Teresita asks.

"It couldn't have been more awful," I begin. "A couple of years ago, Doc Taylor dropped me off here after taking me with him to see a patient. I wanted to study new specimens with the microscope, and he had another house call to make. I went around back to get the spare key and let myself in, and that's when I found her, Agnes Taylor, dead. She was lying on her back. There was nothing I could do to save her. A neighbor boy came by to deliver groceries and saw her, too. He dropped the bags and ran. I stayed with her until the doctor got home. I can still see her there like it was yesterday."

Teresita pats my hand. "It must have been very traumatic for you," she nods. "You've had troubles in your short life, but you've overcome them, yes? And you will overcome some more. Evangelina, I asked you to come out here because you wrote in your note to Cora that you wanted to speak to one of us in private."

"Yes, I did. It's just that—I'm nervous. What if the truth hurts my family? Or people treat me like an outcast when they find out?"

"President James Garfield once said, 'The truth will set you free, but first it will make you miserable.' Only the bearer of the truth knows if it's right to tell. What do you think is right?" asks Teresita.

I press my fingers to my lips. *It's now or never.* "Sheriff Pearl tried to . . . he tried to . . . violate me when I was in jail."

"Oh, my dear girl. I was afraid you might say that. You were alone and defenseless inside that cell. Keeping you there the way they did was a miscarriage of justice in and of itself. You said, 'He *attempted* to violate you.' Do you mean he did not complete the act?"

"No, ma'am." I squeeze my hands together to keep them from trembling. "But it terrified me. He said he'd hurt my family if I told anyone."

"Did anyone witness this?"

"Josiah, the deputy on the nightshift did. There was a drunk man next to me one of the times, but he was asleep and snoring."

"And you've told no one else?"

"No," I whisper. "I've seen the sheriff outside my window late at night. He's been watching me."

"Evangelina, one thing is for certain. Sheriff Pearl will pay his penance in the next life, and you will have justice for what he did in this one. When we first met, I told you I was thrown from a horse when I was a young girl. Do you remember?"

"I do," I reply.

"What I did not tell you is that I was running away from a cruel and bitter man, just like Stanley Pearl, only this man raped me. I managed to get away the second time, but my horse hit a hole in the open field and broke her leg in the dark of night. When she stumbled, I flew off and landed on a large outcropping of rock, breaking my back and three ribs. I never told a soul why I was on the horse that night, and for years I grew angrier and angrier. I grieved over what I had lost, and the memory haunted me.

"Finding the fight within me proved to be the cure," she says. "I founded La Liga, so the vile and violent get their due. You'll never forget what happened or how it made you feel, but you have the power now, not him."

A clap of thunder jolts us without warning, and the skies open up, typical in the Texas springtime: sun one moment and flooding the next. I look at Teresita for a second before running down the steps and letting the rain soak me through. Heaven sent me a cleanse after all. I hold my arms out and twirl around and around.

"Oh, there you two are!" Cora says, flinging open the back door. She is wearing a clean eye patch. "What on earth are you doing out there, you crazy girl! Have you lost your mind? Come in and dry off, for goodness sake."

I head back up the steps. "What happens next?" I ask Teresita.

"We build a fool-proof plan. Sheriff Pearl has it coming, and he'll never know until it hits him. Anarosa Montemayor, the Loma mayor's daughter, provided a written statement that Sheriff Pearl raped her in her teens. She has yet to press charges, but we are working with her and her father on that. We also have a witness who heard the sheriff speaking with Doctor Morley about the charges against you. The witness wrote down the sheriff's exact words," Teresita says as she pulls a piece of paper from the pocket in her skirt.

She reads, "'I thank you for bringin' her to us, doc. It don't matter if she's guilty or not, and I don't wanna know. Them Mexicans ain't welcome here, not even the women and children. If watching her twitch from the end of a rope don't send a message, what will?'"

ڶ ڶ ڶ

I dry off and change clothes, and we gather in the living room.

"There is no way to tell if her vision will return to its normal state," Doc Taylor tells me. "The abrasion caused an infection which may have changed the structure of the corneal lens."

"I am sorry about all this," Cora says to me. "I take responsibility for what's happened."

"You understand you may have permanently lost some or all of the vision in your right eye?" Doc Taylor asks.

"Yes, sir, I do," she says.

"I'll give you something to fight the infection, but at this late date, I cannot guarantee it will make much difference in the outcome."

"I understand, sir," Cora says.

"Did any of you see the man who threw the rock?" Teresita asks us. "Or did anyone outside the home see it?"

"I ran after the man but was only able to see the back of him. His horse had a distinctive mark," Joaquín adds. "That's how Cora identified the man as Humphrey Chestnut."

"That will not be enough to prove it was him," Teresita concludes. "Plus, he has the protection of a badge. Ignorance and power are a dangerous mix."

CHAPTER 20

Social News

I use a feather duster to clean the window sill and shelves. The clinic and everything in it gives me a feeling of comfort. I've spent countless hours and learned most of what I know about medicine in here.

There are the exam table and Doc Taylor's desk, messy with books, papers and bottles. Two chairs against the wall for patients or anxious family members to sit on while they wait. A spittoon for men and the occasional woman who comes in with their mouths full of chewing tobacco, something Doc Taylor frowns upon and makes them spit out. A separate smaller table covered with a white sheet and a doctor's standard tools is next to the exam table. His framed diploma and medical license hang above the desk.

"Evangelina? You down there?" I hear him call from the top of the stairs.

"Yes, sir. Doing a bit of cleaning," I reply.

"You know you're not my housekeeper anymore. I plan on hiring someone soon—perhaps Myrna, the young lady across the street."

"I have time on my hands, and I'd rather be busy than sit and think for too long."

"One day, you're going to get back to all this," he says, motioning around the room. "Why don't you sit down. I have news for your eighteenth birthday tomorrow. It's a day early, but I don't want to wait."

I sit down in one of the patient chairs.

"There is no conceivable way the oleander syrup you gave Ramona Healy led to her death," he says.

"You're sure?"

"I spent hours at the Goldendale Library researching herbal remedies. Three medical journals and two separately published studies confirmed that it would take much greater concentrations of oleander to poison someone. You gave Mrs. Healy three spoonfuls of the syrup. With the proportions of water to seeds and flowers you used, it would take ten times that much to have an adverse effect, even someone with her slight frame."

"That's wonderful!" I say and hug him around the neck.

"It gets better," he adds. "I telegraphed a laboratory in Virginia that specializes in toxic substances. They confirmed my findings. You did not, in any way, harm Mrs. Healy. You provided care and comfort, that is all."

"Doctor, you are my angel on earth. I can't thank you enough!"

"Let's get you out of this mess, and then you can thank me by finishing your schooling and joining my medical practice. How does that sound?"

"I beg your pardon?"

"I'm getting on in years, and I owe it to my patients to make a plan for my replacement. When you are ready, we can practice medicine as partners, and when it's my time to retire, you can stay on—if that's what you want. But there's no obligation to do so."

"Some of your patients would not like that very much," I say, "but it's a nice dream, isn't it?"

"Attitudes and beliefs can change. People who don't trust you or say you're somehow less than them don't know you. Once they do, they'll see you as I see you. You'll be an excellent doctor someday, and the people of this town will be lucky to have you."

There's a knock on the downstairs door, undoubtedly the first patient of the day.

"I'll see you upstairs at lunchtime," I say.

"Evangelina? I brought you something." He walks to his roll-top desk, opens the bottom drawer and pulls out something wrapped in brown paper.

I pull the paper off what feels like a heavy book: *The University of Texas Journal of Medicine.*

ॐ ॐ ॐ

I sit at the dining table with my new book and see *The Seneca Press* sitting nearby. Before I delve into the eight hundred and seventy-four pages of my birthday present, I lazily open the newspaper at the fold. There, on the bottom right corner are Selim and a striking young woman with large, attractive eyes, long, thick hair and enviable lips curved into a charming smile.

SENECA SOCIAL NEWS
The Families of Fatima Itani and Selim Njaim
Proudly Announce Their Upcoming Marriage
Private Ceremony
August 21, 1915, at 3 pm
Al-Omari Mosque
1106 Edmonds Avenue

Don't over-react.

The parents put the announcement in the paper, not Selim. Maybe he saw it, told them the truth and they've called off the wedding.

Selim and I are getting married in two hours.

CHAPTER 21

He Can't Erase What He Saw

I decide to wear Enrique's old clothes on the way there and change into the white dress before the ceremony. I part my thick hair down the middle and weave a ribbon into two braids. I twist the braids across the top of my head and pin the ends down, forming something of a crown. I don't do fancy hairdos. This is as fancy as it gets.

ڶ ڶ ڶ

I arrive at the barn door. There's no sign of Selim. I walk along the north side and peer around the corner when Selim gently grabs my arm and pulls me in.

"Happy eighteenth birthday!" he says.

"And what a birthday it's going to be," I say. "How many people get a wish come true as a birthday present?" I kick the dirt floor with the tip of my shoe. "Selim, did you see yesterday's newspaper?"

His chest deflates. "Yes, my mother showed it to me. If I'd known beforehand, I would have stopped her, or I would have at least warned you. Fatima's parents placed the advertisement."

"She's beautiful," I say.

"I do not love her, Evangelina. I love you."

I step forward and lay my cheek against his chest. "But you think she's beautiful . . ."

"I think you're beautiful. We're about to be married." He folds his arms around my back and holds me tenderly. I sigh a breath of relief. *Selim is the oyster and I am the pearl and I am safe.*

"I thought you should wait before telling your parents, but it's not fair to let them go on planning for a wedding that's never going to happen," I say. "It's not fair to Fatima or her family, either."

"This week, I will tell them this week."

"Good," I say quietly. "I will tell my family, too. We'll already be married by then, and there'll be nothing they can do to stop it.

Selim kisses the tip of my nose. "Let's do it."

        🚲 🚲 🚲

Andrés Villanueva opens the door to his cabin, lantern in hand.

"Welcome, Evangelina," he says. "And to you, sir," he says, nodding to Selim.

A young man I don't recognize steps out onto the porch. He removes his scuffed brown cowboy hat and looks at me with wide eyes.

"This is Cyrus Longoria," Señor Villanueva says.

"Hello," I say to Cyrus. "I'm pleased to make your acquaintance. You're probably wondering why I am wearing men's clothing, and I would happily tell you, but it's quite a long story, and we're short on time."

"Honored to meet you, Miss," he says, bowing his head.

"The pleasure is mine," I reply. "May I ask how you two met?" I ask.

"When I left the priesthood, I became a farrier," Señor Villanueva answers. "Cyrus and his father, Ramón, been coming to me since Cyrus was knee-high. There isn't a soul in these parts who doesn't need their horses shoed, except the few pompous asses driving Cadillacs and Model-Ts in town," he says. "Excuse my language."

"Señor Villanueva asked if I'd talk with you," Cyrus says. "My mother would want me to tell the truth."

ॐ ॐ ॐ

Selim and Señor Villanueva go inside the house to give us some privacy.

Cyrus speaks English and Spanish, but the two of us stick to Spanish. His Mexican father insisted that he learn both. He tells me what happened on the day his mother died.

In the early morning hours of May 7, Ramona Healy went into labor. Terrified that he'd have to deliver the baby himself, Cyrus set out to find someone else willing to do the job. Not knowing this, Ramona Healy asked the neighbor, Mrs. Graham, to get help. I arrived first. Doctor Morley showed up and ordered me to get out. Cyrus saw me leave.

The doctor made it clear that Cyrus was not to go inside under any circumstance. He tried to busy himself by chopping wood and skinning a rabbit, but his mother's screams were coming through the walls. He peeked through the window.

Now he can't erase what he saw.

An hour later, he cleaned up the blood.

❦ ❦ ❦

Mercedes Villanueva sits in her little rocking chair with her corn husk doll tucked under her arm. She's filling in her clothes better, and her stomach pain is a thing of the past.

"What's her name?" I ask, pointing to her doll.

"Belinda," she says.

"Really? My favorite doll is named Belinda, too! I brought her with me from Mexico. Would you like me to listen to your doll's heart?"

"Does she have a fever?" asks Mercedes.

"I don't think so, but let's check to be sure." I feel the doll's forehead and put my stethoscope on its chest. "She's in perfect health!" I declare. "You must be taking good care of her."

"Yes, Doctor Evangelina."

"Mercedes feels much better, thank heavens," Señor Villanueva says.

Mercedes strokes my face with her tiny hand. "You are very pretty, and that man is very handsome," she swivels to point at Selim. "Is he your husband?"

"Funny that you should ask that," Selim says. "Evangelina, I'll go grab your bag. I am sure they won't mind if you change in here."

"I've been looking forward to this. I haven't done a marriage ceremony in many years," says Señor Villanueva.

❦ ❦ ❦

A quilt hangs in the corner of the house, forming a triangular space for me to change. I pull off Enrique's clothes and set them on a small wooden chair against the wall. I open the green embroidered bag with the stiff bottom and pull out the white dress Elsa borrowed from the dress shop, one final favor the owner couldn't deny after letting Elsa go. I hold it up against the wall with one hand and use the other to smooth out the wrinkles without success. Wrinkled it is! A pair of white stockings, bloomers, a petticoat and Elsa's too-big high-heeled black shoes complete my wedding attire. With no mirror in the house, I can only hope that I look presentable.

I step out of the curtained corner to a waiting Selim, now in brown trousers, a white shirt, dark orange suspenders and a matching tie. My body warms at the sight of him.

"You look stunning," he says.

"Why, thank you!" I say, giving him a little curtsy.

He holds his hand out. "Walk with me."

Flickering oil lamps form a three-quarter circle under a tall twisty oak tree.

Selim takes me to the outer edge of the circle and stops.

"Wait here," he says and rushes over to the carriage rider box, where he leans in and pulls out a bouquet of roses. They smell sweet and clean, like nature's blessing.

We join Señor Villanueva inside the circle. Little Mercedes brings another oil lamp and sets it down, making a fully enclosed ring of light. With stars as our witnesses, the former priest opens his Bible.

"Are you ready?" he asks.

Selim and I nod.

"Let us begin. We gather here to unite these two people in marriage. Their decision to marry has not been entered into lightly, and today they declare their private

devotion to each other. Marriage is a sharing of respon-
sibilities, hopes and dreams. It takes effort to grow
together and offer unconditional, unselfish love, even in
the best of circumstances. Evangelina and Selim, marriage is a holy commitment to honor and care for one
another, cherish and encourage each other, through sor-
rows and joys, hardships and triumphs, for all the days
of your lives."

He looks to Selim. "Selim, please take Evangelina's
hands."

I lower my hands to meet Selim's upward turned
palms.

"Selim, do you take Evangelina as your wife . . ."

The sound of gravel underfoot starts soft and grows.

"Well, well, lookit what we have here! Why it's the little murderer and her Ay-rab lover," says Sheriff Pearl.
He and Humphrey walk toward us with their guns
drawn.

Selim shields my body with his. Señor Villanueva
swoops Mercedes up in his arms.

"Don't be afraid, *m'ija*," he tells her. "I won't let them
hurt you. Gentlemen, my name is Andrés Villanueva,
and I can explain . . ."

"Nobody didn't ask you nothin'," Humphrey snarls.

"Put your hands up, both of ya's," the sheriff shouts
and waves his rifle back and forth between Selim and
me. "What is all this?" he says, jerking his head toward
the oil lamps on the ground. "Is this a damn weddin'?"
He roars with laughter. "You gotta be kiddin' me! Well,
I'm sorry ta break up yer romantic li'l party, but yer both
comin' with me. I told Judge O'Leary not ta let ya outta
my sight. Patrick O'Leary's gonna eat crow fer his supper tomorrow!"

I step out from behind Selim. "Sheriff, let me ex . . ."

"Yer gonna hang for sure, now," Humphrey sneers. "And your man ain't gonna see the light'a day neither."

"Gentleman, please put your guns away. We are unarmed, and there's a child here," Selim says evenly.

"Shut yer mouth," the sheriff growls. "I got some unfinished business with yer pretty li'l bride, and yer both under arrest!"

By "unfinished business," does he mean . . .

A wave of anger I've never known explodes. "Leave us alone, you son of a bitch!" I scream.

The sheriff slaps me so hard that I stumble backward and hit the ground.

Selim lunges toward me with outstretched arms, and the sheriff whacks him in the chin with the end of his rifle.

⅊ ⅊ ⅊

Selim and I spend the night talking, which feels so strange—him in his cell and me in mine, able to hear but not see each other. I talk, but mostly, I cry. And cry. More than anything, I wanted to seal our bond as husband and wife in this life before I have to leave him for the next.

⅊ ⅊ ⅊

Teresita and Joaquín stand outside the jail cells.

"Evangelina, we just heard," she says.

"I only let 'em in here, 'cause he's yer legal counsel, an' I felt sorry for the hunchback," says Sheriff Pearl standing nearby, biting into a chicken leg and wiping his hands on his pants. "Otherwise, I woulda tossed 'em out like any other mangy dogs."

"Selim, you may need to have that wound stitched up. I'll ask Doctor Taylor to come by," says Teresita. "Did the sheriff do this to you?"

"Yes, ma'am," Selim says.

"How did they find us?" I ask Joaquín.

"We don't know," he says. "You're going to have to fill us in."

"You been meetin' in Franklin Carlson's barn, and his son's been watchin'," the sheriff comes over and interrupts.

I did see a light in old man Carlson's window that night!

"Ole Franklin Jr. read Cora's article, if ya wanna call it that. He figured it was you meetin' up with this Arab. Franklin thought he'd get some kinda reward, which he ain't."

"What happens now?" I ask Joaquín.

"I don't anticipate being able to get you out of here again before or during the trial," Joaquín answers. "Teresita, Doctor Taylor and I have been working hard and have news to share with you. When we're alone, you'll need to tell us why you were found just outside of Fox Grove, less than five miles from the Healy home. It could look suspicious to a jury. Why Fox Grove of all places?"

"She took the risk not for her benefit, sir. She was caring for a patient," Selim says.

"There wasn't no patient! This girl was tryin' ta marry that fool!" Humphrey says. "But we stopped it cold, didn't we, sheriff?"

"Why don't you shut your mouth?" Selim yells.

The sheriff bangs his baton on Selim's cell door. "What's yer daddy gonna say when he finds ya here? Huh? Ya think this is gonna help his sales?"

"Sir, we have a right to speak privately with our clients," Joaquín says. "I suggest you leave the building for a short while, perhaps twenty minutes. You can stand just outside if you want. Or, release Evangelina and Selim so we may talk with them elsewhere. You can leave their cuffs on."

"Did ya hit yer head, boy, 'cause yer not thinkin' straight. Ya may be her legal counsel, but I'm in charge here, an' I ain't leavin' the damn buildin'!" His yellow-stained eyes grow and nearly stand out of his head.

"Sheriff, I assure you that we will address your racist behavior and appalling treatment of my client in court," Teresita says icily. "As Mr. Castañeda already explained, Evangelina has a right to a private conversation with her legal counsel. So, if you would leave the area, I presume you have work to do at your desk."

"What're ya gonna do? File charges 'cause I called ya a few names? If that's what yer talkin' about, yer gonna be filin' charges against half this town. You don't have no authority here. I don't care one whit how big yer ranch is or how much money you rollin' in. I'm the sheriff, and I can say or do . . ."

He stops mid-sentence and swivels his square head over his shoulder.

"What in the hell? Who are those people marchin' up the street?" he says, stepping around the half-wall toward the door.

What people?

Teresita's eyes crinkle at the edges.

"What is it?" Selim asks.

"Reinforcements," Teresita says.

"What's Cora Cavanaugh doin' with them people? And what's that on her eye?" the sheriff bellows.

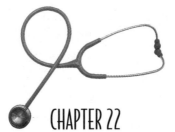

CHAPTER 22

We Demand

Specks of dust drift and fall through the air as the sheriff throws open the massive front door of the jail.

"Who in the hell are you people?" he screams. "I'm the law 'round here! You turn yerselves 'round and go on back to where ya came from!"

"Let Evangelina go!" someone yells.

"Milton? Is that you? What're ya doin' with the likes of these people? Miss Hayden? That goes for you, too. What is this? Whaddya all want?"

"Excuse me," Joaquín says to Selim and me as he moves toward the front door. "I'll be outside with Cora and the others."

"What's going on?" I ask Teresita.

"Cora's articles have given your case the exposure that we'd hoped for," she answers. "La Liga's board reached out to some of the most influential leaders in Texas, Mexican and Anglo alike. People are coming in to show their support. We timed it for today in anticipation of the trial."

"Teresita? The sheriff said he has some 'unfinished business' with me," I say.

"The moment we learned you were back in jail, Joaquín filed papers with the judge about concern for your safety. He's seen the publicity around this case grow, and he doesn't want to make any mistakes. We sent a dispatch this morning requesting additional guards. Law enforcement officers from Loma will be with you twenty-four hours a day, and I requested two in particular with whom I've worked before. The sheriff's people will be here as well, but you won't have to be alone with them, ever again."

"Thank you, Señora. What about Selim?" I ask. "He didn't break the court's order; I did."

"We'll take care of Selim. Now, I really must go."

I move to the edge of my cell and hold out my hand. Selim's fingers brush across mine.

"I don't want to leave if you have to stay," he says.

"Selim, you're only here because of me," I say. "I convinced myself that we could do it without getting caught. It was wrong of me. I'm sorry."

"Thank you all for coming!" Teresita shouts outside. "Evangelina de León is innocent!"

The crowd cheers.

"Evangelina is in jail not because she's guilty but because she's Mexican. Innocent Mexicans across the state are being falsely charged, tortured and killed. If you feel powerless against those with more money and power, hear this! You are *not* powerless! The government counts on your fear and your silence, but we will not be silent! We demand equal opportunity for life, liberty, dignity and justice! Repeat after me! We demand!"

"We demand!" the crowd shouts.

"Equal opportunity!" she yells.

"Equal opportunity!"

"For life!"

"For life!"

"For liberty!"

"For liberty!"

"For dignity!"

"For dignity!"

"For justice!"

"For justice!"

"You listen ta me!" the sheriff roars.

"Listen up, everybody!" Humphrey echoes.

"This here's an unlawful disturbance a the peace, and I'll arrest every one a yas," the sheriff screams. "Get the hell outta here! Now!"

"What're you gonna do? Are you really going to arrest *all* of us, sheriff?"

It's Cora!

"There's a whole crowd here," she shouts. "And it's only gonna grow. How many jail cells you got in there?"

"I read what you wrote, Cora. Lies, all lies! Don't listen ta this woman! Y'all like sheep ta the slaughter. She's a menace ta society, and y'all are makin' fools of yerselves. Yer breakin' the law here! Now, git on home!"

"We will meet right here tomorrow morning at the same time," Cora shouts. "We will not be bullied into submission. The trial of the century begins in three days!"

⏞ ⏞ ⏞

Teresita, Joaquín and Cora step inside, their faces sweaty and flushed.

"Hooo-weee!" Cora shouts, wiping her forehead with a handkerchief. "Quiet little Seneca's gettin' rattled, and I love it! The sheriff looked downright thunderstruck!"

"I wish you could have seen the looks on those people's faces," Joaquín says to Selim and me. "I counted thirty-eight. They came from all over to support you."

"Where are they now?" Selim asks.

"We've arranged for them to stay with the locals," Teresita answers. "They'll come in waves. None of them can stay for long, but when one wave leaves, another will arrive."

"I wish I could have been out there to see it," Selim says.

"Joaquín? I have crucial information about my case," I say. "Can I speak with you now, while Humphrey and the sheriff are still outside?"

"Cora, Teresita, will you be so kind as to wait for me at Lonnie's? We can have lunch when I'm finished here . . . Oh, and bring something back for Selim and Evangelina."

"You know I want to hear everythin', but I understand . . . attorney-client privilege and all that nonsense," Cora says, shaking her head. "I hate it when someone knows somethin' I don't know. Let's go get some of that fried chicken," she says to Teresita. "I've been smellin' it for hours!"

"We've eaten at Lonnie's many times," says Teresita. "What I want is a plate of *enchiladas, frijoles* and rice," Teresita says. "Next time, we eat in the Mexican neighborhood. You can try *machitos*," one of my favorites.

"What is that?" Cora asks.

"Goat innards," Teresita says. "Like haggis in Scotland. Don't you hail from there? *Machitos* are a northern Mexico specialty. They're especially good with blood gravy."

"I'll stick with fried chicken and peach pie!" Cora responds.

"I'll join you as soon as I can," Joaquín says.

"What is it you want to tell me?" he asks.

"You asked earlier why Selim and I were at the Villanueva home. I asked him to drive me to see patients outside of town. We used the carriage to keep me concealed. He did nothing wrong. I begged him to do it."

"They wouldn't have gotten medical care otherwise," Selim adds. "She risked everything to help them. It was my choice to help her. She didn't beg me at all. The second patient would have died if she hadn't examined him."

"Humphrey was right about the marriage ceremony," I tell Joaquín. "Andrés Villanueva is a former priest. With my uncertain future, we took the chance while we could."

"You two are married now?"

"The sheriff came before we said our vows," says Selim.

"Thank you for being honest with me, both of you. I will see if I can get Selim released within the next forty-eight hours," Joaquín says. "No promises, but I will try."

Joaquín leans down to pick up his briefcase.

"There's one more thing," I tell him. "While we were there, Cyrus Longoria spoke with me."

"Ramona Healy's son?"

"Exactly."

"How is it that . . . I wanted to interview him myself but couldn't get a hold of him. I thought he was hiding out somewhere."

"The two patients I visited live near Fox Grove. One of the patient's fathers knows Cyrus. It's a small community around there, even smaller than Seneca, and everybody knows everybody."

"I don't know whether to scold you or thank you," Joaquín says.

"Cyrus says Jedidiah Morley caused his mother's death. We'll need Doc Taylor to verify that."

"Why didn't Cyrus come forward with this before?" Joaquín asks.

"The doctor threatened to accuse Cyrus's Mexican father of breaking into his clinic for cash and medicine. Cyrus knew what that would mean for his father. He'd just lost one parent and didn't want to lose the other."

"What exactly did he see?"

"Selim? Are you in there?" someone calls.

Selim's mother and father enter, his mother in a long black dress and gray shawl draped over her head and neck. His father wears trousers that gather at the ankle, a white shirt, a dark sash wrapped tightly around his middle and a waist-length jacket.

"We heard what happened!" his mother cries. "That you tried to marry this girl!" She points at me. "A known murderer! Fatima's parents are devastated! Fatima fell to pieces when she found out. We are in the middle of planning a wedding! You've shamed our family. Look at you! I said it couldn't be true, but there you are, behind bars like a common criminal!" she shouts. "We told you to stay away from her! You're a fool to have disobeyed us." She lifts a layer of the shawl from around her neck, pulls it over her nose and mouth, and weeps.

Joaquín mouths the word "goodbye" and leaves the building, tipping his hat toward Selim's parents on his way out.

"Mama, Baba, let me explain," Selim pleads. "I have not been honest with you, and for that, I apologize. I love Evangelina, and she loves me. If obeying you meant leaving her, I knew that I could never . . ."

"Stop!" his father commands, his nostrils flaring. "We do not want to hear your dishonorable words. We must pray."

He and his wife bow their heads.

"Did you not hear me? I love her," Selim says defiantly.

"I do not know you anymore, Selim," his father says. "We brought you and your brother here to make a better life, and you have forsaken our sacrifices."

They lower themselves to their hands and knees, and his father murmurs a prayer only the two of them can hear.

"You are a stain on our family, Selim," his father utters, pushing himself up to stand. "The only way to rid ourselves of it is to cut it out."

Selim's mother moans. His father jerks his head toward the door and walks out, pulling his wife behind him. "You must be strong, Hamia," he tells her. "Do not look at him. He is dead to us."

"Don't do this!" Selim calls to his parents, but they are already gone.

🚲 🚲 🚲

Juan de los Santos, a bear-sized man in uniform with hands the size of tea kettles arrives at the jail with a court order.

On this day, July 2, 1915, it is hereby decreed that two (2) law enforcement officers from Loma, Texas, will guard prisoner Evangelina de León until such time that her murder trial is over and a verdict read.

Signed, the Honorable Judge Patrick O'Leary
Patrick O'Leary

Humphrey swaggers in carrying a chair for the guard.

"Don't ya try nothin'," he says to the officer. "You dohn scare me."

Officer de los Santos assures me he'll be there throughout the night. I sit against the wall and close my eyes.

"Selim? I am sorry about your parents," I say. "I would give anything to make it different."

"I know," he whispers.

I wait for him to say something else, but he never does.

殂 殂 殂

The following morning, they let Selim go.

CHAPTER 23

Rice and Beans

Sheriff Pearl walks in with the newspaper in hand. He reaches inside and pulls out a leaflet.

"Read this," he says. "*The Gazette* published Cora's lies about yer case. Now they've come ta their senses an' printed the truth. All the clowns ya brung here to stampede the streets ain't gonna change the facts."

The Goldendale Gazette
Special Edition Insert
By The Gazette Editorial Board

DEATH OF AN INNOCENT
"WOLF IN SHEEP'S CLOTHING" TO BE TRIED
FOR WITCHCRAFT AND MURDER

July 3, 1915 One of the most sensational trials in our history begins the day after tomorrow in the honorable Patrick O'Leary's court. Evangelina de León is charged with witchcraft and the murder of Mrs. Otis Healy. Donald Mitchell, Attorney at Law, will serve as the prosecuting attorney. The facts of the case are as follows:

The victim, Mrs. Ramona Healy, lived with her husband, Otis Healy, and teenage son Cyrus in an idyllic country cottage near Fox Grove. On that fateful day, May 7, 1915, Otis Healy was not at home.

Eight months with child, Ramona Healy went into labor at approximately 1 o'clock that morning. At 4 pm, a neighbor, Mrs. Erasmus Graham, visited the Healy home bearing fresh bread and found Ramona Healy in considerable pain, agitated and fearful for her unborn infant. Being a good Christian woman, Mrs. Graham left, without hesitation, to search for help.

In her frantic search, she knocked on another neighbor's door. It was there she came upon a Mexican girl, Evangelina de Leon, stitching up nine-year-old Esteban Garza's foot at the dilapidated home of Jose Luis Garza and his wife. Carol Anne Graham inquired about Miss de Leon's capacity to assist with childbirth, to which de León responded that she had adequate experience with traditional birth in the United States and primitive Mexican care in her country of origin. Mrs. Graham weighed her options and decided that she had no other choice but to escort her to the Healy home despite her reservations about the Mexican girl's qualifications and intentions. They arrived around 5 pm. Mrs. Graham stated that she would have stayed to assist Ramona Healy herself had she not had four children, ages 8, 6, 5 and 3, at home in need of careful supervision.

We now know that Mrs. Graham's reservations turned out to be well warranted. Miss de León, a 17-year-old Mexican immigrant barely out of secondary school, falsely claimed that she had medical expertise. A wolf in sheep's clothing, she performed routine healthcare mostly for other Mexicans. Some who mistakenly placed their trust in her suffered the consequences of inexcusable malpractice, according to multiple sources.

When the kindly neighbor Mrs. Graham left to find help, she was unaware that Ramona Healy's son, Cyrus, had already left home to search for a qualified physician, which he found in Jedidiah Morley.

The doctor, with more than two decades of commendable and even heroic service to local communities, entered the premises and witnessed the murder in progress. His exact words follow.

CAUTION: Doctor Morley's account may be difficult for some to read and could cause harm to those with tender hearts and weakened physical constitutions. Read at your discretion.

"Upon approaching the home, I saw through the window, a figure hunched over the patient. Not knowing who it was, I entered quietly, so as to not be detected, and saw Mrs. Healy, lying flat, in a defenseless and semi-conscious state. The accused chanted gibberish and moaned like a tortured creature sent from the bowels of Hell.

Mrs. Healy shook violently, and foam emanated from her mouth. I rushed forward and pushed the girl away, but it was too late. Ramona Healy looked at me with terrified eyes and drew her last breath. I faced an almost unbearable decision—try to resuscitate Ramona Healy or save her unborn child. The mother had no pulse, and the baby had just moments to live. In the end, I saved her unborn son. Percival Healy was born that night to a murdered mother. The widower, Otis Healy, has taken to calling him Percy, a name his deceased wife had chosen.

After tending to the infant, I examined the home. On a side table, next to Mrs. Healy's lifeless body, I found a cup with poison in it. Ramona Healy suffered a long and painful death, a death of Evangelina de León's doing."

Read *The Goldendale Gazette* for continued updates on trial proceedings as Donald Mitchell, Attorney at Law, seeks justice for Ramona Healy. The crime is punishable by death by hanging.

I crumple the paper and toss it in the bucket.

"Sheriff Pearl, we beg you to let us in to see Evangelina," I hear Mamá plead.

"Mamá!" I call out.

"Fools never learn," he says. "If ya want to talk to 'er, you can do it from outside, like ya did before!"

"Sheriff," Mamá continues, "we know there is no rules about visit Evangelina."

The daytime guard, Senovio Rivas, the other Loma police officer brought in to protect me, rises from his chair and walks around the half wall.

"Sheriff Pearl," he begins, "Miss de León's attorney stated to me that there are no legal restrictions regarding which visitors can enter during regular business hours and which ones cannot."

"For yer information, it wasn't me who agreed ta lettin' ya in here, an' now ya see fit to give me guff?" Sheriff Pearl says.

"I have the judge's orders in my pocket if you'd care to see them—again," Officer Rivas counters.

Seconds pass.

"I'm givin' 'em ten minutes back there," the sheriff grumbles.

"I will give you some privacy. I'll be just outside if you need me," Officer Rivas says to my parents.

"Just because I'm lettin' you two and the old man in there," Sheriff Pearl says, "don't mean I can't listen to what you say. Remember that."

Old man?

Mamá rounds the corner. Abuelito hobbles behind her with his cane, followed by Papá.

A prickling sensation starts in my head and rolls down into my toes. I throw my arms open to hug him, then remember that I'm behind bars.

"You came!" I cry. "How did you . . . How are . . . ? I can't believe you're here! I've missed you so much!"

"*M'ija*, what a relief it is to see you," Abuelito says in Spanish. "Your *mamá* wrote to us of your troubles, and I knew I had to come," he says, his voice shakier than I remember. "René accompanied me here by train, then turned around and went back to Francisca and the children."

"You are an answer to my prayers," I say, reaching for Abuelito's hands. "Beans and rice, together again as they should be.

"What is wrong with your hands?" I say, examining his fingers and palms. "Your fingers are as big as sausages."

"Nothing, *m'ija*, just some swelling from sitting too long," he says.

"We would have come sooner had we known what was going on," Mamá says, her eyes wet with tears, her hair gathered into a collapsing bun. "Your papá went to Sierra City to ask about a foreman position at a ranch there. Your little brothers and I went with him. It took a full day to get there and another to get back. I should have stayed behind! I should have been here when they brought you back to this wicked place."

"No need to apologize," I say. "Teresita brought two officers from Loma to guard me as soon as she heard."

"God bless Teresita," Papá says.

"We heard you left Doc Taylor's home in the middle of the night to tend to patients. Is this true?" says Mamá.

I nod.

"Where is Selim?" Mamá asks. "I thought he would be here with you."

My heart races.

"Joaquín got Judge O'Leary to release him. The judge didn't need a second fight with Joaquín. He's got enough trouble on his hands with my trial starting the day after tomorrow and protesters crowding the streets. I hope you don't hate me."

"Nonsense, *M'ija*. This is a hard time for you," says Abuelito. "I think your parents will agree, the best thing we can do is to love you without judgment. Whatever happened between you and this young man, Selim is a discussion for another time."

"Y'all have to go," Humphrey announces. "You been eatin' too many beans," he says, waving his hand in front of his nose.

Papá strides over to Humphrey and faces him. "I no like you," Papá says and pushes his finger into Humphrey's chest.

"Dohn'choo touch me!" shouts Humphrey.

"Adán, be careful," Mamá says.

"You have no honor. May God has mercy on you," Papá adds.

"You wanna say that to me?" Sheriff Pearl growls. "I didn't think so. Now, get out. You had more than yer ten damn minutes."

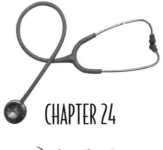

CHAPTER 24

Who I Am

"Guilty," the judge booms as his gavel comes down. My parents jump up from their seats in the first row. "Witches can't die!" Papá screams. My mother falls to the ground. Domingo rushes forward and grabs my arm. "Does this mean you can't be my sister anymore?" he sobs. Selim stands with his parents and an olive-skinned beauty wearing a white gown and lace head covering at the back of the courtroom. I try to catch his eye, but he turns away.

A cloaked figure glides in and pulls me through the side door exit. The crowd boos. At the foot of the gallows platform, Teresita motions for me to walk up the steps.

Abuelito stands head and shoulders above the crowd. The sheriff sits on his horse nearby, smoking a cigar.

The noose slips over my neck. Immediately to my left, a wooden platform drops, exposing a square hole. Doctor Taylor waits in a surgical gown below.

La Llorona removes her hood. I knew it was her from the start. It's always her. The sound of a thousand trains screaming to a stop explodes from her mouth with a ribbon of butterflies that flutter out.

The onlookers cover their ears; the littlest children cry, Ramona Healy appears from the beyond and pushes me. I wait for the snap of the rope.

&ᵇ &ᵇ &ᵇ

Drenched in sweat and out of breath, I sit up, open the window and try to shake the cobwebs from my head.

There's a pattern with my La Llorona dreams. Whenever I feel guilty about something, she comes in the night. I've destroyed the lives of those I love. Of course, she couldn't resist.

The sun streams through the window, and the birds outside sing back and forth in their annual ritual to find a mate, build a nest and raise their hatchlings. Such happy sounds on an otherwise worrisome morning. I clasp my hands in prayer, stand up and decide to get on with it.

I change into the ensemble Elsa brought for me: a long white cotton skirt with two layers of wavy ruffles at the hemline and a white Mexican blouse with colorful flowers stitched around the neckline, across the back and around the wrists of the gathered long sleeves. I undo the damp braid I made last night and shake my wavy hair out.

My family and friends arrive.

"I gave this to your abuelita on our tenth anniversary," says Abuelito, handing me a small wooden box. "She would want you to have it."

Inside sits a silver butterfly brooch.

"A *mariposa*," I say, wiping away a tear. "Thank you, Abuelito. I'll cherish it always." I pin the butterfly just above an embroidered red flower near my left collarbone, a perfect place for it to land.

"You sure you wanna wear that?" Cora asks. "It's beautiful and all, but it's not exactly courtroom attire. It could draw unwanted attention."

"This is who I am," I reply.

Cora nods. "All right, darlin'. I'm proud of you."

Humphrey handcuffs and leads me outside. We stand on the top step facing the street. A crowd of people of every skin color holds their signs high.

Verdict: INNOCENT!
FREE Evangelina!
Senecans for Evangelina
Justice for ALL

People look at me expectantly. Children squirm in their parents' arms. I try to calm my nerves.

"You're gonna have to be bold to get through this thing," Cora told me when all this started. Here I go.

"We, the people!" I shout over the stirrings of the crowd.

"We, the people!" they shout back.

"Demand justice!"

"Demand justice!"

"Come on," Humphrey growls and forces me down the steps.

"Without regard!" I continue as he pushes me ahead.

"Without regard!"

"To race, color or faith!"

"To race, color or faith!"

The crowd follows us, chanting with me.

New people filter in from every direction, holding a different kind of sign.

LOCK HER UP!
DEATH TO WITCHES
JUSTICE FOR RAMONA HEALY

Victor Hughes, my old schoolmate, holds a metal megaphone.

"An eye for an eye!" he shouts.

"An eye for an eye!" half the crowd repeats.

"Witches must die!"

"Witches must die!"

The two sides chant louder and louder, drowning each other out.

Victor crosses in front of me and spits. The glob from his mouth misses my shoe and lands on Humphrey's.

☙ ☙ ☙

Joaquín meets us at the door to the courthouse, a familiar place since the school is on the second floor. The court looks mostly the same as the last time I saw it in 1912. Two rectangular oak tables, each with two tall chairs, face the judge's seat in the center front of the room, one table for the defense and one for the prosecution. Sitting on a raised platform along the sidewall is a long table with simple wooden chairs. The twenty-four eyes of twelve Anglo men study me as I enter the room. Some examine me like a side of beef hanging in cold storage. A few have "you should be ashamed" expressions, and one man leisurely runs his tongue over his lips.

A gold-framed portrait of the Texas Governor hangs behind the judge on a dark paneled wall. An American flag hangs in folds against a pole in the left front corner of the room and the Texas flag on the other side.

Joaquín leads me to the defendant's chair. The crowd of people that walked behind us files in, one by one, into the rows of wooden benches, their signs of support and blame left outside.

Judge O'Leary pounds his gavel. "Order in the courtroom!" he shouts.

Mamá dabs her eyes with a handkerchief in the front row. Papá wraps his arm around her slumped shoulders. Tomás looks around the room, squeezes his eyes shut, then takes hold of Mamá's arm. Domingo tries to wink at me but closes both eyes in the process. Selim, Abuelito, Elsa and Cora sit quietly, eyes forward. Men wearing large "PRESS" buttons on their lapel jackets fill the second row.

"Hear ye, hear ye!" shouts a short round man in dark pants, a blue buttoned shirt and a red scarf tied around his neck. "Be it remembered that on this day, the fifth of July in the year of our Lord, one thousand, nine hundred and fifteen, before the Honorable Patrick O'Leary, in Seneca, Texas, this trial shall commence.

"The jurors of the people of Haller County, Texas, shall decide if Miss Evan-jell-ina duh Lee-on, of Mariposa, Mexico, is guilty or innocent of the charges that she deliberately, maliciously and feloniously used the Satanic rituals of witchcraft to affect the death of Ramona Rose Healy on the seventh day of May, in this year of our Lord, one thousand, nine hundred and fifteen."

"All rise so that the Honorable Patrick O'Leary may address the court," the scarved man announces.

The shuffling sounds of people rising from their seats fill the room. An infant cries. A mother shushes and soothes. The judge stands and speaks, but his voice echoes as if he's in a far-away canyon.

I see myself sitting on the flat rock near the ranch house in Mariposa, *my* flat rock, by the swirling Río Bravo, throwing stones into the water and listening for the splash. I stand by the headstone at Abuelita's gravesite in a field of bluebonnets and sing softly to her. I look out over our orchards. I walk alongside Mamá, carrying a basket of citrus to give away at church. I watch Elsa and Papá dance at her *quinceañera* under a canopy of paper flowers dangling on strings that sway in the breeze.

When my time comes, bury me next to Abuelita, in Mariposa, where my heart lies.

"Mr. Mitchell, you may proceed with your opening statement," Judge O'Leary says.

"You may be seated," says the man in the scarf.

"Evangelina, are you all right?" Joaquín whispers in my ear.

"Yes," I reply, nodding. "I'm fine."

"I need you to pay close attention throughout the trial," he says gently. "Whenever there is a break, we will discuss what happened in the period before it."

Donald Mitchell stands, buttons his jacket and adjusts his small rectangular glasses. His closely cut white hair stands out against his navy suit and red bowtie.

"May it please your Honor, the court foreman and gentlemen of the jury, Haller County accuses Evan-jell-ina duh Lee-on of murdering Mrs. Otis Healy on May 7th of this year. The law requires that I prove, beyond doubt, that she went to the Healy home with the express intent of killing Ramona Healy and her unborn child.

"We have several degrees of homicide in this state. With homicide, the accused can be charged with murder in the first degree or murder in the second degree. The difference between the two stems from the intent or lack thereof. Murder in the first degree equals intent. Murder in the second degree equals death without pre-meditation, deliberation or plan. In this case, the evidence will show that while the infant, Percival Healy, survived, Ramona Healy did not because Evan-jell-ina duh Lee-on poisoned her.

"She brought the poison with her knowing that she intended to use it. In other words, it was no accident; it was a cold, calculated killing.

"You may or may not believe in backwoods witch-craft, but the prosecution will show that Doctor Jedidiah Morley of Fox Grove saw the accused putting a Mexican curse on the victim. At that very moment, the victim lay defenseless and gasping for air."

I turn around and look at the first row. Mamá buries her head in Papá's shoulder.

"The very act of placing what we shall, from here onward, call 'a curse,' real or not, will show the intent to kill," Mr. Mitchell continues. "Autopsy findings will show that the poison Evan-jell-ina duh Lee-on adminis-tered attacked Ramona Healy's lungs and stopped her heart.

"The Prosecution will also show that the defendant misrepresented her medical background giving the vic-tim a false sense of safety, and, that in fact, she has a known history of malpractice, maiming those entrusted to her care and quite likely causing the death of yet another victim."

Conversations erupt across the benches behind me.

"You heard correctly!" Donald Mitchell booms. "The prosecution contends this murder may not be her first. An eyewitness saw Evan-jell-ina duh Lee-on placing a curse on another defenseless woman, who also died, and that eyewitness will testify before you."

"What is he talking about?" I whisper to Joaquín.

He writes on a notepad between us on the table. "No idea."

"Now, you may think, 'This girl is young, just eighteen years old, seventeen at the time of the crime. How could a young woman in small-town Texas possibly summon within her a desire to murder a woman with child?'" Mr. Mitchell asks. "I assure you it's quite possible, and in fact, has been done many times over. Consider the fifteen-year-old serial killer Jesse Palmer of Alabama, who killed at least nine children in his basement. And May Westervelt in our neighboring state of Louisiana, who at the tender age of thirteen murdered her mother and step-father while they slept."

A few women begin crying.

"Silence!" the judge scolds. "There will be no disruption in this court!"

"Mr. Mitchell, you may continue," says the judge.

"Evan-jell-ina duh Lee-on may have been on the young side the day of the tragedy, but I assure you, she was and is quite capable of murder," Mr. Mitchell says. "A girl from Mexico arrives in Texas, uneducated, unable to speak English, and takes all that our great and noble country has to offer, only to murder a law-abiding, vulnerable, American citizen. The county will prove, beyond doubt, that Evan-jell-ina duh Lee-on murdered Mrs. Otis Healy for no other reason than she wanted her and her unborn child dead. She, a self-anointed, lying, scheming Mexican witch, who comes from a family of the same, wanted them to die. Doctor Jedidiah Morley and others will testify to that fact and convince you that the only true and correct verdict is guilty of murder in the first degree and that Miss duh Lee-on should pay for her crimes, without delay, through death by hanging. Thank you for your keen attention."

Donald Mitchell strides back to the prosecution's table.

"Mr. Castanedda, you can make your opening remarks now," the judge says.

Joaquín stands, pauses, then moves closer to the jurors but faces the audience. His dark gray suit and navy blue tie look neatly pressed, his dark wavy hair slicked back with hair cream. His brilliant blue eyes scan the room.

"Good morning. My name is Joaquín Castañeda, legal counsel to Miss de León. In his opening remarks, Mr. Mitchell used character assassination, untruths and opinion to outline the county's case against my client. The difference between his approach and mine is that I will present undeniable facts and credible witnesses. You will come to know Miss de León not as an impostor and a witch but as an innocent, competent, compassionate and accomplished young woman who herself has been unjustly vilified and the subject of abuse at the hands of Haller County officials.

"Evangelina de León was at the home of Ramona and Otis Healy on the afternoon of May 7th. That is the only information the defense will not dispute.

"Miss de León, a seventeen-year-old living in Seneca had, in May of this year, four years of medical mentorship and practice under the instruction of Doctor Russell Taylor, the most trusted physician in Seneca and, some might say, in all of southeast Texas. That may seem impossible to you, a teenager practicing medicine, but Evangelina de León is no ordinary teen.

"In the past two years, she has administered patient care, often free of charge. That is what she was doing on May 7th, stitching up a boy's foot, when Mrs. Graham, the Healy's neighbor, arrived, pleading for help. Miss de León went gladly, confident in her experience assisting with childbirths at Doctor Taylor's clinic and delivering babies on her own in many of southeast Texas' rural communities, such as Fox Grove.

"When she arrived, Ramona Healy was in stable condition. As labor progressed, Miss de León used widely accepted methods of natural healing and prayer.

"Gentlemen of the jury, I ask you. Have you ever heard of murder by massage, herbal tea and prayer? The prosecution's assertion that Miss de León was using witchcraft and poison to kill Ramona Healy is not only utterly false, but it's also absurd.

"Furthermore, Miss de León was not there when Ramona Healy died. I guess Mr. Mitchell forgot to mention that. I repeat: Miss de León was not there when Ramona Healy died. Doctor Jedidiah Morley was. Doctor Morley unintentionally killed Ramona Healy, then used lies and threats to cover it up. We will demonstrate this to be the truth."

I hear the scratching noises of the reporters' pens scribbling away in their notebooks behind me. The rest of the audience sits silently except for the occasional cough or sneeze.

"Lastly," Joaquín continues, "we will provide examples of a disturbing string of racially motivated crimes underway across Texas. Before this trial is over, the defense will leave you with little doubt that Evangelina de León's arrest and shocking treatment at the hands of local law enforcement are a part of the same alarming trend of bigotry and violent vigilantism. In accusing Miss de León of a crime, Doctor Morley and Haller County assumed you would disregard the facts and convict because of Miss de León's race. It will be up to you to demonstrate with your verdict that 'with liberty and justice for all' means just that. Thank you for your time."

Joaquín returns to the defense table. "What do you think?" he whispers.

"Brilliant," I say.

"That's what I keep telling Cora, but she says I'm only smart enough to be a smart aleck," he says and winks.

"Hear ye! Hear ye!" the man in the scarf calls. "We are now adjourned for a short recess. The Honorable Patrick O'Leary will promptly commence proceedings again at 10 am, sharp."

A flurry of words and movements break out. People talk about the merits of each side's arguments or sprint for the water closet.

"Hey, smart aleck!" Cora says to Joaquín. "Good work up there!"

My family moves in for a round of hugs. Selim looks on from behind until Abuelito nudges him closer to me. Selim responds with a forced smile on his worried, handsome face.

CHAPTER 25

Shock and Displeasure

"The county will call its first witness," the man in the scarf announces. Joaquín said the man is called a "bailiff," a term I'd never heard until today.

Mr. Mitchell rises from his chair. "As its first witness, Haller County calls Hamish Cavanaugh to the stand."

Cora jumps up from her seat. "What on God's green earth is he here for?"

"Sit down and control yourself, Miss Cavanaugh," the judge says.

"Why is he a witness?" I write on the notepad.

"I wish I knew," Joaquín writes back. "Cora will be furious!"

Cora's father enters from the double doors in the back of the room, wearing brown checkered pants, a cream vest and a long brown suit jacket that stops just above his knees. His bushy red mustache covers all but his lower lip.

"Please enter here," the bailiff says and opens a small door leading to the witness stand. "Please place your right hand on the Bible. Do you swear to tell the truth and nothing but the truth, so help you, God?"

"Yes, of course," Hamish Cavanaugh says.

"Gentlemen of the jury, my first line of questioning will paint a picture of the accused's past malpractice. You will see how Miss duh Lee-on misrepresented her abilities and how that resulted in disastrous consequences for those who entrusted her with their care.

"Mr. Cavanaugh, you are the founder and executive officer of Cavanaugh Fine Fabrics, are you not?"

"That is correct," Mr. Cavanaugh says.

"You employ upwards of one hundred people in this area?"

"Yes, sir, one hundred and eleven at present."

"Most around these parts know of your reputation as a highly successful businessman and that you've had an indisputably positive impact on this thriving town, but please tell us about the lesser-known side of you, your family."

"My wife, Fiona, died in childbirth twenty-two years ago. I never remarried, and Cora is our only child. We left Scotland and arrived in New York when Cora was three years old. We came to Seneca soon after and have lived here ever since."

"Has your daughter had any recent health problems?"

What is he getting at?

"Yes, I'm afraid so."

"Will you please describe this health problem?"

"Cora visited the home of Doctor Russell Taylor, where Miss duh Lee-on was staying under house arrest. Cora supports Miss duh Lee-on, much to my shock and displeasure. Doctor Taylor was not home at the time."

"When did this visit occur that you speak of?"

"Approximately three weeks ago."

"Please continue."

"Cora came home from her visit with a patch on her eye looking haggard and pale. She said that a window broke and glass got into her eye. Believing Miss duh Lee-on to be a competent medical professional, Cora allowed her to look at her eye more closely and prescribe an ongoing regimen of care."

"And, why would Cora believe Evan-jell-ina duh Lee-on to be a competent medical professional at only seventeen years of age?"

"Because Miss de León convinced her so. Miss duh Lee-on overwhelmed my impressionable daughter over multiple visits to the jail."

Joaquín pushes his chair out and stands. "Objection! This is an inflammatory smear on my client," he says.

"Objection overruled," the judge answers.

Joaquín sits and writes on the notepad. "Unbelievable!"

"Mr. Cavanaugh, what has happened since Miss du Lee-on first administered to your daughter's injured eye?"

"She's gone blind," he says.

I squeeze Joaquín's arm.

"And you believe that if Cora had seen a true and competent doctor, she would still have her sight today?"

Joaquín stands up so quickly his chair topples backward. "Objection! Speculation!" he says, holding up his hands and shaking his head.

"Objection overruled," the judge says. "Answer the question, Mr. Cavanaugh. And Mr. Castanedda, I don't know where you normally practice law or what they let you get away with, but in this court, you will follow the rules. Now sit down."

"It's hardly speculation, young man," Hamish Cavanaugh continues, avoiding Cora's spitting-mad glare. "She had perfect vision in both eyes, up until that day. My daughter went blind in her right eye because of that imposter."

"What was the nature of the malpractice?" Mr. Mitchell asks.

"All I know is that girl over there is no medical expert, despite her delusions of grandeur. Cora went there able to see and wound up blind after that imposter touched her. You can see my daughter still has the patch on. I just hope she doesn't lose the eye."

People stretch their necks to catch a glimpse of Cora's face. Some even stand up and step closer.

"Thank you. No further questions," Mr. Mitchell concludes.

"People, people! Return to your seats! This is a courtroom, not a circus tent," the judge orders. "Your witness," the judge tells Joaquín.

Joaquín buttons his suit jacket despite the high temperature in the room.

"Mr. Cavanaugh, did you speak with your daughter about the treatment she received from Miss de León regarding her injured eye?"

"Not directly," Cavanaugh answers.

"How do you know then if Miss de León's treatment of the eye is what caused the vision loss?"

"Our housemaid, Caledonia, told me. She and Cora are very close and speak daily."

"Is it possible, sir, that something else caused your daughter's vision loss other than the medical care that my client administered?"

"Of course not."

"Is it *possible*, Mr. Cavanaugh?"

"Is it in the realm of possibility? Yes. Is it the truth? No."

"I see. Are you completely certain that your daughter lost all the vision in her right eye?"

"She's blind in that eye or partially blind. What difference does it make? She's impaired."

"Mr. Cavanaugh, why haven't you spoken with your daughter directly about this if you are so concerned about her welfare?"

"We have conflicting schedules and no opportunity to speak."

"And yet you live in the same house. Mr. Cavanaugh, when was the last time you spoke to your daughter?"

"I don't have an exact date," he says.

"I'll re-frame the question. Can you give us an estimate of how long it's been since you've spoken with your daughter? Days, weeks, months?"

"I can't recall," Cora's father says. "I've seen her struggling to go up and down the stairs! She dropped an expensive crystal vase yesterday, broke it into a hundred pieces. My daughter, while impressionable, is exceptionally coordinated, and that never would have happened before. She's damaged goods now! How will she ever run a household in that condition? What man would want her?"

"No further questions, your honor," says Joaquín who turns and walks back toward the defense table, pressing his lips together as if suppressing a smile.

Imagine the look on Mr. Cavanaugh's face when he finds out about her and Joaquín!

Hamish Cavanaugh steps down and files down the aisle past his daughter.

"You lying son of a bitch!" Cora hisses at her father, who does not so much as turn in her direction.

"I'll clear this up when I bring Cora to the stand," Joaquín writes.

"The prosecution calls Willie Falkirk," announces Mr. Mitchell.

"Who is Willie Falkirk?" I write.

"They don't have to provide a list of witnesses before-hand," he writes and draws a frown face. "They don't have our list either. It'll work to our advantage later," he writes, followed by a smiley face.

A boy in a tweed cap, tan pants, white shirt and sus-penders strolls up and takes the oath.

"Take your hat off, son," the judge instructs.

"Sorry, sir," the boy responds. "I mean, judge, your honor, sir."

"Willie, will you tell the jury how old you are?" Mr. Mitchell asks.

"Thirteen, sir," he says, pushing his floppy brown hair off his forehead.

"Have you ever seen the accused, Evan-jell-ina duh Lee-on before today?"

"Yessir," he answers.

I recognize him!

"When did you see her, and under what circum-stances?"

"I saw her two years ago on Doc Taylor's back porch. She was holding Mrs. Taylor's dead hand and mumbling gibberish to her. I mean, her hand wasn't dead; the old lady was dead."

The boy who dropped the groceries!

"Let's back up, shall we? You were eleven years old when this incident with Mrs. Agatha Taylor occurred?"

"Yes, sir, but I never knew her first name."

"Why don't you tell us what you were doing at Mrs. Taylor's home?"

"She hired me to get her groceries or go to the pharmacy and pick up a special kind of lotion she liked for her feet. She gave me money to buy stuff and an extra nickel for my time. I kicked the front door with the tip of my shoe a few times with two bags of groceries in my arms, but nobody answered, so I went around to the back of the house. And there she was."

"What did you see?" Mr. Mitchell asks.

"Mrs. Taylor, lying there, dead as the mouse my cat Chester dropped at our doorstep this morning."

"And, you're sure it was Mrs. Taylor?"

"Yes, sir. I saw her lots of times. She gave me lollipops sometimes when I passed her house on the way to school, but that was just when I was a little kid. I don't eat lollipops anymore since I'm all growed up."

"On that day, the day we were just discussing, when you found her on the porch, how did you know she was dead?"

"She was flat on the ground, and I couldn't see any breath going in and out o' her, and her skin looked all gray. She didn't move neither."

"To be clear, when you say she was 'flat on the ground,' you mean she was lying on the porch floor?"

"Yes, sir, that's what I meant."

"And what else did you see?"

"That girl over there," he says, standing up and pointing at me. "She was holding something in her hands and all bent over poor Doc Taylor's mother."

"You may sit back down, Willie. What was in her hands?"

"It was some kind of skull."

I want to scream!

"And what else?"

"The girl with the skull spoke some kind of talk I couldn't understand, and she said the same thing over and over again. She was talking to the devil."

"Speculation!" Joaquín shouts.

"Sit down! Your belligerent tone does not bode well with me, Mr. Castanedda," bellows the judge.

"And what did you do then?" continues Mr. Mitchell.

"I dropped the groceries and ran home."

"What did you think Miss de Lee-on was doing all hunched over Mrs. Taylor like that?"

"She was killin' her with a witch's spell. My best friend, Charlie Burton, told me all 'bout witches like he's some kinda expert."

"Willie, I have one more question for you," Mr. Mitchell says. "What did you do when you got home? Did you tell your mother or father or anyone else?"

"No, sir. I thought the witch would come after me if I did, so I didn't say nothin', not even to Charlie, but I drew a picture of it 'cause I couldn't get it out of my mind. I got it right here, if you wanna see it." He pulls a folded paper from his pants pocket.

"Will you hold it out for the jury to see, Willie?"

The boy unfolds the paper depicting a female with a long black braid, holding a skull and kneeling over another woman on the ground. It hardly looks like an eleven-year-old could have drawn it, but he holds it up proudly with both hands for the jurors to see.

"Gentlemen of the jury, I give this to you as evidence of Willie Falkirk's experience on the day of Agatha Taylor's likely murder. Why else would a boy, eleven years old, draw a horrifying picture of a dead woman and her killer if he did not see it with his own eyes? No further questions, your honor."

"I will interview this Charlie Burton," Joaquín writes on the notepad. "They must have paid that kid to lie."

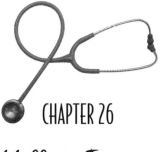

CHAPTER 26

Hollow Justice

Selim, Cora, Teresita and my family join us in the hallway during the second break. Selim stands next to me. I'd grab his hand if I thought it wouldn't draw attention and upset my already upset family.

"*M'ija*, I didn't like the look of that man up there, the one with the red hair. Anyone could see the streak of mean in him," Abuelito says in Spanish. Over the years, he's forgotten most of the English he once knew. "And the boy never looked the judge or the attorney in the eye. I could not understand what they were saying except for a few words. I should have brushed up on my English before I came, but I am old, and my memory fails me," he chuckles. "Your parents can tell me what I missed when we get back to the house. Regardless, I am certain you will be found innocent. I feel it in my bones, *m'ija*."

I lean forward and kiss his soft wrinkled cheek. "You're here, and that is enough for me," I say.

"Evangelina, many of your supporters, are outside," Teresita says. "Would you make a brief appearance? If we want them to stay motivated, they'll need to hear from you from time to time."

"Of course," I say, my stomach flipping at the thought of it.

"Come with me," Teresita says, leading me by the elbow.

Just outside the courthouse steps, a crowd stands along the sidewalk and partway into the street. Many hold up their signs.

I grab Teresita's hand for reinforcement.

"My case is just one of many wrongs suffered by Mexicans and Tejanos in this state and elsewhere!" I shout in a voice so loud that I startle myself. "In a land that says it welcomes the weary and provides equal rights to 'We, the People', they offer us hollow justice or no justice at all. I am 'the people'! We are all 'the people!'"

Some people cheer, others boo. An egg flies from the back and lands on the bottom step.

"Miss duh Lee-on! Did you kill Ramona Healy?" one man with a PRESS button yells.

"Have they charged you with Agatha Taylor's death?" another journalist shouts.

"How long have you been practicing witchcraft?"

"Did you think you'd get away with murder?"

"Miss de León will not be answering questions from journalists or anyone else at this time," Joaquín yells.

"Let's get back inside," Teresita says.

&ð &ð &ð

"All rise for the Honorable Patrick O'Leary," the bailiff announces.

"Mr. Castanedda, you may now question the prosecution's witness, Willie Falkirk Jr.," the judge says.

Willie makes his way back to the witness stand, where he fidgets with his hands and studies his shoes.

"Willie, you said that Mrs. Agatha Taylor was deceased when you arrived. Is that correct?" Joaquín asks.

"Yes, sir, I did."

"Do you know how long she'd been dead?"

"She musta died when that lady started putting a spell on her."

"And you know this how?" asks Joaquín.

"I don't know, mister."

"What time did you arrive at the Taylor home?"

"4 pm."

"And how do you know it was 4 pm?"

"Because I left for the store after school and then went straight over to her house. School ends at 3:15, mister."

"Well, that's curious, Willie, because Doctor Russell Taylor, Mrs. Taylor's son, determined that based on the state of rigor mortis, she passed away between 10 am and 12 noon. Miss de León was in class in this very building from 8 am to 3:15 pm on that day, the same as you. We know this because Miss de León had a perfect attendance record."

"What's rig . . . rigga . . . ?"

"Rigor mortis? It's the degree of muscle and joint stiffness that occurs naturally in a person's body after death."

Willie scrunches his face. "Gross."

The judge bangs his gavel. "Mr. Castanedda, are you morally bankrupt? We have women and children with tender ears in this courtroom!"

"No further questions," Joaquín responds. "However, if I may make a suggestion?"

"You're hardly in a position to make a suggestion, young man," the judge snaps.

"This is a murder trial, your honor. Unsavory details about the case will come to light in due time. You may want to warn those with 'tender ears' and encourage them to leave the courtroom."

"Court adjourned," the judge replies, ignoring Joaquín's suggestion. "We will start promptly at 10 am tomorrow."

"And one other thing, your honor, if I may, my last name is pronounced Cah-stahn-yeh-dah. The wavy line above the 'n' denotes the *enye* sound."

"Son, we speak English here, so you will answer to whatever I call you," Judge O'Leary snipes.

挅 挅 挅

I'm escorted back to jail. Selim enters through the back door, where Officer de los Santos shakes Selim's hand and joins Josiah in the office area.

Selim hands me a white rose. "For you," he says.

"Thank you," I say, bringing it up to my nose. "I'll ask Josiah to put it in water. It was good to see your face in the courtroom today," I tell him. "I know it must be awkward sitting next to my parents and Abuelito."

"Not at all. We talked about—the weather, of course," Selim says, taking a seat. "Best keep it simple for now."

"Any word from your parents?"

"My parents won't even look at me. I took as many of my things as I could and moved into Lonnie's barn. He offered me a job. I can't cook much except for a few Lebanese dishes, but he's teaching me."

"So, you're cut off from the family business, too."

Selim closes his eyes for a moment and clasps his hands in his lap.

"Evangelina, someone set my father's wagons on fire."

"What?"

"There's nothing left, the carriages, the merchandise, all of it."

"When did this happen?"

"Last night," he says. "Seneca has a volunteer fire department, but they never came."

"And you think someone set the fire deliberately?"

"They found cans of kerosene. It was no accident. I went over there as soon as I heard, but my father only shouted at me, that it's my fault for . . ."

"For what? Standing by me?" I say and lower myself to the ground.

"There's no way to know if that's the rea . . ."

"It is. I'm sure of it. First, my father lost his job, then Elsa, and now your family is caught up in this. I am so sorry, Selim. Your family must be in terrible distress."

"They'll need my help, but they'll never ask for it. Their pride will get in the way of letting me back in."

"What will you do?" I ask.

"I don't know. I told my father that I loved him. I'd never done that before," he says, looking blankly at the brick wall behind me. "He pretended that he didn't hear." Selim turns his attention back to me. "I don't want to talk about it anymore, okay? Teresita said that Jedidiah Morley would be on the witness stand tomorrow. Lonnie's giving me the day off, but that won't happen again for a while. The restaurant is busier than ever with the protestors in town. I'm learning to be a cook now, but I'll do better for us in the future. Once we decide where we want to live, I'll see about opening a hardware or grocery store. That's what I'm thinking, anyway. We can talk about it after they let you go."

We say our I love yous and goodbyes. I eat the cold quesadilla and plum that my parents brought by earlier and lie down with a light quilt Teresita supplied. With Officer de los Santos nearby, I fall asleep as soon as I pull the quilt over my shoulders.

۶ ۶ ۶

The trial begins promptly at 10 am.

"This should be interesting," Joaquín says. "What lies will the good doctor tell? Brace yourself. Listening to him could be hard."

"The prosecution calls Doctor Jedidiah Morley to the witness stand," announces Donald Mitchell.

Doctor Morley, whom I only saw once on that fateful night, walks up the aisle wearing a white lab coat. Doc Taylor said he's forty years old, but Morley's thinning light hair combed over his balding head, round spectacles, goatee and potbelly make him look older than he is.

"Do you swear to tell the truth and nothing but the truth, so help you, God?" the bailiff asks, holding out the Bible. The doctor places his right hand on it, closes his eyes and murmurs what I presume to be a prayer that goes on for at least a minute.

"I do," the doctor says and sits.

"Theatrics," writes Joaquín on the notepad.

"Before we start," the judge announces, "today's testimony may reveal information that could distress the fairer sex and children with sensitive constitutions. Given this court's obligation to reveal the truth, the attorneys and witnesses will not hold back in their descriptions of any unpleasantness. If knowing this, you would like to excuse yourself; you may do so at this time. I will not tolerate interruptions, such as fainting or sniveling during the proceedings. Ladies, did you hear me?"

A handful of women and children make their exit.

"Thank you, your honor. Your concern for the delicate and impressionable minds among us is much appreciated," Mr. Mitchell says, turning to the witness stand.

"Doctor Morley, if you would, good sir, please start by describing your medical qualifications."

"I earned my medical degree from the Tennessee College of Sciences in 1892, graduating in the top five percent of my class. I started my medical practice in 1893 in Morton, Tennessee. I arrived in Alden, Texas, in 1912. I had a successful practice there before moving to Fox Grove in late April of this year."

"And what prompted your move to Fox Grove?"

"Miss Mathilda Mathison, a young lady from Fox Grove and I plan to marry this September."

"My congratulations to you both. If I am doing my math correctly, you have practiced medicine for twenty-three years. In your estimation, how many patients have you treated?"

"Well over 2,500 unique persons," he says, looking up to search the faces in the fully filled room, perhaps to see if they look impressed.

"How many babies have you delivered?"

"I'd say around three hundred. That's an approximation, of course."

"Very well. Will you describe for the jury what happened on May 7, the day of Ramona Healy's death?"

"It started like any other day in the clinic. I saw three patients before lunch and three afterward. As we were closing up the office for the day, a young man of about fifteen years came through the door, pleading with me to help his mother. He said she was in the throes of childbirth, alone, and the baby was coming prematurely. Naturally, I grabbed my medical bag and followed him to the home on horseback, three or so miles from Fox Grove in a heavily wooded area."

"What happened after you arrived?"

"I told the boy, Cyrus was his name, to wait outside. He had said that his mother was alone, so I was shocked when I opened the door and saw a girl bent over the patient. I thought she might be a neighbor or a relative. I walked in quietly so as not to disturb and allow me to observe what was going on."

"Yes? And what then?"

"From the moment I opened the door, I noticed a pungent, sickening smell in the home. I looked around to find the source and saw two disturbing things. First, there appeared to be a burning root of some sort sticking out of a hole in a fist-sized stone. The smoke coming from it irritated my throat."

"In what way?"

"It began to close in on me, as if it was inducing a gradual suffocation."

"You said there were two things that disturbed you. The smoke was one. What was the other?"

"Candles, as many as thirty, lit throughout the small cottage. Between the foul-smelling smoke and the candles, I thought I'd walked into one of Grimm's fairytales."

"For those who may not be aware, what is a Grimm's fairytale?"

"Children's stories, many of which end with violence and death."

One woman stands up and leaves hand-in-hand with a young girl in a pink dress and matching bonnet.

"What else did you see?" Donald Mitchell asks.

"I walked within ten feet of the girl. She stood up menacingly over Mrs. Healy, absorbed in some kind of, well, what I can only describe as Satanic chanting and moaning. She held a skull in her hands, not of a human but a small animal such as a possum."

"Objection!" Joaquín says. "The witness answers as if it is a fact that Miss de León was engaged in a Satanic ritual. I ask that Mister Morley's last answer be stricken from the record."

"Overruled. You may broach this subject in your cross-examination, Mr. Castanedda," the judge responds. "You may continue, Mr. Mitchell."

"Thank you, your honor. Doctor Morley, in what condition was Mrs. Healy at the time you arrived and saw Miss duh Lee-on engaged in the alleged witchcraft?"

"She died shortly after I arrived," says the doctor.

"Based on your twenty-three years as a licensed physician, can you say, with no qualms whatsoever, that Ramona Healy died with Miss duh Lee-on standing over her before you ever touched the patient?"

"Yes, sir. Her final breath was what we call the 'agonal breath.' It's the last sudden gasp, a reflex of the dying brain. It happens after the heart has stopped beating and has a distinctive sound."

"She was alive and well when he tossed me out!" I write on the notepad.

"Cyrus Healy's testimony will corroborate that," Joaquín writes back.

"You are a man of science, doctor. Do you believe in witchcraft?"

"Certainly not. However, it was clear that Miss duh Lee-on's actions were intended as witchcraft to hasten Ramona Healy's untimely death. The fact that she had the burning root, the candles and the skull with her when she arrived prove, in part, intent to kill."

Joaquín stands abruptly. "Objection! Your honor, many of the doctor's statements are the very definition of speculation!"

"Denied!" the judge shouts. "I'm running out of patience with you, Mr. Castanedda."

Joaquín sits back down and tightly grips the arms of his chair.

"If the burning root and supposed Satanic curse did not kill Ramona Healy, what did?" Donald Mitchell asks.

"Poison. I found a teacup with poison in it, left near the deceased. An autopsy, performed by myself, determined the cause of death to be prussic acid combined with oleander. A person can die within minutes of ingesting prussic acid, and oleander can increase its effects. Whalers added the acid to the tips of their harpoons to slow the whales enough that they could finish the job. You can imagine, then, the effect on a human."

Prussic acid?

"How do you know someone else did not feed her the prussic acid?"

"Her son Cyrus had been gone for more than an hour before arriving with me. Otis Healy was working many miles away, and Mrs. Erasmus Graham, the neighbor, would not have been anywhere near the home when Mrs. Healy took her last breath. Plus, the poison left in the cup was still warm, I presume to make it seem more like tea. That leaves one culprit and one culprit only."

"And that is whom?"

"Evanjaleena duh Lee-on."

"Do you have a copy of the autopsy report to release as evidence?" asks Mr. Mitchell.

"Yes, I've released it to the court clerk, who will make it available to the jury."

"Thank you, doctor. Now please describe for the jury how you saved Mrs. Healy's unborn son."

"With the mother dead, I had no choice but to use forceps to remove the infant from the cervical canal."

"What are forceps, and how does a physician use them?"

"They're specially made medical tongs with rounded ends that go around the infant's head. With the forceps in the right position and at the right time, an experienced physician can pull a newborn safely from the cervical canal, which was the case with baby Healy. I checked his vital signs, swaddled and lay him on his dead mother's chest, figuring it would be the last time mother and son would have together."

Sobs and sniffles bounce around the room. I turn around and see one woman in the third-row slumped sideways. My family and friends shift in their seats and whisper to each other. Mamá cries quietly.

"What other evidence do you have to prove your claims?"

"I have the skull Miss duh Lee-on was holding to summon the devil. She left it behind in her hurry to leave."

Mr. Mitchell walks to the defense table and pulls an object wrapped in paper out of a cloth bag.

He holds it up and turns around slowly to let the jurors and audience see the skull in his hands.

The audience lets out a collective gasp.

"Is this the skull you saw in Miss duh Lee-on's hands?"

"Yes, the very same."

"I have no further questions, your Honor," says Mr. Mitchell.

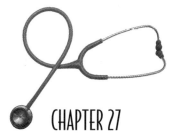

CHAPTER 27

Approach the Bench

"You may begin your cross-examination, Mr. Castanedda," the judge says.

"Thank you, your Honor. Mr. Morley, you said . . ."

"*Doctor* Morley," he interrupts Joaquín. "You may call me *Doctor* Morley."

"Doctor Morley, I stand corrected. You said that you left the town of Alden for Fox Grove to marry Miss Mathilda Mathison."

"That is correct," Doctor Morley replies.

"I wanted to interview Miss Mathison in preparation for trial and searched for her myself. I checked available Fox Grove public records and interviewed townspeople, some of whom have lived their entire lives in Fox Grove. To my surprise, I was not able to locate documentation that a Miss Mathilda Mathison lives there now or has resided there in recent memory."

"You must be a very poor researcher, Mr. Castanedda. I saw Mathilda just the other day. She is new to the town."

"You may call me Mr. Castañeda. I'll sound it out for you again: Cahs-tahn-yeh-dah. That's not too difficult, is it? Is Miss Mathison here, in court, to support you?"

"She is not."

"Oh, I see."

"Objection! What does any of this have to do with this case?" Mr. Mitchell says.

"Sustained! This line of questioning is not pertinent, Mr. Castanedda."

"I'll move on," Joaquín says. "Doctor Morley, during your time in Alden, did you have any patients who suffered medical impairment while under your care?"

"Of course, that happens to every physician. We are not gods. Some things we can heal and others we cannot."

"I will rephrase the question, Doctor Morley. Have you ever had a patient suffer *permanent* health damage or death due to your medical malpractice?"

"No!" he thunders.

"What about Mr. Edward Schiff?" Joaquín asks.

"What about him?"

"Did you do nothing more than apply simple splints to his two broken legs because you assumed that he would not survive his injuries from a chimney collapse?"

"I applied splints to the broken legs, which was the best course of treatment for the man."

"Did Mr. Schiff survive his injuries?"

"Yes."

"And did he live his remaining days, unable to walk on malformed legs and in unspeakable pain?"

"That's a false characterization."

"No, it is not, sir. I saw and spoke with Edward Schiff last week. Did his family not accuse you of medical malpractice, insisting that you recklessly chose the less expensive option of splinting his legs? Any responsible physician would have set the bones, wrapped the legs in plaster or employed a surgical approach. You set the badly broken legs in splints because you did not want to waste your time or money on a man you thought would die!"

Donald Mitchell waves his arms in the air. "Your honor, what does this line of questioning have to do with this case? We're not here to talk about a man with broken legs!" he shouts. "He slanders my client to make up for the weakness of his case!"

The judge's face looks like a swollen tomato, with two squiggly veins popping out at his temples.

"Castanedda, what is your point? I'm about ready to toss you out in contempt," the judge says.

"Your honor, Miss de León would not be here had Doctor Morley not accused her of murder. My questions relate to his credibility. Surely you cannot fault me for that. Mister Mitchell did the same thing in his questioning of Hamish Cavanaugh."

The judge crosses his arms. "You may continue, but stick to the relevant points," he says.

"Yes, your honor. Doctor Morley, were you nineteen-year-old Francine Deveraux's physician at the time of her pregnancy last year?"

The doctor's eyes search his attorney's face, then settle on a heavyset man in striped overalls—the only person standing up.

"Yes, I was the treating physician throughout her pregnancy," he answers.

"Were you the treating physician at the time of her death?"

"I was," he says.

"What was the cause of Francine Deveraux's death?"

Doctor Morley presses his lips together, glares at Joaquín and adjusts the position of his lab coat.

"Doctor Morley, please answer the question," Joaquín says.

"During the second phase of Miss Deveraux's labor, her heart rate rose to a dangerous level, which caused catastrophic seizures. The cause of death was apoplexy," he spits out hastily.

"You killed my wife!" the man in the audience screams.

The judge bangs his gavel. *Whack! Whack! Whack!*

"Order in the court! Remove that man!" the judge shouts.

"I buried my wife and daughter because of you!" the man yells and storms toward the witness stand.

The bailiff and a man in the juror's box spring into action, grab the man by the arms and force him to turn around. The bailiff slaps on handcuffs and pushes the man toward the exit door.

"My wife bled to death! I saw it! I saw it!" the man screams one final time before he's shoved out.

The courtroom erupts in chaos.

"Order! Order! This courtroom will come to order!" The judge yells and slams his gavel repeatedly. "Ladies and gentlemen, settle down! Members of the jury, you will disregard that man's outburst," the judge says. "Valerie? I mean, Miss Hudson? Strike the incident from the record," he says to a woman with a startled expression sitting at a small desk with a typewriter.

When the commotion quiets down, Joaquín approaches the witness stand.

"Who is Betty Pérez?" he asks Doctor Morley.

"A nurse in Alden whose employment I terminated for gross misconduct."

"Nurse Betty Pérez submitted a signed and verified written statement contradicting your account of Francine Deveraux's death."

Joaquín holds out a folded piece of paper. "Would you read Miss Pérez's statement aloud for the jury?"

"What kind of sideshow are you running here?" Doctor Morley asks the judge.

"Your honor, I ask that you put a stop to this distraction," Mr. Mitchell says.

"The statement from Nurse Pérez will paint a clear picture of how Doctor Morley's actions led to Francine Deveraux's death and that of her unborn child."

"He is not on trial here. *Your* client *is*. The victim in this matter is Ramona Healy, not this Francine Deveraux. Have you ever studied the law, boy?" the judge replies.

"Your honor, when it is our turn to call witnesses, I will show the direct connection between Mrs. Deveraux's death and Ramona Healy's. The jury must hear the content of Miss Pérez's note."

"I do not care, counselor! Put that damn piece of paper away, at once then approach the bench," says the judge and pulls out a handkerchief to wipe his perspiring face. I cannot hear what he says to Joaquín.

"We are adjourned for a short break. This court will resume at 11 o'clock," the judge announces.

Teresita walks over to the railing that separates the defense table from the audience.

"What did he say?" she asks Joaquín.

"He is charging me with contempt. If I don't pay a six-dollar fine by tomorrow morning, I will no longer be able to serve as Evangelina's legal counsel. He called me a 'degenerate,'" he chuckles.

"I will take care of the six dollars," Teresita says. "To be clear, he is not throwing you out?"

"No, just the fine," Joaquín replies.

"Keep up the pressure, Joaquín, but don't get thrown out! How you strike that balance, I have no idea, but I'm sure you'll come up with a way," Teresita offers.

"I agree with Teresita. Please don't get thrown out!" I say.

"Don't worry about that; I've got this under control. After the break, I'll ask Morley some more questions. I'm not done with him yet," answers Joaquín.

CHAPTER 28
Nuttin' Like That

"Doctor Morley, before the break, you stated that you moved to Fox Grove from Alden in anticipation of marriage to Miss Mathilda Mathison and that you administered responsible and appropriate medical care to Edward Schiff and Francine Deveraux. Is that correct?" Joaquín begins.

"For the second time, that is correct," the doctor says.

"Isn't it true that you moved to Fox Grove, not because of an upcoming marriage to someone I can find no record of, but because the citizens of Alden ran you out of town?"

"Don't you speak to me like that. You have no earthly idea what you're talking about!" Doctor Morley shouts.

"Did you get run out of Alden after two or more cases of medical malpractice?" Joaquín presses.

"I most definitely did not!"

"I would like to submit, as evidence, a newspaper article from *The Caruso Courier*, the town just east of Alden, about residents' claims of medical negligence and Doctor Morley's sudden resignation and immediate expulsion from the area. The investigation revealed that Francine Deveraux bled to death while in labor due to an experimental medical practice Doctor Morley used called 'twilight sleep.'"

"Objection!" Donald Mitchell yells. "These claims are not proven in a court of law. They came from a damn newspaper!" He pauses and points at me. "And he has not shown how any of this relates to Ramona Healy's murder by *his* client!"

"Your honor, this relates to Ramona Healy's death because she bled to death after Doctor Morley used the same experimental practice he used on Francine Deveraux. We will bring evidence to bear that shows this to be true."

"This man will stop at nothing to ruin me!" the doctor bellows.

The judge hesitates before responding. "I'll allow it. Mr. Castanedda may continue his line of questioning, Donald," he says.

Jedidiah Morley stands up abruptly and turns toward the judge.

"I will not be treated . . . in this regard . . . by the likes of *him!*" he says.

"I want to hear where this leads, doctor. Sit down and answer the question," the judge orders.

The doctor sits and straightens his back so his upper half appears taller.

"Doctor, who did the autopsy on Mrs. Healy?" Joaquín asks.

"Me."

"If you did the autopsy, and you were the one with her at the time of death, how likely would it be that you would find yourself at fault for her passing?"

"Shut up, you ass!"

"I have no further questions," Joaquín says.

Doctor Morley steps down from the witness stand and walks down the aisle briskly.

"Court adjourned," the judge announces.

"The trial of duh Lee-on versus Haller County will begin at 9 am tomorrow," the bailiff declares.

Joaquín and I head for the hallway through the side door.

Selim reaches me first. "How are you doing? Is there anything I can get for you? Something to drink?"

"I had some water in the courtroom, but thank you. I'm fine," I answer, reaching out for him, then think the better of it.

"How about something to eat?" Selim asks. "I just wish I could do something for you."

"I can see it in his eyes, *m'ija.* Your friend is a kind young man," Abuelito says, patting my cheek then reaching up to pat Selim's.

ॐ ॐ ॐ

Josiah escorts me back to the jail a few short blocks away from the courthouse. Selim stops by with a piece of fried chicken and pickled okra that he made himself at the restaurant. I sit on the floor and eat part of a chicken leg and pick at the okra. I'm up to ninety pounds, which makes Doc Taylor happy.

The night's quiet ends when we hear the whinny of a horse and a man's harsh voice. Officer de los Santos steps outside to see what the commotion is. The moment he exits the front door, the back door opens.

"You shut up!" the sheriff hisses at Josiah.

The sheriff whips around the corner and rattles my cell door. "Don't choo even think about crossin' me, girl. I heard yer crooked lady friend's been askin' questions an' spreadin' lies about me. I can arrange some time with you alone afore I hang ya. How'd ya like that? Jus' the two of us in a place o' my choosin'. Josiah's a coward, and he won't tell nobody." He slams his palms on the bars and exits the way he came.

Moments later, Officer de los Santos returns. "It smells... like sweat. Did someone come in while I was outside?" he asks.

Josiah peeks around the corner at me.

I shake my head. "No, sir," I say, my knees feeling loose and wobbly.

&ofb; &ofb; &ofb;

The protesters, now nearly doubled in size since the first day of the trial, follow us from the jail to the court-house.

"It's almost time to start. We best head inside," Joaquín says. "I've got all sorts of surprises for Mr. Mitchell coming up."

Judge O'Leary and Donald Mitchell talk to each other and laugh in the doorway leading to the judge's chambers. I imagine them sitting around at night, slapping each other's backs over a glass of whiskey.

The bailiff enters the room, and people take their seats.

"Okay, Mr. Castanedda, it's your turn. Call your first witness," the judge says.

Joaquín calls Cora as the defense's first witness. She saunters in wearing bright red pantaloons and a red, white and blue striped jacket. I wear the same white skirt and embroidered blouse that I've worn since the trial started. Elsa brought me a bright pink Mexican dress from her closet, but Humphrey wouldn't allow me to take it. He flirted with Elsa, despite the look of disgust on her face, then shooed her away like a mangy alley cat when she refused to acknowledge him.

The bailiff swears Cora in.

"The next time you enter this court, I expect you to dress proper, Cora. Whatever that is that you're wearing is a downright disgrace," the judge snorts. "It assaults one's basic sensibilities. We have standards here."

"Patrick, where is it written that men can wear pants, but women cannot?" Cora says.

"Settle down now, Cora," the judge replies. "I'm only sayin' it doesn't look ladylike. Mr. Castanedda, please proceed."

"Good morning, Miss Cavanaugh. On the first day of trial, your father, Hamish Cavanaugh, said you'd lost the vision in your right eye due to Miss de León's negligent medical care. Do you know that to be true?" Joaquín begins.

"No, sir. It is not."

"What happened the afternoon Miss de León treated you for an eye injury?"

I was sittin' on Russell Taylor's livin' room sofa, enjoying conversation with Miss de León when Humphrey Chestnut threw a rock through the window."

"How did you know it was Mr. Chestnut? Did you see him in the act?"

"I did not, but a witness saw Humphrey fleein' the scene on his horse, Thunder. Everybody in town knows that horse because of his unique markings."

The audience stirs at this revelation.

"Objection!" yells Mr. Mitchell. "Who is this eyewitness? What proof do we have of this, and what does it have to do with this case?"

"I'll move on," Joaquín responds. "What caused the injury to your eye, Miss Cavanaugh?"

"A particle of glass from the broken window. Miss de León did everythin' she could to help me. She examined it thoroughly, instructed me to rinse it out, put a patch on it and gave me instructions for what to do afterward, but I didn't follow them. I didn't lose any sight in that eye because of her. Humphrey Chestnut threw that rock, and I'm sufferin' the consequences of my stubborn pride."

"So, your father's assertion that it was Miss de León who caused your . . ."

"False. My father heard what I said to one of our staff at home and assumed things he shouldn't have. Miss de León instructed me to see Doctor Taylor afterward, but I never returned to the clinic, even when my eye showed signs of infection. I didn't keep the patch on either. I had a lot of writin' to do, and the patch was makin' it hard to do my work. My eye is the way it is because I'm bad at followin' directions. My father was flat wrong, and I told him so, right before I packed my things and moved out yesterday."

"Did your father ever speak with you directly about your eye? Ask how it happened? Ask how you were feeling? Ask if it was healing?"

"Objection!" Donald Mitchell says. "Which of those questions does he want her to answer?"

"Sustained. Rephrase the question," says the judge.

"That's fair. Did your father ever speak with you directly about your eye?" Joaquín asks.

"We haven't spoken for months," Cora says.

"No more questions, your honor," Joaquín says.

Mr. Mitchell approaches the witness stand. "Miss Cavanaugh," he begins, "did you or did you not receive care from Evan-jell-ina duh Lee-on after broken glass landed in your eye?"

"I did."

"And are you or are you not partially blind in that eye?"

"I am partially blind, that is, but I'm hoping it gets . . ."

"Did your father recently find you stealing a valuable from his property?"

"I did no such thing!" Cora says.

"Did he not approach you about stealing a pearl necklace from the premises?"

"Oh, that. Yes," Cora says.

"So, you did steal it?"

Joaquín bolts up and out of his chair. "Objection! This line of questioning is wholly irrelevant!"

"Your honor, the jury should consider the credibility of her testimony in light of this revelation about the necklace," says Mr. Mitchell.

One corner of the judge's mouth lifts in amusement. "Overruled, please continue, Mr. Mitchell," he says.

"Miss Cavanaugh, do you admit to stealing the necklace?"

"No, of course not. It was my mother's. I knew my father would never give it to me. He'd rather it sit in a jewelry box than let his only child have it. I do hope to be married one day, and when I do, I want to wear it," she says, glancing at Joaquín. "So yes, I took it. She would have wanted me to have it."

"Did your father purchase the necklace, or did you?"

"He did, but it belonged to my mother," Cora says. "I never knew her and had nothing of hers to call my own."

"When your father first asked you about the missing necklace, did you acknowledge that you took it?"

"No! He would have been furious, and at that moment, I didn't have the energy for a fight. I planned to tell him when . . ."

"The simple truth is that you stole your father's property, then lied to cover it up. Correct?"

"I disagree with that characterization," Cora says.

"Who else was with you on the afternoon of your eye injury?"

"Ummm—I think it was just Miss de León and me."

"Was Mr. Castanedda, the defense attorney, sitting right there, also in Doctor Taylor's living room?"

"I cannot recall."

"Are you and Mr. Castanedda seeing one another romantically?"

"We are acquaintances, sir."

"A Mrs. Yvonne Barry reported that she saw Mr. Castanedda placing his hand on your forearm at Lonnie's Deli, and so did the rest of the patrons I interviewed."

"Joaquín and I are friends who happen to care about one another. Is that a crime, you nitwit?"

"No further questions for Miss Cavanaugh," Mr. Mitchell says.

Cora steps down, her shoulders back and chin high.

"The defense now calls Charlie Burton to the stand," Joaquín announces.

A tall, lanky boy with red hair and freckles settles into the witness chair after being sworn in.

"Charlie, your friend Willie Falkirk told this court yesterday that he never spoke to you about Mrs. Agatha Taylor's death, two years ago. Is that true?"

"No, sir, it ain't."

"So, Willie *did* speak with you about her death."

"Yessir."

"When did he speak with you, and what did he say?"

"He came ta my place right after he saw 'er on the back porch. He was so scared he said he nearly wet hisself. He never seen a dead person afore."

"Did he say anything about Miss de León being there?"

"He said a girl from school was holdin' the dead lady's hand an' sayin' the Lord's Prayer. The girl was cryin'. Not the dead one. The live one. Her, right there," he says and points at me. "I knowed her from school, an' Willie done pointed 'er out the next day."

"Did Willie mention anything to you about an animal skull or a witch's curse?"

"No, sir, he didn't say nuttin' like that, an' I woulda 'membered if he did. Us boys like skeletons an' such, and he didn't say nuttin' 'bout no skull."

"And, why did you come here today, Charlie?"

"'Cause my momma said if I dint tell the truth, my daddy'd whip my behind with a switch from here ta kingdom come. She said I ain't supposed to hang 'round with Willie no more."

"Thank you, Charlie. No more questions."

"No questions, your honor," Mr. Mitchell says.

CHAPTER 29

Make Your Voice Heard

Cora struts around outside the courthouse during the lunch break, handing flyers to reporters and anyone else who'll take one. Teresita tells me that a translation will follow for Spanish speakers.

I get a flyer and sit in the defense's meeting room.

The Truth Will Prevail–
Justice for Evangelina de León
Part III
Guest Opinion by Cora Kay Cavanaugh

July 5, 1915. Seneca, Texas. It's been a trying day for eighteen-year-old Evangelina de León, falsely accused of witchcraft and murder. The opening day of trial, prosecuting Attorney Donald Mitchell painted Miss de León into a perverse picture of lies, deceit, medical negligence, evil and murder. He did so with the dishonorable and false testimony of Hamish Cavanaugh and thirteen-year-old William Falkirk, Jr.

We must join forces to bring an end to the injustices and racial violence plaguing Mexicans and

Tejanos across the state. Make your voice heard! Support Miss de León and her cause. Do not patronize the following Seneca businesses, proven to mistreat customers and employees based on race.

- Coughlin's Apothecary—fired an employee in March 1915 for speaking Spanish on her lunch break.
- Glennwood Hotel—written policy forbids staff from renting rooms to non-Anglos.
- Seneca Meat Market, Reilly's Paint Supply, Grandma Annie's Bakery, Anderton's Corner Store—display window signs: "No Negroes, No Mexicans, No Dogs."
- Haller County Bank—bylaws forbid non-Anglos from opening bank accounts.
- Cavanaugh Fine Fabrics—pays foreign-born employees half of what their Anglo counterparts make; labor pool includes foreign-born and Negro children as young as 5-years-old.
- Contact La Liga Protectora Mexicana in Loma, Texas, if you've experienced discrimination based on race or national origin. Send a detailed letter with your contact information to:

La Liga Protectora Mexicana
c/o Teresita Olmos
1111 Virginia Street
Loma, Texas

Teresita and Joaquín come in with ham sandwiches and a box of vanilla sugar wafers for our lunch. Teresita tells me the boycott is a temporary but necessary step in raising awareness for our cause and forcing the changes we want to see.

Joaquín says Doctor Taylor will come to the stand next.

⁂

Joaquín approaches the witness stand.

"Doctor Taylor, given your profession, I'd venture to say that most everyone in this town knows who you are. But for the record, would you please describe your background, including your education and current role in the community?"

"I was born in Philadelphia and moved to Seneca as a boy with my parents Julius and Agatha Taylor. I attended school in this very building and completed two undergraduate degrees at the University of Texas in biology and mathematics. Within three years, I received my medical degree from the same institution. I opened my medical practice in Seneca thirty years ago."

"Tell us how you came to meet Evangelina de León."

"She came to me in the spring of 1911, asking for help with an emergent medical need at the family home, which required multiple follow-up visits. It was during one of those visits that I hired Miss de León as a part-time housekeeper. She quickly took an interest in my medical practice. Over time, I began mentoring her. Four years later, she had patients of her own and continued assisting me in the clinic. Of course, she is not able to perform surgeries or diagnose complex illnesses, but she was and is quite competent at routine care."

"Please tell us about Evangelina de León's patients and their experience with her."

"Evangelina began seeing patients approximately eighteen months ago. She took on the more straightforward cases. Many of them have written her thank-you letters, some of which I brought with me today," he says, fishing a stack of folded papers out of his suit pocket.

"Please enter these into evidence," Joaquín says, handing the papers to the bailiff.

"I am sorry to bring up a sensitive subject, but I'm afraid I must," Joaquín says. "The prosecution brought a witness, a Master Willie Falkirk, to testify that Miss de León caused your mother, Mrs. Agatha Taylor's death. Do you know of evidence that corroborates that assertion?"

"The assertion is not just false, it's impossible," Doctor Taylor replies.

"And how do you know that?"

"On that day, I picked Evangelina up at school, and she joined me for an in-home patient appointment. At 4 pm, I dropped Evangelina off in front of the house to study some new lab specimens I'd received and left to make one more house call. When I arrived home the second time at 4:45 pm, I learned from Miss de León that my mother had died. The body temperature and level of stiffness, otherwise known as rigor mortis, indicated that she'd passed four to six hours earlier."

"Thank you, Doctor Taylor. Please accept my condolences. To be clear, you are saying that your mother, Agatha Taylor, died while Evangelina de León was in this very building, attending classes."

"Yes."

"Thank you. Will you explain Miss de León's competence in assisting women in childbirth?"

"Indeed. I looked through my files and confirmed that Evangelina assisted me with sixteen recorded births over two years. She had patients in the more rural areas around town and, on her own, or with her mother's help, delivered seven healthy babies."

"So, you would say that Evangelina de León is a competent practitioner of midwifery?"

"For straightforward cases, yes. For more complex cases, I would need to take the lead."

"Fair enough. Doctor Taylor, what do you know about Miss Ramona Healy's death?"

"Initially, I knew only what Evangelina told me. A neighbor of Mrs. Healy's pleaded with Evangelina to look in on her, and she did so, knowing that she did not have enough time to come and get me.

"Evangelina checked Mrs. Healy's vital signs as soon as she arrived, and they were within the normal ranges for a woman in her condition. Evangelina continued to monitor the vital signs throughout her time there. Mrs. Healy became restless with worry and significant back pain, and Evangelina massaged her with warmed oil to calm her nerves. She also gave her chamomile and raspberry teas to speed the softening of the cervix and dull the pain. As the pain progressed, she offered the patient three teaspoons of oleander syrup, a natural pain reliever. Finally, they prayed together."

"Could any of the things you mentioned have caused or contributed to Ramona Healy's death, including the incense or candle Doctor Morley spoke of?"

"Certainly not. Evangelina used natural substances, none of which would have caused harm to mother or child," Doctor Taylor says. "These are well-documented facts based on medical science, not opinion."

"What do you think caused the death of the patient?"

"I was not able to ascertain the exact cause of death until recently."

"Why is that?"

"Doctor Morley conducted Mrs. Healy's autopsy and determined the cause of death to be prussic acid poisoning. Due to the suspicious nature of the death, I was able to secure Otis Healy's permission to conduct a second autopsy."

"Objection!" Donald Mitchell shouts.

"On what grounds, Don?" the judge asks.

"The prosecution was not made aware of this . . . this s-s-s-second autopsy," Mr. Mitchell stammers.

"Your honor, we were not required to notify the prosecution about the second autopsy," Joaquín says evenly. "It was a private matter between Doctor Taylor and Otis Healy. Mr. Healy asked Doctor Taylor to verify the cause of death, and he agreed. I have his signature allowing him to proceed with the examination of the body."

Joaquín steps over to the defense table, grabs a thick envelope and hands it to the bailiff.

"There are three official documents in that envelope which we will soon explain," says Joaquín.

The judge sits up in his seat and rubs two fingers over the space between his eyebrows. "Objection overruled," he says.

"Doctor Taylor, what did you determine as the cause of death?" Joaquín continues.

"The patient bled to death. Morphine and scopolamine were found in Mrs. Healy's system, indicating the doctor used these medications to induce a coma-like state in which the woman feels no pain, and the doctor uses forceps to pull the infant from the birth canal."

"Objection!" Donald Mitchell tries again.

"On what grounds?" asks the judge.

Mr. Mitchell stands up silently, his mouth opening and closing like a fish.

"Your honor and gentlemen of the jury, Doctor Taylor has evidence of these claims," says Joaquín. "The autopsy results are in the envelope I just gave to the bailiff," Joaquín says.

"Objection overruled," the judge says, frowning at Mr. Mitchell.

"The prosecution asserts that Ramona Healy died from prussic acid poisoning. Did you find any level of prussic acid in Ramona Healy's bloodstream or tissue?"

"I did not," Doctor Taylor answers.

"How would the jury know that your findings are accurate, and Jedidiah Morley's are not? It's your word against his."

"With Otis Healy's written approval, I had an independent physician, Doctor Waylon Rucker from Goldendale conduct a third study to determine the cause of death, and his findings mirror mine. His report is the second document in the envelope."

"Now, can you explain what 'twilight sleep' is?"

"Twilight sleep is a pain relief method for women in childbirth discovered by the Germans approximately ten years ago. The combination of morphine and scopolamine reduces a mother's pain and her memory of birth all together.

"Unfortunately, there are more than one hundred documented cases of twilight sleep patients entering a state of psychosis, thrashing around, banging their heads on walls, clawing at themselves and screaming continuously. In those cases, nurses had no other choice but to tie the women to their beds or put them into straitjackets to prevent further injury. Two dozen of these patients died from excessive blood loss.

"Being that it's advertised as 'painless childbirth,' women in the US are demanding it, not knowing the potential dangers. American doctors are traveling to Germany to observe the procedure and offering it to their pregnant patients upon their return."

"What would be the benefit of offering twilight sleep to pregnant women?"

"It would mask a woman's pain as intended and make them forget the entire childbirth experience. What woman would not want to avoid the pain of childbirth if they could? A doctor's caseload of pregnant women would increase, perhaps exponentially, leading to more income; however, the risk to their patients would also increase."

"Would you ever consider using twilight sleep with one of your pregnant patients?"

"No, the benefits are not worth the risks I just described."

"Were you aware that Jedidiah Morley traveled to Germany on the *RMS Victoria* steamship last year?"

"No, I was not."

"The ship's passenger log with the date and Dr. Morley's name is the third and final document in the envelope. No further questions, your honor."

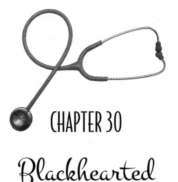

CHAPTER 30

Blackhearted

"I had no idea you've been arranging all this, the third autopsy, finding out about Doctor Morley's trip to Germany. It's astounding!" I say to Joaquín in our meeting room.

"Doctor Taylor proved to be an exceptionally knowledgeable and believable witness," Joaquín replies. "But I expect a challenging cross-examination from Mr. Mitchell."

Teresita knocks softly and enters the room. "It seems the Seneca Mayor wants to speak with me," she says. "Our boycott of local businesses has gotten his attention. I'll be heading over to City Hall soon. I also just learned that Nicolás Montemayor, the Loma Mayor, has arrived with his daughter, Anarosa."

"Am I allowed to be hopeful yet?" I ask.

"You can be whatever you want," says Teresita, "but me, personally? I won't allow myself to feel one way or the other. Despite Joaquín's outstanding work thus far, there are still battles yet to come; I am certain of that."

"After Doctor Taylor's cross-examination, I'll call Sheriff Stanley Pearl to the stand," Joaquín says. "Are you ready?"

"Are you going to ask him about . . . everything?"

"You agreed that Stanley Pearl deserves punishment for what he did to you. A black-hearted man with a badge is a dangerous one. If we don't stop him, someone else will suffer the same fate," says Teresita. "The jurors must know what you endured."

"How much time do we have before we have to go back in?" I ask.

"Another fifteen minutes," Joaquín says.

"Will you please bring Abuelito, Elsa and my parents in? They should hear it from me first."

"Certainly," Joaquín says. "We'll let you have some privacy."

"Teresita? If you can get a message to Selim at Lonnie's after the hearing today, I would appreciate it. I need to speak to him about all of this in person. I just hope I get to him before someone else does."

I brace myself for what I've been dreading. I rehearsed what to say, but now I can't remember it. I touch the butterfly pin on my blouse and run my finger lightly over the wings.

Mamá, Papá and Abuelito enter the room, and I burst into tears.

&8 &8 &8

"Your witness, Mr. Mitchell," the judge announces.

"Doctor Taylor, you said that your mother died hours before Miss duh Lee-on discovered her body on the porch," says Mr. Mitchell.

"Yes, that is right," Doctor Taylor replies.

"Did you do an autopsy to determine an exact cause of death?"

"No, it was not necessary. I believe my mother died of natural causes due to old age. She had a history of heart troubles."

"What was her age at the time of death?"

"Seventy-two."

"Had she been well in the weeks before her death?"

"To my knowledge, yes, although the gradual slowing of heart rate was a constant concern."

"Did you have any indication that morning that she was not feeling well?"

"No."

"Did you speak with her that morning?"

"Yes, we spoke at the breakfast table."

"What did you speak about?"

"I cannot recall, but I imagine it was an ordinary conversation one might have with their elderly mother, errands to run, the weather, ordinary things."

"So, by your own admission, she felt fine, and you spoke with her that morning. And yet, you did not do an autopsy to determine the exact cause of death. Is it true, then, that you cannot say with a hundred percent certainty, as a medical expert, what caused her death?"

"That is correct, and speaking as her son, not her physician, I am comfortable with that."

"Is it possible that she died after ingesting poison?"

"That would be improbable."

"That does not answer the question. I asked if it is possible."

"Yes, I suppose it is possible, but that's an illogical sugg . . ."

"Do you keep medications and chemical compounds in your office that could cause a person's death if administered improperly?"

"Technically, the answer is yes. In reality, that has never . . ."

"Would Evan-jell-ina duh Lee-on have had access to these substances on the date of your mother's death?"

"If you are inferring that . . ."

"Doctor Taylor, Jedidiah Morley found Evan-jell-ina duh Lee-on bent over Ramona Healy's lifeless body reciting some form of Mexican gibberish. Willie Falkirk also found Miss duh Lee-on hunched over your deceased mother while reciting gibberish. Doesn't that strike you as an unlikely coincidence?"

"Your question includes a false premise, Mr. Mitchell. Evangelina was reciting a Catholic prayer, not 'gibberish,' as you call it."

"Were you present to hear these Catholic prayers?"

"No, sir."

"So you weren't there in either case, but you insist that Miss duh Lee-on said Catholic prayers, contradicting the two *eyewitnesses* who said it was some attempt at Mexican hocus pocus."

"Is there a question, Mr. Mitchell?" Doctor Taylor asks.

"Yes. Do you keep track of all your medications and chemical compounds?"

"In what way?"

"Do you know exactly how much you have at any one time?"

"I track which medications I prescribe to patients and in what dosages."

"Of course, but if someone were to take pills or a liquid from one of your shelves and use it to poison someone, would you know?"

"I would think so."

"You think so. Thank you for that definitive answer. Earlier today, you said that Evan-jell-ina duh Lee-on gave Ramona Healy oleander syrup to ease her pain. Can oleander cause illness or death?"

"Yes, but only in larger quantities than what she administered."

"Do you know if any of the dried oleander you kept at your clinic has gone missing in the past two months?"

"I have not checked on my supply of oleander as I have not used it in . . ."

"Do you keep prussic acid in your clinic?"

"Yes, but I rarely use it for . . ."

"Do you know if you have any less now than you did, say, before May 7th, the day of Ramona Healy's murder?"

"I have not opened the bottle in years, so I presume not."

"In essence, you *presume* someone has not taken oleander and prussic acid from your clinic, but you do not *know*. Would you say that you are friends with Miss duh Lee-on?"

"Yes. I've come to know Miss de León quite well over the years."

"Have you told Miss duh Lee-on that you care for her, even love her, as you would a daughter?"

"Yes."

"Did you pay Doctor Waylon Rucker from Goldendale to do the third autopsy on Ramona Healy?"

"Of course, I did, and Otis Healy contributed what he could. Doctor Rucker is a certified physician, and I asked him to travel to Seneca. It would be entirely unprofessional to ask a doctor to take three days away from his practice and not compensate him for his time and service."

"I see. Given the nature of your relationship with Miss duh Lee-on, one you just described as 'fatherly love,' why wouldn't the jury conclude that you paid Doctor Rucker to corroborate your findings, thereby undermining Doctor Morley's?"

"Objection! Mr. Mitchell is speculating about the intent, integrity and professionalism of Doctors Rucker and Taylor," Joaquín says.

"Mr. Castanedda, approach the bench," the judge snarls.

Joaquín speaks quietly with the judge for an uncomfortably long time then takes the seat next to me.

"He's charging me with contempt for my continued objections, which he insists are unfounded and disruptive," he says calmly. "He alluded to the content of Cora's flyer. This may be his way of making us pay for the negative publicity and the boycott."

"This? This *what*?" I ask.

"He's throwing me out for the rest of the day."

"Can he do that?" Every inch of me starts to tremble.

"I asked if we could delay the rest of today's proceedings until tomorrow, and he refused."

"What do we do?"

"I'll request twenty minutes to find Teresita. I don't know of anyone else who could represent you with no advanced notice. I've never experienced anything like it before. It's outrageous."

"Mr. Castanedda. I have asked you to leave the courtroom until tomorrow," says the judge. "What is your plan for the remainder of the day? You have another witness standing in the wings, ready to testify. If the defense does not bring him to the stand today, as documented on the court docket, the chance to do so will be gone."

"Who's going to defend her now?" Selim shouts. "This isn't fair!"

"Sir, you will leave this court peacefully, or you will be forcibly removed and fined an additional sum in contempt of court," the judge says.

I look back at Abuelito for some look of reassurance, but he's sleeping.

"I'll do it," I tell Joaquín.

"Do what?"

"I'll question the sheriff myself," I say.

"Your honor, if you please, may I have ten minutes with my client to confer on our next steps?" Joaquín asks.

"I'll give you five," the judge responds.

Joaquín puts his hand on top of mine and squeezes. "Are you sure you want to do this?" His blue eyes have never looked so bright.

"You can pick back up tomorrow, where I leave off," I say. "Stanley Pearl must pay for what he's done."

"What if you break down or freeze up?" asks Joaquín.

"I can do this," I say, totally and completely unsure if I can.

"Without knowing court procedures, the judge could eat you alive—and enjoy it."

"Does Teresita know court procedures?"

"I'm one of four legal specialists at La Liga. Teresita directs the entire organization and serves as its spokesperson. She does not pretend to know the law."

"Then I'm just as qualified to defend myself as she is, if not more so. The sheriff assaulted *me*. He traumatized *me*."

"Very well, but this scares me to no end," Joaquín says.

"Of course, it does, but it scares me more," I say.

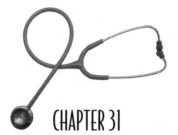

CHAPTER 31

Blossom

"Are you quite ready now, counselor?" the judge asks, looking at the wall clock.

My intestines clench and unclench. *What am I doing?*

"With the change in today's hearing, I respectfully request a fifteen-minute break to prepare my questions," I say.

"I just gave you and your lawyer five minutes," the judge replies. "You do understand that in defending yourself, you are accepting the potentially disastrous consequences of your actions. Experience compels me to tell you that defendants who represent themselves make serious mistakes that are used against them. I advise you to put this idea out of your head. You have no earthly idea what you are doing," the judge says. "I advise you to dismiss today's remaining witness and start again tomorrow," he continues.

"Thank you, your honor. I understand, but I want to keep going."

The judge bangs his gavel. "Given Mr. Castanedda's dismissal for the remainder of the day, I am granting a fifteen-minute recess. Against my advisement, Miss duh Lee-on will represent herself when we return."

த் த் த்

I find Joaquín in our meeting room.

"I'm so glad they didn't throw you out of the building!" I tell him.

"They did, but I snuck back in a side door. Let's review the questions I planned to ask the sheriff. You may need to adjust depending on how he answers," he says.

The door opens a crack. "I can't believe you're goin' to do this!" Cora says. "You are a tiny but mighty woman! Make that bigot pay for what he's done! What a story this'll make! You're gonna be a legend!"

"Thank you, dear," Joaquín says calmly. "Would you please ask the family to resist the urge to visit Evangelina? She and I have a lot of ground to cover."

"Oh, yes, sorry," she says and backs out as she blows me a kiss. Or was it for Joaquín?

He slides a folder across the table. "I have all my notes written here, including the questions I prepared for the sheriff. We've discussed bits and pieces of this already, so you should be familiar with most of it. The goal with Sheriff Pearl is not to prove that he's guilty of anything. Your job is to establish that you're a victim of racial injustice and mistreatment. If it goes well, you'll generate a motive for your arrest. You do not have to address the assaults. We'll deal with that soon, and I'll re-emphasize the racial injustice in my closing statement."

"I want to do this, but I can't believe I am doing this. It's the last thing I ever would have expected. Not even in my La Llorona nightmares," I say.

Joaquín pats my shoulder. "She haunts your nightmares, too, eh? I don't know if there's a Mexican kid anywhere who hasn't been spooked by those stories. Look. All you can do is the best you can do," he says.

I smile. "Abuelito used to say that."

"Your abuelito's a wise man," Joaquín says.

"I need a few minutes alone to read the file before I have to go back in," I tell Joaquín.

"Of course. I'll wait just outside the door in case you have questions. When it's over, find me and let me know how it went. Evangelina, I believe in you," he says.

ക ക ക

I make my way down the hall with the bailiff trailing behind. There's a sign on a door to my left: "Water Toilet—No Negroes—No Mexicans."

"Please excuse me for a moment," I say to the bailiff.

"The judge is expecting us," he says. "You know you're not supposed to go in there, but there's no time for the outhouse. Make it quick."

I open the door and practically jump inside. My stomach twists and I wretch. My knees feel weak and wobbly as I rinse my mouth in the sink.

The bailiff leads the way to the courtroom. With his back turned, I grab a pen from inside Joaquín's notebook, cross out "No Negroes—No Mexicans" and write the word "HUMAN" before the words "Water Toilet."

Abuelito stands next to the courtroom door. I put my arms around him and feel my body soften. We separate;

he holds my hands and looks at me with a gleam in his eyes.

"Your hands still feel swollen, Abuelito. The doctor should examine you," I say gently.

"I am old, *m'ija*. It happens to all of us. When your father told me that you agreed to question the policeman, the pride inside of me swelled so great, I thought I would burst. When you were just a little thing, I told your *abuelita* that one day, you'd blossom from a shy girl afraid of her own shadow into a woman with enough intelligence and courage to change the world. I've always known it. And here you are. You are changing the world, *m'ija*. You are up to the challenge. I may not be able to understand much of what is said in the courtroom, but know that I am with you in spirit, always, no matter what happens."

☙ ☙ ☙

"The defense calls Sheriff Stanley Pearl," I say as loudly as my soft voice will go.

Sheriff Pearl strolls toward me dressed in uniform, his gun in its holster. I look up. *Lord, give me strength.*

"Patrick, what in the hell is goin' on here?" the sheriff asks as he sits down.

"I threw Miss duh Lee-on's attorney out for contempt," says the judge. "She has chosen to represent herself for the remainder of the day."

"Well, ain't this a nice surprise?" the sheriff says.

The bailiff swears the sheriff in, with the sheriff saying, "You bet yer ass I do. I'm the sheriff here," to the question about swearing to tell the truth.

"Sheriff," I begin. "Can you tell the jury how many Mexicans and Tejanos have spent time in the Seneca Jail over the past year?"

"What's that gotta do with anything?" he retorts, folding his arms across his chest.

"Excuse me, but doesn't he have to answer?" I ask the judge.

"Where are you headed with this, young lady?" the judge says.

"Your honor, we believe the charges against me have everything to do with my race. The question is revelant . . . ummm . . . *What is the word? What is the word?* The question has to do with race," I say and heave out a sigh.

"Answer the question, Stanley," the judge says. "Let's put this to rest."

"What's the question?" asks the sheriff.

"In the past year, how many Mexicans and Tejanos spent time in the Seneca Jail?" I ask.

"Miss duh Lee-on, please clarify if you mean January through today, 1915, or over the past twelve months from 1914 into 1915," says Judge O'Leary.

"I am sorry, your honor. I mean the past twelve months."

"How would I know?" the sheriff grumbles.

"Because your deputy, Josiah Martin, tracks each prisoner who enters and exits the jail. I have his records here, which say that seventy-two total prisoners of all races spent time behind bars in the last twelve months." I scan the paper in my hand. "Of the seventy-two, twenty-three were Mexican or Tejano, and thirty-two were Negro." I look at Josiah's notes again. "Forgive me . . . uh, I meant thirty-two were Mexican or Tejano, and twenty-three were Negro. That's forty-four percent Mexican or Tejano."

"What're ya babblin' about, girl?" the sheriff asks.

"I'm sorry, I need a minute," I say. *Where was I?* I flip the paper over and read Joaquín's notes on the backside.

"Get on with it," the judge says. "You're wasting people's time, and most importantly, mine."

"Yes, sir," I reply.

"Yes, *your honor*," the judge says.

"Yes, sir, your honor. Sheriff Pearl, records at Seneca City Hall estimate that about eight percent of the people who live here are Mexican or Tejano."

"So?"

"Why would eight percent of the population make up forty-four percent of the prisoners?"

"Maybe you should be askin' the Mexicans why they commit so many crimes," he says, putting his elbow on the side of the witness stand and leaning over casually.

"None of the Mexicans or Tejanos had a trial, but all were found guilty. Some went straight to the Loma prison, while others were shot or hung for crimes that were never proven. It seems that justice for all in Seneca means justice for Anglos. Would you agree with that statement, sheriff?"

"Am I on trial here, Patrick?" the sheriff shouts.

"What are you sayin'?" the judge yells. "How dare you slander this court!"

"During my time at the Seneca Jail, do you remember calling me a 'mongrel' and a 'Mexican whore?'" I ask.

Images of him stumbling into my cell flash before me. My knees threaten to give out, so I straighten and lock them into place.

"No!" he snaps.

"Do you remember saying the following to Doctor Jedidiah Morley?"

I flip through Joaquín's file, and a handful of papers drop to the ground. The bailiff rushes over to help me pick them up.

Some in the audience snicker.

Where is it? Where is it?!

I shuffle the papers, find the right one and read.

"I thank you for bringin' her to us, doc. It don't matter if she's guilty or not, and I don't wanna know. Them Mexicans ain't welcome here, not even the women and children. If watching her twitch from the end of a rope don't send a message, what will?"

"That's a lie!" the sheriff shouts.

"Deputy Josiah Martin, your own employee, wrote those words down at the jailhouse after you said them to Doctor Morley."

"Objection!" Donald Mitchell shouts.

"Patrick? May I have a word with you?" says a stately-looking man as he walks up the center aisle.

"Nicholas? What are you doing here?" the judge asks.

"We should discuss it in your office, Patrick," the man says. "Trust me. It would be in your best interest to do so *immediately*."

"This court is adjourned for a recess!" the judge shouts.

The bailiff whispers in the judge's ear.

"What? You can't be serious," he says. "Oh hell, we're done for the day! Go on home, everybody!"

CHAPTER 32

The Lion

We stand outside the front entrance to the building. "What a day! What a day!" Cora says enthusiastically. "I mean, you didn't know what you were doin' before you went in there, and you still stuck it to that racist bastard. It was like the lion and the mouse," she gushes. "And I'll be damned if you weren't the lion!"

Joaquín springs up the building steps, two at a time. "How did it go?"

"I stumbled some, but I still wish you could have been there," I say, suppressing the urge to jump up and down.

"Looking at these smiles, I'd wager that it went well," he replies. "I promise we'll discuss today's proceedings in detail later, but there's something important I must tell . . ."

"Sheriff Stanley Pearl?" Someone shouts over the boisterous mix of a hundred people moving about, talking and shouting.

Sheriff Pearl and Donald Mitchell stop in place on their way down the steps.

Josiah stands at the street level, facing the sheriff.

"You been talkin' behind my back, Josiah?" the sheriff seethes.

"You are under arrest for the violation of Miss Anarosa Montemayor and two-time assault of Miss Evanjaleenuh duh Lee-on," Josiah says, clapping a pair of handcuffs on the sheriff's right wrist. The sheriff looks straight at him, mouth open, stunned.

"What in the hell is this?" Donald Mitchell says.

"Come with me, sheriff," Josiah says while pulling the sheriff's gun out of its holster and sticking it inside his own. "Give me your other wrist," Josiah orders.

"I won't do no such thing!" the sheriff growls.

Josiah quickly grabs his left wrist and smacks on the other handcuff.

"Do you want to hire me as your attorney?" Mr. Mitchell asks as the sheriff is pushed forward and walked across the street toward City Hall. "Stanley, do you want me to come with you?"

"Yes!" the sheriff shouts.

What is happening?

Someone puts their hand on my shoulder from behind.

"It's all starting to come together," says Teresita, coming around to face me. "Justice. Do you see it? I do. I see it in the handcuffs on that bigot's wrists. Let's go inside through the back door so that we can talk. The crowd's getting more disruptive by the minute."

We move toward the back of the courthouse. Reporters surround us and shout questions.

"Why is the sheriff in handcuffs?"

"Did you and the sheriff have relations?"

"Why is Nicholas Montemayor here? Did you kill somebody in Loma?"

"Guard the door," Teresita says to Officer Rivas.

"There is trouble for the sheriff for what he do to my daughter?" Mamá asks.

"The Loma Mayor, Nicolás Montemayor, came to file charges against Stanley Pearl on behalf of his daughter, Anarosa," says Teresita, switching over to Spanish. "She only recently told him what the sheriff did to her years ago. Joaquín filed charges on Evangelina's behalf for what occurred while she was in the sheriff's custody. Her courage to come forward gave Anarosa the courage to do the same."

Papá pulls me in and holds me close. "I'm sorry I could not protect you, *m'ija*," he says softly and weeps. "I want to tear that man apart."

"We've got statements from Anarosa, her friend Beatrice who saw Anarosa and Stanley Pearl immediately following the incident," says Joaquín. "The man in the cell next to Evangelina's gave a statement about what he heard, and so did Josiah Martin."

"If the deputy knew, why didn't he say something?" Papá asks.

"The sheriff threatened Josiah Martin and his family as he did with Evangelina," Teresita replies.

"When we assured Josiah that the sheriff would be arrested and kept at the Loma jail, he agreed to give us a statement," Joaquín adds. "And he's willing to testify."

"Why the Loma jail?" Papá asks.

"Right now, Seneca has no sheriff," Joaquín says. "Evangelina will be back at Doctor Taylor's on house arrest, only this time, officers Rivas and de los Santos will be there to make sure she stays there. No more sneaking out in the middle of the night!"

"Where are Elsa and Abuelito?" I ask, looking around.

"Elsa took your *abuelito* back to the house," Papá says. "Despite all the excitement, he couldn't keep his eyes open."

"I'll ask Doc Taylor to look in on him, just to be safe," I say. "I bet Abuelito hasn't seen a doctor in years."

"Closing arguments tomorrow," Joaquín says. "It's going to be a big day. If you'll excuse us, Evangelina and I have some preparations to make. Officer Rivas can take her back to the doctor's house when we're through."

"See you soon," I say. "Hug Abuelito for me," I tell my parents. "Teresita, please make sure Selim comes to Doc Taylor's after work. I must tell him about the sheriff."

歠 歠 歠

Selim sits across from me, his elbows on the kitchen table, his head hanging low. When he looks up, there's a rage in his eyes that startles me.

"If that son of a bitch weren't already in jail, I swear he wouldn't live to see another day."

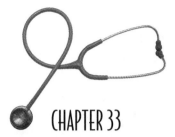

CHAPTER 33

My Momma Taught Me

I slept like I haven't slept since I was a child. La Llorona didn't so much as make a peep in last night's dreams. I even ate a full breakfast this morning.

Selim has to work again today. Elsa's staying home with Abuelito, Tomás and Domingo, and Doc Taylor has patient appointments, his first with Abuelito, as I requested. None of them will be at the trial to hear closing arguments.

⁝ ⁝ ⁝

Restless strangers, angry opponents and friendly supporters cram the courtroom like matches in a matchbox. Twice as many reporters than before sit in the front rows. *What do they see when they look at me? A harlot, a witch and a murderer, or an innocent victim of assault and a wrongful arrest?*

"The defense calls Cyrus Longoria to the stand," Joaquín says.

Cyrus enters the room in dark blue pants and a checkered red and white shirt. He looks straight ahead until he reaches the witness stand.

"Place your right hand on the Bible," the bailiff says. "Do you swear to tell the truth and nothing but the truth, so help you God?"

"Yes, sir," Cyrus says.

"Cyrus, thank you for being here today," Joaquín says. "As you know, I'm going to ask you a series of questions related to your mother's death."

"Yes, sir," Cyrus says.

"Speak up, boy," the judge commands.

"Yes, sir," Cyrus repeats in a voice not much louder than before.

"The prosecution claims that on May 7th, 1915, Miss Evangelina de León attempted to put a witch's curse on your mother and poisoned her with the intent of causing her death. Is that what you believe?"

"No, sir."

"Why not?"

"Because I saw my mother's death and can tell you that it didn't happen the way they say."

"When you say, 'they,' do you mean Attorney Donald Mitchell, sitting right there at the prosecution's table?"

"Yes, sir, and the doctor who killed her, Doctor Morley," Cyrus responds.

"Objection!" Donald Mitchell shouts and pounds the table.

"Sustained. Miss Hudson, strike the witness' last statement from the record," the judge says.

Joaquín steps right up next to the witness stand.

"Cyrus, tell the jury exactly what happened on that day."

"I ran off to find help for my momma. She'd been trying to have that baby for hours, and she was hurting real bad, and the baby wasn't coming out. Her husband Otis wasn't home, so it was just momma and me. I guess momma asked Mrs. Graham to find help, too, only I didn't know it. She asked Mrs. Graham after I'd already left for town."

"And did you find help?"

"Yes, sir, I did. I must have asked five or six people walking around town, but they couldn't help. Then, the man at the candy store said there was a new doctor in Fox Grove, just started a month or so before. I found him in his office and asked if he'd come with me."

"Cyrus, what happened when the doctor went into your house, and where were you at that time?"

"He told me to stay outside, given my momma was in a womanly state, and it wouldn't be proper for me to see any of it."

"You said you saw your mother die. If you were outside, how did you see anything, and what did you see?"

"After the doctor went inside, I heard him yelling at someone, and I wondered if he was yelling at my momma, so I looked in the window," Cyrus says. "It turned out he was yelling at a young lady. He called her a 'fraud' and a 'field rat,' and I could see the look on my momma's face. She was scared and asked the young lady to stay with her."

"Your mother asked Miss de León to stay?"

"Yes, sir, she did."

"Did you see Miss de León holding a skull in her hands or hear her chanting something in a language you could not understand?"

"No, sir. She was praying to God and holding my momma's hand."

"What happened then?"

"Doctor Morley ordered Miss de León out, and she gathered up her things and left. After that, I started chopping wood, the way Otis, my step-daddy, told me to before he left for the Gulf. I heard my momma screaming, but I wasn't too worried. I thought all ladies scream when they're pushing babies out. But my momma kept on screaming, and it went on for at least another hour. I went behind the house to skin a rabbit I shot the day before. When momma wouldn't stop screaming, I looked through the window again. I was worried about her, you know?"

"And what did you see when you looked through the window?"

"I saw my momma rolling back and forth in bed. Her mouth stayed open wide, her back arched, and she scratched her face. She screamed all the while. There was blood all over the sheets and floor."

"How much blood?"

"I've never seen that much blood in my whole life. I couldn't move, and I didn't know what to do, anyway. My momma looked white as a ghost. Then she took one long breath, like a growl and a breath at the same time," he says, wiping tears away with his sleeve.

Joaquín hands Cyrus a handkerchief. "Do you need a drink of water? Would you like to take a minute's rest?"

"No, sir. I'm fine. I think my momma died after she took that breath. She got real still and didn't make any sounds at all. The doctor put his fingers on her wrist and put his ear to her mouth. Then he picked up something metal, like a long silver tool split in half with two big loops at the end."

"What did he do with that silver tool?"

"He stuck it inside my mother's private part. I couldn't look anymore after that. I sat down and leaned against the house. I couldn't help it, but I cried and couldn't stop. I was pretty sure my momma was dead. I wanted to yell for help, but what good would that do? The doctor came outside about ten minutes later and asked me what I saw."

"And what did you tell him?"

"I said I saw nothing but heard my momma screaming."

"And what did he say?"

"He told me to burn the sheets and my mother's nightgown. He said that if I talked to anyone about what happened, he'd tell the police that my father stole medicine from his office."

"And how did he know about your father?"

"I told Doctor Morley about my father on the ride back to the house, but I wish I never did."

"Tell us briefly about your father."

"His name's Ramón Longoria. He came to Texas from Mexico as a teenager. He was my mother's first husband, and he lived on the other side of Fox Grove."

"Why would Doctor Morley accuse your father of something he did not do?"

"He wanted to scare me, of course."

"Speculation!" Donald Mitchell screams.

"Overruled," the judge says, his hands folded across his chest and his head shaking slowly back and forth. "You may continue, Mr. Castanedda."

"So, Doctor Morley threatened you to keep quiet or else," Joaquín says. "Why are you telling us now?"

"My momma taught me to tell the truth. Coming here today is what she'd want me to do. My father's moved back to Mexico now. I hope to join him real soon, maybe after the war."

"Cyrus, do you think Miss de León killed your mother?"

"No, sir. I do not."

"Do you think Doctor Morley killed her?"

"Yes, but I don't think he meant to. He was just trying to get her to stop screaming, but she bled and bled until she couldn't bleed no more."

"I have no further questions, your honor," Joaquín says. "I leave it to Mr. Mitchell for cross-examination."

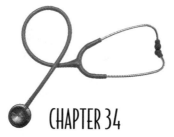

CHAPTER 34

Three Straightforward Steps

"Mr. Longoria, may I call you that?" Donald Mitchell asks.

"Nobody's ever called me that, but you can if you want to," Cyrus answers.

"We've been through this whole trial and still don't know much about your mother. I don't think that's right. Why don't you tell us about her?"

"Oh, I could go on a long time about that. My momma was the best momma a boy could ask for. She was real patient. I had chores I was supposed to do every day, but I'd forget from time to time. When I was little, she made me a calendar of my own with tiny drawings on it to help me remember, like a log for when I was supposed to gather firewood or a bucket for when I should haul water in from the well. She made the tastiest rabbit stew with turnips and carrots, and she had the prettiest voice you could ever imagine. She sang to me at night when I was a boy. I told her she was good enough to be on a big stage, but she said that would be like bragging about it, and she didn't think it was the Christian way, to brag. The day before she died, she gave me this red and white shirt I'm wearing now. She traded someone two loaves of bread for it. You should have smelled her bread when it came out of the oven. And the taste? It was like a slice of heaven. She was a good reader, too. She'd read to me every night, like *The Story of King Arthur and His Knights* and *The Call of the Wild*. She did lots of voices, too, to keep my interest, as I was known to fidget from time to time."

The sound of sniffles comes from every corner of the room. I hold my breath to keep from bawling. *I only wanted to help her, and she was so frail and scared.*

"Thank you for sharing those memories with us, Cyrus. The fine woman that your momma was cannot get lost in these proceedings. She is the true victim and deserves our respect. Now, I'm afraid I must switch to a more serious and unpleasant matter, all right?"

"Yes, sir."

"Earlier, you said that you did not think Miss duh Lee-on was holding a skull in her hands when you looked through the window. Are you willing to swear on that?"

"I didn't see a skull, and I think I would have noticed it."

"You also said you think she was praying with your mother. What prayer was she saying?"

"I didn't hear it exactly."

"Whether you believe in witchcraft or not, is it possible then that Miss duh Lee-on was attempting to put some kind of curse on your mother?"

"I don't think that's what it was because my momma was saying something along with her. They were saying it together."

"But it's possible?"

"Yes, sir. I suppose."

"You testified that you saw a lot of blood."

"Yes."

"Did you see what caused all this blood that you speak of?"

"No, sir."

"Did you see Doctor Morley do something that caused you concern?"

"No, sir, I did not."

"And you say that you burned the alleged bloody sheets?"

"I did, sir."

"Well, you must have bloody clothing. By that, I mean your own clothing. If you were cleaning up that much blood, surely you have bloody socks, or bloody pants, or maybe blood stains on the mattress or bedposts. Can you produce evidence of any bloody clothing or other items from the home?"

"I burned everything, sir, and wiped down the rest."

"But you said that Doctor Morley asked you to burn the sheets and your mother's clothing."

"I burned everything that had blood on it, even the mattress. Otis told me to burn all of it."

"How about bloodstains on the floor?"

"Otis replaced the floorboards there, sir. It was the first thing he did when he found out about momma. The floorboards look new in that spot now."

"And where is he now? Your step-daddy?"

"Back on the Gulf at the seafood plant, sir. He had to go back soon after momma died, right after he found a wet nurse to take Percy."

"Cyrus, you say Miss duh Lee-on did not kill your mother, and yet, Doctor Morely says the autopsy proved she died by poisoning. Can you be certain that Miss duh

Lee-on did not feed your mother poison at some point during her time there?"

"No, sir. I don't know about any poison. Miss duh Lee-on was alone with my mother before Doctor Morley and me arrived."

"No more questions, your honor."

"We will return this afternoon for closing arguments," says the judge. "Return promptly at 1 pm. Those who arrive late will be locked out. I want no interruptions."

⚄ ⚄ ⚄

I ask to be alone in the little room. We're nearing the end. *Have we done enough? Will they look past what they see to the inside of me?*

I lay my head on the table and doze off. I wake up when Joaquín pats my arm and tells me it's time.

⚄ ⚄ ⚄

"Gentlemen, you may begin your closing arguments," says the judge. "Mr. Mitchell?"

"Gentlemen of the jury. We've given you a great deal of information to think about and synthesize, so I'm going to describe your job in three straightforward steps," says Donald Mitchell. "First, discuss the evidence. Think of yourselves as judges, judges of the facts. Second, consider the testimony of each witness and assess their credibility. Third, return a verdict. The jury must come to a unanimous conclusion. While the job before you is a serious one with serious consequences, the process for getting it done is as simple as one, two, three.

"You've heard from multiple witnesses throughout this trial, so let me remind you of the essentials. Evan-jell-ina duh Lee-on used backwoods Mexican witchcraft on twenty-nine-year-old Ramona Healy to hasten her death, and therefore, end baby Percival's life. You may not believe in witchcraft, but your belief about such things is of no consequence in this context. What's important is that Miss duh Lee-on thought she was using witchcraft, complete with candles, incense, chanting and a skull, all of which she believed would ensure Ramona Healy's death and that of her unborn son's. These facts prove intent to kill or murder in the first degree."

Mr. Mitchell clasps his hands behind his back, walks toward the jury and bows his head in concentration.

"I ask you, what is the likelihood that Doctor Jedidiah Morley, a respected medical professional, and Willie Falkirk, a local teen with no reason to lie, would see someone commit the same heinous actions in two separate incidents? Keep in mind, the doctor and the teen have never met before. Yet, both testified under oath that they saw Miss duh Lee-on bent over dead bodies, those of Agatha Taylor and Ramona Healy, holding a skull and chanting gibberish that neither of them recognized. Both women had been in relatively good health before Miss duh Lee-on arrived on the dates of their respective deaths.

"Jedidiah Morley conducted an autopsy as he's done hundreds of times without question or error and proved, without a shadow of a doubt, that Ramona Healy died from ingesting prussic acid and oleander. Evan-jell-ina duh Lee-on had access to prussic acid and oleander at Doctor Russell Taylor's office. I have here, for the jury, the cup that carried the deadly contents," he says and grabs a folded white cloth on the prosecution table.

"To this day, the cup smells like almond. Do you know what prussic acid smells like? It smells like almond, gentlemen! It comes in the form of a transparent liquid and has little taste. That's why murderers prefer it. Mix it with hot water and a pinch of sweetener, and the victim doesn't suspect a thing. Imagine Ramona Healy taking the cup from the defendant's hands, not knowing that she would soon be foaming at the mouth and that, her heart, lungs and brain would cease to work. And if Doctor Jedidiah Morley had not come in time, the unborn child would have succumbed to the devil's wishes, delivered at the hands of Evan-jell-ina duh Lee-on!

"If I may, your honor. I'd like the gentlemen of the jury to hold and smell the cup that delivered the deadly substance."

"You should have presented this evidence during testimony, Mr. Mitchell, but I'll allow it," the judge says, nodding in approval.

"Gentlemen, the small amount of prussic acid remaining in the cup was tested and confirmed by Doctor Morley. The remaining almond *smell* cannot cause you harm."

Donald Mitchell hands the cup to the bailiff, who gives it to the first jury member.

"Finally, and as if that was not enough, just this past week, Evan-jell-ina duh Lee-on broke a legal agreement with Haller County that allowed her to leave the Seneca jail and stay in the home of Doctor Russell Taylor. The deal was written and signed with two conditions. One, she would not practice medicine, and two, she would not leave Doctor Taylor's house. And? You guessed it: she did both! This young woman, who the defense would have you believe is an upstanding citizen and capable medical practitioner, broke her agreement with the county within two weeks of signing it. And not only that! She broke the trust of Doctor Russell Taylor, the man who loved and treated her like a daughter. Plus, she got a twenty-one-year-old Arab male, her betrothed, involved in the scheme, endangering his life. More evidence that Evan-jell-ina duh Lee-on has no conscience. Indeed, one of the patients she visited in the dark of night had both his legs amputated below the knee after Miss duh Lee-on administered her supposed care!

"You may wonder what the motive was for this crime," Mr. Mitchell continues. "Why would Evan-jell-ina duh Lee-on kill Ramona Healy? Because Evan-jell-ina duh Leon believes she's a witch, folks! Witches think they're agents of Satan! Why would a then seventeen-year-old, now eighteen-year-old with no formal education in her primitive country of origin come here and pretend to be some kind of doctor? Easy victims, folks. Get them to trust you, just like Evan-jell-ina duh Lee-on did with Hamish Cavanaugh's daughter. Cora Cavanaugh herself testified that Miss duh Lee-on 'took care of her' when she got glass in her eye. And what did she get for trusting her?

"Cora Cavanaugh told you that it was her own negligence that led to the blindness, but the defense has since learned that Miss Cavanaugh is romantically involved with Mr. Joaquín Castanedda. Yes, *that* Joaquín Castanedda. Isn't it possible that it was Evan-jell-ina duh Lee-on's negligent care that led to the blindness, and

Cora Cavanaugh lied on the stand to help her Mexican Don Juan's lost cause?

"The defense tried to distract you. They created something of a three-ring circus with Sheriff Stanley Pearl. Don't be fooled. The defendant's guilt has nothing to do with the sheriff. It has to do with Ramona Healy, a defenseless woman in the prime of her life, a daughter, friend, wife and loving mother. There can be no justice for Ramona Healy. She's with the angels and watching us now. You must find the defendant guilty for those Ramona Healy left behind, especially young Percival Healy, who'll never get a chance to love or be loved by his mother. It'll be his justice most of all. Thank you."

CHAPTER 35

No Doubt Whatsoever

"Gentlemen, Donald Mitchell gave you three steps to doing your job as jurors, and while his directions were neat and tidy, there's something of critical importance that he forgot to mention," Joaquín begins. "In step three, he said you must agree on a verdict. Of course, you must agree on a verdict; everyone knows that. But, to come up with a verdict of 'guilty,' all of you must be one hundred percent positive that my client is guilty. That means no doubt whatsoever. If even one of you has a hint of doubt, you must find her 'innocent.'

"He also commented about the complexity of the case and the significant amount of information you must synthesize to reach the correct verdict. And it is precisely for those reasons that you must find Evangelina de León innocent of all charges.

"Nothing about this case has been straightforward. At every juncture, the defense has introduced testimony and evidence that contradicts that of the prosecution. Mr. Mitchell painted Miss de León as an imposter, someone with virtually no training who brought unsuspecting people into her lair to harm and kill, and yet, Doctor Russell Taylor, a physician of high repute, told a very different story. He explained how proud he was of Evangelina's studies and the progress she had made. Doctor Taylor told you of his confidence in her ability to start seeing patients of her own. He produced letters from patients thanking her for her outstanding care.

"The prosecution brought young Willie Falkirk to the stand, who said that Miss de León killed Agatha Taylor, that she held a skull and chanted a witch's curse. But Charlie Burton, Willie Falkirk's best friend, said that Willie told him an entirely different story. Doctor Taylor also contradicted Willie's story when he said that the level of rigor mortis in his mother's body proved that Evangelina de León could not have caused or contributed in any way to Agatha Taylor's death.

"Doctor Jedidiah Morley said he saw Miss de León chanting gibberish and holding a skull, but Cyrus Longoria, the deceased's son and eyewitness, told you otherwise. Doctor Morley said Ramona Healy died from prussic acid poisoning; however, two separate and independent autopsies done later showed no prussic acid in Ramona Healy's body. The actual cause of death was massive blood loss.

"Doctor Taylor told you about a medical procedure discovered by the Germans called 'twilight sleep' and how it's become popular in the United States as a means to reduce the pain and memory of childbirth. He also explained the dangers of twilight sleep, which can cause, among other things, enough blood loss to bring about death. Doctors Taylor and Rucker found morphine and scopolamine in Ramona Healy's tissue samples, those being the two medications used to induce twilight sleep. Doctor Morley traveled to Germany on the *RMS Victoria.* Upon his return, he used the twilight sleep methodology on numerous pregnant women, including Francine Deveraux of Alden and Ramona Healy of Fox Grove.

"Cyrus Longoria, Mrs. Healy's son, testified that he saw his mother bleed to death under Doctor Morley's care and that Doctor Morely threatened to put Cyrus' father in jail to scare him into silence.

"If ever there was a case where members of a jury must admit doubt, this is it. Doctor Morley showed his true colors when he called Evangelina a 'field rat.' He caused Ramona Healy's death, albeit unintentionally, and blamed it on a young Mexican woman, knowing that a sheriff with a history of hatred for foreigners and Negroes would support his false claim, no questions asked. He knew that a Mexican getting a fair and unbiased trial was as likely as snow in a Texas summer. And that would be *if* she got a trial at all. All across Texas, Mexicans and Tejanos face harassment, torture and execution for crimes they did not commit. Most go without the benefit of formal charges or a fair and impartial trial. They're simply rounded up and beaten, shot, burned or lynched.

"Two days ago, a boy found seventy-four-year-old Rodolfo Muñiz of Goldendale dead, tied to a tree with a beer can shoved in his mouth. Had he committed a crime? Neighbors say the only time he left his home was to walk to and from his mailbox. Who killed him in such a cruel manner? Two Anglo men bragged about the killing in a local saloon, but Goldendale law enforcement says they do not intend to conduct an investigation.

"Ten Mexican men recently were pulled off a Texas train near Loma and shot in front of their families by the Texas Rangers. An entire train full of passengers witnessed it! The victims, the Rangers said, had robbed a bank, only, no such robbery ever occurred.

"Right here in Seneca, twenty-year-old Modesto Domínguez got dragged to death behind his horse less than a month ago while out looking for work. Two witnesses saw three young men, Reggie Brooks, Caleb Hawthorne and Tom Shaughnessy, shake a branch at the horse, causing it to buck, then cheered when the horse took off with Mr. Domínguez trailing behind. The death was declared an accident by the sheriff's office.

"Manuel Ybarra's sister found her brother in a field with a gunshot wound in the back of his head, left there for the vultures. Earlier that day, an Anglo man named Buck Milton confronted Mr. Ybarra, an American-born citizen of Mexican descent, a Tejano, because he wanted Mr. Ybarra's land. Mr. Ybarra would not agree to sell it and wound up dead.

"Authorities tell us these cases are closed! No investigations, no arrests, no justice for Mexicans or Tejanos.

"The statistics Miss de León cited are worth repeating. Approximately eight percent of Seneca's population is Mexican or Tejano, but they made up forty-four percent of the jail population in the past twelve months. That deserves a future investigation, but it provides context for this case. Sheriff Stanley Pearl and guard Humphrey Chestnut repeatedly called Miss de León and her parents racist names. They nearly starved Miss de León and ignored her cries for basic decency. She endured two lascivious assaults at the hands of this town's sheriff while locked in a cage for a crime she did not commit. We brought you the written testimony of Deputy Josiah Martin, who heard Sheriff Pearl say, 'I thank you for bringin' her to us, doc. It don't matter if she's guilty or not, and I don't wanna know. Them Mexicans ain't welcome here, not even the women and children. If watching her twitch from the end of a rope don't send a message, what will?'

"Those who have wronged Evangelina de León are counting on you to believe the unfortunate, unsubstantiated, *un*truth that's common in these parts, that she's guilty, by virtue of her race. It's up to you to prove them wrong. You must agree, this case is, at best, full of doubt and bigoted motivations by officials, and Miss de León has suffered enough. The only correct verdict is innocent of all charges. Thank you."

The commotion in the courtroom is more than I can bear. I hug my family and friends and ask Joaquín to answer the press' questions without me. Josiah whisks me away and takes me back to Doctor Taylor's house, where I can rest.

⇢ ⇢ ⇢

I open my heavy eyelids and wipe the drool from my mouth. It's 7 pm, three hours since I arrived at the house, ran upstairs and practically threw myself into Agatha Taylor's bed.

"Evangelina! Sorry to wake you, but Joaquín just came by," says Doc Taylor. "The judge wants you back in court."

"So soon? Is that good or bad?" I ask.

"I wish I knew," he says.

⇢ ⇢ ⇢

Teresita sits on one side of me with Joaquín on the other. We hold each other's hands and squeeze tight.

The group of reporters stands in the wings with note-books and pens at the ready.

The bailiff hands a piece of paper to the judge.

Judge O'Leary reads it, drops his head and scowls. "Gentlemen of the jury, your note says here that you are at an impasse."

I let go of Joaquín's and Teresita's hands. *Will they send me to the gallows if there's an impasse?*

"Yes, your honor," says a gray-haired man in the jury box.

"You have been deliberating for a measly three hours, Jacob," says the judge.

"Yes, your honor. Within the first hour, it became crystal clear that three jury members did not agree with the other nine. Those same three indicated they would not listen to the deliberations or budge, citing their God-given right to act on principle. Based on that, I did not see how any further discussion would change things."

"That is unacceptable, Jacob," says Judge O'Leary. "As the jury foreman and a former city council member, I expected better leadership. Or at least that you would have tried longer before attempting to force a mistrial. I will speak with the jury and provide explicit instruction tomorrow. Haller County will not be made a mockery in the eyes of Texas.

"This is a hanging case, gentlemen, and not a time for ambivalence, stubbornness or incompetence. You *will* reach a unanimous verdict, however long it takes. I cannot believe you yanked me out of bed for this non-sense. It is now past my bedtime, and I am going home. Report for duty tomorrow at 9 am, at which time I will privately address each of you to ensure an understand-ing of your obligations to this court and Haller County."

CHAPTER 36

Rise

Selim and I sit on the porch steps of Doc Taylor's house just before sunrise, knowing it could be the only time we'll have to be alone, maybe for forever, although neither one of us says it out loud.

"Can I put my arm around you?" he asks.

I grab his arm and guide it around my back. Selim pulls me in close enough for my side to join with his like one pancake poured too close to the one next to it.

We sit, content to hold hands in silence, but the gray, white and pink chickadees have other ideas. They hop from tree to tree, chirping their good morning song. A hawk glides overhead, screeching and searching for its breakfast. Petals of white magnolias drop from their branches to the grass below.

"Do you see the sun peeking out?" Selim asks, looking straight ahead.

"How could I not?"

"Do you see the clouds above it?"

"Yes."

"I predict those clouds will disappear soon. It's going to be a sunny triumphant day, one for the ages, one we'll celebrate into our old age and tell our children about."

"What will you do if I am found guilty?" I ask. "You must have thought about it. Will you marry Fatima and get your family back? I wouldn't blame you if you did. I'd smile down on you from heaven and send my angel wishes for your happiness."

"I will never be in my family's good graces again, and you are the only one I want to marry. There won't be another."

"I wouldn't want you to be alone for the rest of your life. I'd want you to find love again. You'll make a wonderful husband and father.

"What will you do if they find me innocent?" I ask.

"The better question is, what will *you* do *when* they find you innocent, not *if* they find you innocent?"

"Teresita said she plans to open a new chapter of La Liga Protectora in Goldendale. Joaquín will lead the staff and volunteers there. Many of the clients in Loma have injuries from the Mexican Revolution, and the Goldendale office will be no different. I want to be a part of it. I have something to contribute, a purpose to fulfill."

"What about going to school and becoming a physician?"

"Working at La Liga doesn't mean I can't also go to school and become a doctor. But before that, I want to finish what we started at Señor Villanueva's, under the oak tree, surrounded by all those lanterns."

"Nothing would make me happier," says Selim.

A carriage approaches and the man inside gawks at us, maybe because a Lebanese male is sitting side by side with a Mexican female, or perhaps because I am recognizable around here for all the wrong reasons.

Either way, Selim does not care. Before the carriage passes, he leans in and kisses my cheek so that the man can see.

❧ ❧ ❧

We join Doc Taylor at the dining table set with small china plates, forks and a pineapple cherry cake he bought at the bakery. It smells good.

"You should eat something before you go back to the courthouse," he says. "I'll pour you each a glass of milk, and I have oatmeal on the stove."

"What do you think it meant when the man said that three jurors would not change their minds? Do you think it was nine in my favor and three against or the other way around?" I ask.

"You and Joaquín did an outstanding job with your case, so I'd like to think the odds are in your favor," Doc Taylor says.

"I told him to come and get me at 10 o'clock this morning. I want to be there when the jurors reach a verdict."

"The verdict may not even come today," Selim says. "Are you sure you don't want to wait here? I can stay with you. I got a friend to take my shift at the restaurant."

"Why don't you come with me to the courthouse?" I ask. "We can wait there together."

"Anything you say," Selim says.

"Will you be stopping by my aunt and uncle's house to see Abuelito? I'd feel better if you did," I ask Doc Taylor.

"Yes, yes. I'll head over there now."

"Tell him I'm still wearing Abuelita's butterfly pin for luck."

⚘ ⚘ ⚘

An hour passes.

A second hour passes.

Then a third.

A fourth.

The wait is agonizing. I brought my medical journal and try reading but don't comprehend a thing.

Five hours after we arrive, we're summoned back into the courtroom. I feel unsteady and put my hand against the wall for balance. Joaquín and I sit down at the defense table.

"Hear ye! Hear ye!" says the bailiff. "All rise for the Honorable Judge Patrick O'Leary."

I push myself to a stand, keeping my fingertips on the tabletop.

"Have the gentleman of the jury reached a verdict?" the judge asks.

The courtroom goes completely silent, even the babies and children.

"Yes, your honor, we have," says the foreman.

The bailiff grabs a paper from the foreman and takes it to the judge, who opens and closes it.

I study his face. *Do I see sparks of anger in his eyes? Is that a frown?*

"What say you?" the judge asks.

"We, the jury, find the defendant, Evan-jell-ina duh Lee-on, innocent of all charges."

I turn to hug Joaquín, but it turns into more of a collapse, and he has to hold me up.

"You are free to go, Miss duh Lee-on," the judge says. "Now, everyone, get out of here. This case is closed!"

"You did it! It's over!" Selim yells.

"Congratulations, Evangelina," says Teresita. "You and Joaquín should be extremely proud of yourselves. I know I am."

"Congratulations, you two!" says Cora. "This is . . . this is so . . . so damn excitin'! I'm beyond thrilled for ya'll!"

Tears roll down Mamá's face as she steps in and wraps her arms around me. Behind Mamá, Papá smiles, but he has a deep crease between his brows.

"Is something wrong?" I ask.

"*M'ija*, God answer our prayers, and we cannot wait to bring you home," says Mamá.

"Where's Abuelito?" I ask, looking around. "Did Doc Taylor see him this morning?"

Mamá's chin wobbles, and tears stream down Elsa's cheeks.

"What's happened to Abuelito?!" I shout.

"I'm sorry, *m'ija*, but he's gone," Papá says.

The noise in the room fades to nothing.

Rock throwing contests that he'd always let me win.

Walking hand in hand through our orchards.

Teaching me how to cast a fishing line and groom a horse and peel an orange.

Talking about the honeybees, the armadillos, the flowers that bloom before the vegetables grow, the colors of the sunrise.

Smelling sweet pipe tobacco on his shirts and in his hair.

Listening to his silly made-up stories at bedtime.

His jokes, his patience, his wisdom.

Like rice and beans.

"No!" I scream.

"I'm sorry, *m'ija*. Doctor Taylor arrived at your *tía* Cristina's house to do the exam, and your *abuelito* had already passed," Mamá says. "He died in his sleep."

"He must have known his time was near. He wrote each of us a note. The doctor found them scattered on the blanket that covered him," Papá says and fishes an envelope out of his pocket.

I unfold the paper with Abuelito's shaky handwriting.

M'ija, the Lord is calling me home, and your abuelita is waiting for me there. We've been a perfect pair, you and me—like rice and beans, and I couldn't be more thankful! I will never stop loving you and will always be with you in spirit. I am confident you will be found innocent, and when you are, you'll be free to go wherever you want and with whomever you want. You will have faced the challenge bravely and won! Rise! Open your wings and fly, m'ija. Where will you command the wind to take you?

Yours eternally,
Your abuelito

☊ ☊ ☊

We spend the next five minutes hugging and drying our tears, but I have one thing left to do here before I head home and fall to pieces in thanks and grief.

The group of us walks to the top step of the courthouse. The clouds have gone. It's a sunny and triumphant day.

A crowd of people mills around the street. I recognize a man from a wedding photo I saw on his fireplace mantle. Otis Healy looks directly at me with the same photo of him and his late wife, Ramona, in his hand. He blinks slowly and nods, pressing the photo to his chest.

Selim links his arm through mine. Joaquin stands on my other side.

"There she is!" shouts one reporter. People scramble over each other to get up close.

I form a fist with my right hand and raise it high into the air.

Afterword

Evangelina de León, the young Mexicana protagonist of Diana Noble's novel *Chances in Disguise,* is a civil rights champion of her time and ours. Unjustly accused of a capital crime which she did not commit, Evangelina endures and ultimately prevails over the racist legal system with the help of her family, community activists and organizers, and white allies. Every step of the way, representatives of the law—from the crudely racist sheriff and his lackey turnkeys to the smug prosecutor and his friend the unscrupulous judge—strive for the guilty verdict they determine to be true, actual facts aside. Every step of the way, a coalition of those outside positions of institutional power—including the Tejana founder of La Liga Protectora Mexicana, a young Mexicano attorney for La Liga, a feminist Anglo female journalist, and Evangelina's Lebanese secret fiancée—band together to force the legal system to work fairly.

Chances in Disguise is a work of historical fiction set in the conflict-torn Texas-Mexico borderlands of the 1910s, when native-born Tejanos and immigrant Mexicans alike were targeted as criminals by law enforcement simply because of their culture, language and skin color. This situation is not unique to ethnic Mexicans, as African Americans, Asian Americans and Native Americans are likewise racially profiled. But the Mexicano community of Seneca, Texas, is disproportionally affected by the abuse of police authority and the denial of due process by virtue of being the largest non-white population in the area. The large influx of Mexican migrants—war refugees fleeing the Revolution—was seen by Anglo authorities as an unwelcome invasion of racial undesirables who needed to be controlled by the most brutal of methods. They become the convenient scapegoats for all of the region's criminality, with little recourse to a justice system set up to enforce white supremacy rather than administer impartial justice.

In this sense, *Chances in Disguise* offers readers a fictional portrait that illuminates a crucial, if now mostly unknown, decade in Texas history: the 1910s as years of *La Matanza*, or "the great killing time," when law enforcement, particularly the Texas Rangers, willfully and wantonly violated the civil and human rights of the ethnic Mexican communities of South Texas. Between 1910 and 1920, over 1,000 Mexicanos (US citizens and Mexican nationals alike) were murdered under the color of authority, with no semblance of due process by the Rangers, county sheriffs and deputies, municipal police and vigilantes. Misnamed "the bandit wars" in the English-language press of the times, these executions were justified as necessary measures to maintain law and order in the borderlands, as a counter-measure to what was seen as the violent and senseless chaos of the Mexican Revolution.

So, while author Diana Noble has crafted a fictional narrative, the story she tells is rooted in the truth of the moment she depicts. Like Evangelia, ethnic Mexicans were routinely arrested and accused of crimes they did not commit; denied humane treatment and adequate legal representation while in custody; saw their families punished through unproven guilt by association; pressured to falsely confess their guilt; and often convicted upon flimsy or even nonexistent "evidence." And this was just for the comparatively fortunate ones who were not outright killed before any arrest or shot in the back while "resisting arrest" or "attempting to escape." Knowing that local and state officials, up to and including the governor, would protect them from the worst possible consequences, white law enforcement officers were encouraged to act with little morality and no accountability.

At the same time, *Chances in Disguise* demonstrates another truth of those times: the tireless efforts of Mexicano organizers and activists to challenge their community's marginalization and scapegoating. Evangelina's acquittal is less a result of an impartial justice system discovering "the truth" than the concerted efforts of the Mexicano community and allies to secure the impartiality that should have been Evangelina's civil right in the first instance. Just as Teresita Olmos, Joaquín Castañeda, Cora Cavanaugh, Doc Taylor, Selim and numerous protestors work through La Liga Protectora Mexicana to prove Evangelina's innocence, historical figures such as Jovita Idár, Sara Estela Ramírez, Alonso S. Perales and José Tomás (JT) Canales worked tirelessly to organize civil rights organizations to protest racially motivated travesties of justice. They organized conferences such El Primer Congreso Mexicanista to bring activists together and formed groups to protect ethnic Mexican civil rights such as La Agrupación Protectora Mexicana, La Liga Feminil Mexicanista and, in the late 1920s, the League of United Latin American Citizens (LULAC). While ethnic Mexicans faced long odds in seeking justice and accountability from the legal system during the 1910s, they fought those odds with great determination and persistence.

While much has changed since 1915, the very height of La Matanza and the year in which Evangelina's ordeal is set, much more work remains to be done to ensure that the justice system is fair and impartial to all, regardless of race, gender, sexual orientation, socioeconomic class and other social determinants. Questions of racial profiling and the unnecessary escalation of force by law enforcement against communities of color are as are relevant in the 2020s as they were in the 1910s. In this sense, *Chances in Disguise* operates at two distinct but related levels. The first is to restore to public knowledge a critical history of anti-Mexican violence not otherwise taught in the national educational system. The second is to urge a strong, collective response from today's readers to take up the challenge of ensuring justice for all, and not just for the privileged few. A role model in this effort, Evangelina is indeed a strong, feminist hero, as she, together with her community, transforms the challenge of racial and gendered injustice by the legal system into a chance, in disguise, to strive for a better future.

John Morán González, PhD
Co-founder, *Refusing to Forget*
J. Frank Dobie Regents Professor of American and English
Director, Center for Mexican American Studies,
the University of Texas at Austin

About the author

With roots in the south Texas Rio Grande Valley, Diana J. Noble currently lives with her family in the beautiful Pacific Northwest. More information available at www.dianajnoble.com.